Find ~~the~~ ~~luck~~ of the Irish
in these Irish Eyes romances . . .

THE IRISH DEVIL
by Donna Fletcher

and

TO MARRY AN IRISH ROGUE
by Lisa Hendrix

Daughter of Ireland

Sonja Massie

JOVE BOOKS, NEW YORK

If you purchased this book without a cover, you should be aware that this book is stolen property. It was reported as "unsold and destroyed" to the publisher and neither the author nor the publisher has received any payment for this "stripped book."

This is a work of fiction. Names, characters, places, and incidents are either the product of the author's imagination or are used fictitiously, and any resemblance to actual persons, living or dead, business establishments, events, or locales is entirely coincidental.

DAUGHTER OF IRELAND

A Jove Book / published by arrangement with the author

PRINTING HISTORY
Jove edition / June 2000

All rights reserved.
Copyright © 2000 by Sonja Massie.
This book may not be reproduced in whole or in part, by mimeograph or any other means, without permission. For information address: The Berkley Publishing Group, a division of Penguin Putnam Inc., 375 Hudson Street, New York, New York 10014.

The Penguin Putnam Inc. World Wide Web site address is
http://www.penguinputnam.com

ISBN: 0-515-12835-X

A JOVE BOOK®
Jove Books are published by The Berkley Publishing Group, a division of Penguin Putnam Inc., 375 Hudson Street, New York, New York 10014. JOVE and the "J" design are trademarks belonging to Penguin Putnam Inc.

PRINTED IN THE UNITED STATES OF AMERICA

10 9 8 7 6 5 4 3 2

One

"*Angus O'Brien, what* a handsome corpse ye've made! I've never seen ye lookin' finer, lad."

"He does appear peaceful, doesn't he? And youthful as well. Sixteen years old, I'd wager, from the look of him. Not the seventy-six we knew him to be."

"Aye, death becomes him. I wager Angus would've passed on years ago, if he'd only known how attractive he'd be."

The mourners at Angus O'Brien's wake formed an appreciative circle around his body, which was stretched on a wide pine plank, supported at the corners by four chairs and covered with a white linen cloth. A plate of tobacco had been placed at his head to assure that he would never be without a smoke in the hereafter. A nearby saucer held salt, into which had been traced a cross to ward away unpleasant disembodied spirits who might also be attending the festivities alongside the living.

The main room of Lios na Daoine Sidhe, the pub where Angus had spent most of his years, was filled with cigarette smoke and the pungent-sweet aroma of the turf fire on the hearth, along with the wailing and lamentations of several professional keeners. These ladies had been hired to do the job properly, their cries alerting folks near and far that a truly popular fellow had passed.

"I don't think he looks so fine," spoke seven-year-old Sean Kissane, one of the younger citizens of the tiny county Kerry village of Gormloch. The curly-haired youngster stood on tiptoe beside his twin sister, Shauna, as the twosome gazed at their recently departed friend.

"Neither do I," agreed Shauna, wrinkling her pert nose. "'Tis dead he looks to me. Nothin' more, nothin' less. Dead entirely."

"Keep civil tongues in those heads of yers," the twins' mother said, applying a light swat to both of their backsides. "You're to speak kindly of all souls, livin' or dead."

"Leave the wee ones be," the children's grandmother, Norah Delaney, interjected, landing a similar thump on her own adult daughter's behind. "'Tis the truth they're speakin', and we all know it, sure. Old Angus was a fine storyteller in his day, but he was as ugly as a mule and dyin' hasn't improved his condition at all, at all."

Sitting on a stool close to the hearth, Moya Mahoney listened to the exchange and smiled through her tears. Of all the mourners present, her grief was the most acute; Angus O'Brien had been dearer than a father to her, and she had loved him deeply.

With no children of his own or family in Ireland, Angus had depended heavily on Moya, who had nursed him through a lingering illness. And she had held him in her arms as his spirit floated up and away from his body.

His final words on earth had been to her. "Thanks be to ye for everything, lass," he had murmured. "Ye made my last years a pleasure with many a laugh. And yer kindness has made me passin' easier, to be sure."

With that, Angus O'Brien had closed his eyes and slipped from her arms to those of the angels.

And already Moya Mahoney missed him terribly, though he had been absent less than twenty-four hours.

"Did someone think to tie his great toes together?" old Norah asked, lifting one corner of the sheet to peek beneath. "We don't want his restless spirit wanderin' about tonight, makin' a nuisance of itself, scarin' the livin' life outta the rest of us. 'Tis soon enough I'll be joinin' the ranks of the ghosts without Angus coaxin' me along."

"Aye, we bound them together with a stout bit of twine," Gill Doolin, the local publican said as he polished glasses behind the bar. "And knotted it thrice, too. He won't be takin' any journeys anytime soon . . . except the one to Saint Peter's gate."

Another round of Guinness—Angus's beverage of choice—was passed to the adults and lemonades to

the youngsters. Together they raised their glasses in
a toast to assure that his eternal destination was a
happy one.

Conn Hallissey, a handsome fellow known
throughout the county for his friendly smile and fine
tin whistle playing, strolled over to Moya and offered to replenish her glass. When she refused, he
said, "I wish you'd step outside with me, Moya, and
dance a few tunes. That's what ye need to lift your
spirits."

Normally she would have accepted. The agility of
Conn's piping fingers was surpassed only by his nimble feet, and dancing with him was a pleasure, indeed. But not today.

"I thank you, Conn," she said, returning his warm
smile. "Some other time."

He reached over and patted her shoulder. "Aye,
some other time, love."

Conn and several other of the village musicians
filed outside, and in a few minutes, she could hear
the band begin to tune their instruments in the cross-
roads in front of the pub. A night of musical reverie
was sure to cheer Angus on his way.

The sounds of Conn's tin whistle, the fiddle, and
the boom of the ancient Irish drum, the bodhran,
cheered the mourners' sad hearts. Several more cou-
ples left the pub, arm in arm, to warm the leather of
their shoes with a lively dance.

One by one, the children drifted toward the fireplace, an open hearth at the end of the room. Its
glow lit the ancient beams that supported Lios na
Daoine Sidhe's ceiling, one of the few remaining

thatched roofs in the village. Now, in modern times as in olden, youngsters from five to eighty-plus years were drawn to the glimmering hearth, its inviting warmth . . . and the storyteller who sat on a stool before it. For generations, the great seanchais—those folk who had been given the sacred gift of telling tales—had sat in this place of honor. By the mystic firelight they had spun golden webs with their words and snared the imaginations of their listeners with stories older than time.

Only last week, sick as he was, Angus O'Brien had sat in that spot and told the tale of the great Irish hero Cuchulain. Tonight he lay stretched out on a plank with candles at his head and feet, his great toes bound with twine. And his lesson by example wasn't lost on those present: Life was sweet, to be sure, but short.

"Moya, tell us, is Angus in heaven this very evenin'?" little Shauna asked as she sat at Moya's feet and arranged her plaid woolen skirt about her knees with exaggerated feminine grace.

Moya looked down into the dark blue eyes, so full of innocence, gazing up at her, then reached to stroke the girl's shining chestnut curls. "I wouldn't claim to know such a thing," Moya told the child. "'Tis only God Himself who can judge men's souls and determine their destinations. But if it's my opinion you're after, I'd have to say that no finer fellow ever walked the green earth, and if anyone deserves to trod golden streets, surely 'tis Angus O'Brien."

Shauna smiled, comforted. "He may even be doin'

one of his jigs there this very minute and smilin'
down on us all."

"Indeed, he may."

Shauna's twin brother joined her and the other village children on the floor, cross-legged, his elbows
on his knees. "Or maybe he's not in heaven at all,"
he volunteered. "Maybe ol' Angus is in Tir na nOg."

Moya glanced over at Norah Delaney and saw that
the woman's thin lips were stretched in a taut, disapproving line. The children's grandmother was a fine,
upstanding Catholic woman, who hadn't appreciated
Angus O'Brien entertaining her offspring with ancient, pagan tales of that mystic land of Tir na nOg.

Moya's desire to tell the colorful story to the eager
children at her feet warred with her healthy fear of
the elderly woman's sharp tongue. It was a well-
celebrated fact in the village of Gormloch that Norah
Delaney's words could strip the fur off a cat at a
dozen paces and Moya had no inclination to stir that
sort of wrath.

But the tale was such a fine one. . . .

"Ah, Tir na nOg, you say," she murmured, bending her head low to the children, her green eyes aglow
with seanchai magic, the firelight glistening in her
copper hair. "And a wonderful place that is. The Land
of the Ever Young, where no one grows older than
they were on the day they arrived and none suffers
an ache or pain. Where there is nothin' but feastin'
and singin' and dancin' the livelong day, and there
is no night besides."

The children sighed and settled into the story, as
both teller and audience stared into the hypnotic

flames that danced on the hearth, allowing their imaginations to be transported to that mysterious place.

" 'Tis a distant land," Moya continued, "far beneath the sea. You cannot walk there, nor swim. You must ride. You must ride to Tir na nOg on the back of an enchanted white stallion, a horse with giant wings, who wears a bridle of silver and a saddle of gold."

She smiled down at the twins, who, even though they knew every word of the story by heart, hung on her every syllable as if they were hearing it for the first time. "And what mode of transportation must you use to reach Tir na nOg?" she asked them.

"An enchanted white horse," Shauna answered eagerly.

"A *stallion*! 'Tis a boy horse you must ride, not a girl!" Sean added. The other boys nodded eagerly, agreeing with him.

"It doesn't matter if it's a stallion or a mare." Shauna lifted her freckled nose a notch. "Any enchanted horse would fly you there in fine style."

"But this one's a boy. Isn't it, Moya?" said Kevin Doolin, the publican's ten-year-old son.

Moya laughed. "In this story, the horse is a boy," she said. "If you don't quarrel, tomorrow evenin' I'll tell you the frightenin' tale of the Night Mare. If it's brave enough you are to hear it."

"Aye, we're brave enough!" Shauna assured her.

"Far more than brave enough," Kevin added.

"Now tell us more about Tir na nOg," Sean said. "Tell us about Ossian and how Princess Niamh appeared to him, ridin' one of those fine stallions and took him away to—"

"Shh." Moya touched her fingertip to the boy's lips. "'Tis my story and I'll not have you ruin it by tellin' all the best parts before me."

Moya cast a quick sideways look at Grandmother Norah, but she was engaged in conversation with Father Shea in the corner near Angus's body and seemed to have forgotten to be disapproving. Gill Doolin had finished polishing his glassware and was pulling another Guinness from the tap to relieve the parched throats of the mourners. But she could tell he had an ear stretched in her direction to hear the story for himself.

"And after a hard day of fishin' there on the banks of the Killarney loughs," she continued, "Ossian fell asleep. And a deep, sound sleep it was. And when he woke from that dreamless slumber, it was well past midnight. When was it he awoke, children?"

"Well past midnight, ma'am."

"Right you are. And a full moon hung over the black waters of the lough, sprinklin' glimmerin' fairy dust across the surface of the lough, like a thousand million tiny diamonds.

"And it was then that he saw the waves lappin' at the shore, ripplin' across the lough as if somethin' had disturbed the stillness of the dark waters.

"At first, he thought it was a fish, a mighty fish, or some class of sea monster come to devour him in two bites. At the very thought his heart leapt into his throat and did a Kerry jig, right there betwixt his tonsils.

"But then . . ."

The children leaned toward her, hardly daring to breathe.

"Tell us!" Shauna exclaimed.

"Aye," Sean added, "tell us before you're a minute older!"

"But then . . . Ossian beheld—not a sea monster or a fish large enough to swallow an elephant without chewin'—but the most beautiful vision he had ever seen. The sight was so lovely it nearly turned his two eyes to stones.

"It was a horse who had disturbed the black waters of the Killarney loughs. An enchanted stallion, gleamin' white there in the moonlight, sportin' two of the largest wings you ever saw. He rose up from the depths of the lough, with silver bridle jinglin', and headed for the shore, straight toward Ossian.

"But it wasn't the enchanted stallion or even its mighty wings that captured Ossian's eye. No, indeed. 'Twas the beautiful woman upon the horse's back. A princess with long, flowin' golden hair that was twisted with ropes of pearls and other precious stones. Her dress was white, like the horse, and floated around her, finer than fairies' silk. And around her neck was a torque, a thick, golden necklace, like those worn by the ancient kings and queens thousands of years ago, right here in Ireland. And where did those nobles wear such finery, boys and girls?"

"Right here in Ireland," they chimed.

Moya smiled and nodded. "'Tis the very spot, indeed. And what did the princess do? Did she fly away into the night? Did she return to the waters from whence she came?"

Her audience shook their heads.

"No, she did not. She rode directly toward Ossian, beckonin' him as she neared the shore, callin' to him with a voice sweet as that of the ringin' of an angel's bell. 'Come with me, Ossian,' she told him. 'Come away with me to Tir na nOg, the Land of the Ever Young. Life is bright there and more lovely than you can imagine. Only ride away with me and you will see.'"

As Moya continued to weave magic with her words, she felt a sense of peace and happiness for the first time in many months. Angus's illness and his passing had been painful for her, to be sure. And she couldn't bear the thought that tomorrow they would be laying him beneath the sod.

But he had given her so much in his life, countless hours here in front of the fire, so many stories, so much pride in her Irish heritage. And this legacy was hers to bequeath to the future generations. Angus had laid the bard's mantle aside, and in a natural progression, she had picked it up and wrapped it around her own shoulders.

And the tradition would continue; Gormloch's next seanchai was no doubt there at her feet that very minute.

If Moya Mahoney had anything to do with it, this village, this pub, and the old, old stories would endure forever. Forever and a day.

Nothing in her world would change. Nothing at all, at all.

Moya simply wouldn't allow it.

•   •   •

Rory O'Brien glared at his secretary over the rim of his coffee mug and wondered exactly when he had lost control of his office. Fredl Knarr—six feet tall and 237, efficient, no-nonsense pounds of her—towered over him, returning his scowl. If he had stood, he would have been eye to eye with her, but he wasn't about to do so and let her know how effectively she was intimidating him. He might be sitting in the three-thousand-dollar, ergonomically correct executive's chair, but neither he nor she had any delusions about who was in charge here.

Ten years ago, when he had hired Fredl, Rory had been a twenty-four-year-old whiz-kid, fresh out of business college, with enough sense to know that he needed a ruthless, perfectionist, well-organized assistant to help him achieve his financial goals.

Now, with an uptown Manhattan office—filled with contemporary designer furniture, modern museum-quality art, and a breathtaking view afforded by sixty-four stories—Rory had reached some of those goals. And he had to give some of the credit to Fredl. They made a good team.

Too bad they hated each other.

"One of these days, Rory," she was saying in a German accent as thick as his New Yorkese, "they're going to find you sitting at this desk, stiff as a golf club, with a knife sticking out of your back. The list of suspects will be endless."

"And you'll be at the top of that list, you old bat," he said, shooting blue-eyed laser darts at her. "I've already given a lawyer a sealed letter to be opened in case of my untimely death, naming *you* as my killer. You knock me off, you fry in the electric chair."

Fredl sniffed and reached over to shuffle and straighten some papers on his desk. "Electric chair, my butt. They'll give me a testimonial dinner and a platter with your head on it for doing the community a great service."

"Leave those papers alone, woman! I have everything right where I want it!" He swatted her hand away, then ducked as she raised her fist over his head. "Unless, of course, you feel strongly about it," he added quickly.

"I'm looking for that projection sheet you were supposed to give me before noon, the one about the proposed computer plant in Dublin. If you want me to put together a decent prospectus for you by Friday, I have to have it now."

"Never mind. I thought it over and decided to dump the idea."

Fredl stopped tidying and stared at him. "But I thought we agreed it would be a great idea to open a plant in Dublin. Several of your competitors have operations in Ireland and—"

"And spend half the day trying to round up their workers who passed most of the previous evening at the local pub, downing Guinness."

Fredl shook her head and gave him a sad, disapproving cluck of her tongue. "That was a racist comment if ever I heard one, Rory, and it wasn't worthy of you."

"Yeah, well . . . I'm a mick, so I can make derogatory comments about 'my people' if I want."

"Not without getting slapped."

"I won't be threatened with physical violence by someone whose salary comes out of my checking account. You're fired."

She shoved his chair and gave it a half spin. "You can't fire me, boy. I've got the office computer programmed so that if I don't log on every morning at nine o'clock sharp, the whole thing explodes."

Feigning exasperation, he sighed and combed his fingers through his loose, black curls that always seemed to look as though he had just stepped out of a wind tunnel. "It'll all explode, huh?" he said. "What if, on your way to work one day, you get caught in a traffic jam?"

"I'm German," she said with a smirk. "Which means I'm punctual, and I don't allow traffic jams to occur in my presence."

Somehow, he believed her.

"Now who's spouting stereotypical propaganda? I've known a few tardy Germans in my day."

"And I know some teetotaler Irishmen."

"Irish *men*?"

She shrugged. "Okay, women . . . but . . ."

He reached into the upper right-hand drawer of his desk and pulled out several sheets of paper that were clipped together. Holding them out to her, he said, "Here are the projection figures. And I want the prospectus on my desk by Thursday; Friday will be too late."

She snatched them out of his hand. "Don't get hoity-toity with me, kid. You just told me you don't even want it anymore. But I think you need it, so you'll get it."

As he watched her walk out of the office, her gray head high, her back as stiff as her upper lip, he wondered again when she had taken over. Here he was, head of a multimillion dollar corporation, with CEOs and politicians from every continent wooing him. He was rich, powerful, and, according to the society pages, a devastatingly handsome, highly eligible bachelor.

But he was completely browbeaten by his sixty-three-year-old, silver-haired secretary.

A 237-pound German secretary, he consoled himself, *with a nasty temper and massive biceps! Who wouldn't cower?*

It didn't make him less of a man, he figured; Fredl Knarr was just one helluva lot of woman.

But then, Rory O'Brien had always had a weakness for strong-willed women, of all ages, shapes, and sizes. He enjoyed the challenge.

He left his desk and walked over to the floor-to-ceiling windows in the corner of the room, overlooking the river to the east and downtown to the south. Rush-hour traffic was beginning, and streams of white headlights and red taillights flowed through Manhattan's streets and great avenues. Strings of blue lights outlined the massive bridges that connected Manhattan to Long Island and Brooklyn.

From the southern window, Rory could see the city haze settling over the Lower East Side, where he had been born and raised. His tough little neighborhood had been a world away from this uptown office. And Rory felt hardly any connection to that skinny, knobby-kneed kid who had run errands, collected soda bottles, and swept sidewalks for a quarter or two to buy a candy bar or comic book.

Now if he really wanted to, he could buy a confection manufacturer or a publishing company. But he knew those acquisitions wouldn't be as deeply satisfying as that Milky Way had been, savored on the tenement stoop on a sultry July afternoon, along with the latest issue of *Superman* or *The Flash*.

But candy and comics aside, those years hadn't been particularly good ones. Being Irish in a non-Irish neighborhood, with a father who personified the stereotype of a drinking, fighting Irishman, hadn't been easy. There hadn't been very many "O"s or "Mc"s in Rory's neighborhood, and the few who did live there were tormented with "mick" taunts, the insults often punctuated with hurled rocks or rotten fruit. Rory would have given the precious stash of comics under his bed and almost anything else he had to exchange his last name for Giovanni or Horowitz.

The passage of years and his own journey into adolescence and manhood hadn't improved things. His father had died of hard drink, his mother of hard work. But, unlike the cliche Irish Catholic family, Rory had been an only child. Other than an uncle in Ireland, whom he had only met twice—once when he was a child and again a couple of years ago—he had no family. And when he saw all the problems his friends and business associates had with their kin, he was thankful.

Rory tried not to remember those days. He felt far removed from that lonely child who had spent so many solitary hours with only pen-and-ink superheroes for companionship. He was his own man now, living in a far superior world of his own making. And his new life was a million miles from that shabby Lower East Side neighborhood . . . even if he could see the old one from his window.

He heard the phone ring in Fredl's office and he glanced at his watch. Five thirty-seven. Unless it was something important she would probably tell whomever was calling that he was gone for the day. Fredl had strict rules about personal time, hers *and* his. She told him it was for his own good, that he would work himself into the ground if she didn't watch out for him.

A couple of minutes later, he heard a soft, tentative knock on his door. Since when did Fredl the Hun knock before entering a room . . . especially softly?

It opened, and she stood there with a look on her face that told him instantly that something was wrong.

"What is it?" he asked, feeling time slow to a crawl, as it does at moments when a person knows they are about to hear something they don't want to know.

"It's a gentleman from Killarney . . . Ireland," she said, "a priest."

"I know where Killarney is," he replied, slightly miffed. "My family is from that area. But I said I'm putting the Irish project on hold for now. I don't want

you to pursue it any further even if you do think it's
a great—"

"The call isn't about the proposed plant, Rory,"
she said, her voice much more gentle than he had
heard it in a long while. "I think you'd better talk
to him. He's calling about your uncle Angus in Ireland—your father's twin brother. It seems he . . .
well, I'm sorry, dear, but he died."

TWO

Even the skies above were weeping for Angus O'Brien
as his friends carried his coffin to the cemetery on
the edge of the village. The soft rain of the morning had turned into a deluge, adding to the suffering
of the mourners. Some were proclaiming their mis-
eries more loudly than others.

"Isn't this a fine day, with the wind and the
weather, to be carryin' old Angus's carcass on foot
across the bloody countryside?" complained Gill
Doolin, one of the pallbearers. "Angus proves to be
a pain in the arse to the very end, insistin' on a traditional funeral march instead of a proper ride in an
automobile."

"Aye," agreed Tommy O'Sullivan, the village post-
man, who walked behind Gill at the rear of the coffin, "and I'll bet he's up there now arrangin' to have
thunder and lightnin' for the burial itself."

Gill cast a wary glance at the heavens and cleared

his throat. "Well, at least he's not too heavy, bag of bones that he was."

Walking beside them, Moya had ignored the protestations from the beginning of the journey, but her anger finally peaked. "Enough of that!" she said. "You two are lazy as a piper's little finger and as worthless besides. If that coffin's too much for either of you manly men to bear, step aside and I'll gladly take your place."

Neither fellow said anything discernible, but they grumbled into their collars.

Moya squared her shoulders and poked Gill roughly in the ribs with a stiff forefinger. "Angus O'Brien was as fine a man who ever trod the green earth," she said. "'Tis an honor to be carryin' him to his final restin' place. If you don't agree with me, be gone and let a woman take that handle."

As she had known he would, Gill declined. So did Tommy. The grasses of Ireland would be purple with pink stripes before an Irishman would surrender such a duty to one of the fairer sex. Especially if she was the type to remind him—and anyone else within hearing—of his shortcomings in the days to come.

Ahead Moya could see the stone wall that marked the boundary of the cemetery. Nearby, the gray stones of St. Bridget's Church rose in majestic grace. Nearly every citizen of Gormloch had been baptized in that building and had taken his or her first communion there beneath the stained-glass window of St. Bridget, who ministered to weary travelers. Those who were married had been joined in matrimony before the altar, and others who had passed on were buried beneath the thick green sod behind the church, within walls whose stones had been laid centuries before.

Little changed from generation to generation in Gormloch. Technological innovations, of course, altered daily life. Like the rest of the world, the Irish had their automobiles, appliances, televisions, and video games. Renting a movie on Friday night and bringing it home was as popular in Killarney, county Kerry, as in Hoboken, New Jersey.

But some things about the Irish didn't change. And Moya was grateful for that. Steeped in tradition, she and others like her clung to the old ways, the old attitudes, and the old rituals. Those customs provided a certain comfort at difficult times because of their familiarity.

Times like these. Times of sorrow.

They had arrived at the iron gates of the cemetery. Through the ornate metalwork Moya could see the freshly dug earth. The gravediggers had done their job well, and in a few minutes it would be time to say a final good-bye to her old friend.

The rain began to fall even harder and a roll of thunder shook the ground beneath their feet. Several children squealed. The keeners increased their volume twofold.

"What did I tell you?" Tommy said. "Thunder, it is . . . right on schedule. And the lightnin' will soon be arrivin', just you wait and see."

"Aye," Gill replied, wearily, "Old Angus always did have a flair for the dramatic!"

●　　●　　●

Rory O'Brien was sure he had experienced more turbulent trips aboard an airliner, but he couldn't exactly remember when. As the plane touched down on the tarmac at the airport in Shannon, county Clare, he breathed a sigh of relief. He wasn't crazy about flying anyway, and the storm that had been perched over the west coast of Ireland had tossed the plane about so vigorously that even the Irish passengers had quieted their chatter and discreetly crossed themselves just before landing.

They cheered as the plane came to a stop at the end of the runway . . . an even more vigorous accolade than the customary European clapping.

"We would like to welcome you to the Emerald Isle," announced a flight attendant with a lilting brogue. "A hundred thousand welcomes. Thank you for traveling with us and may you enjoy your stay."

"Enjoy my stay, harumph," Rory muttered as he jumped up from his seat, threw open the overhead compartment, and hauled out an overnight bag. Everyone else was taking their good old easy time about getting off the plane, so he brushed by them. If they had nowhere to go and nothing to do, fine. But he had a life. And after he paid his respects to his uncle, he would be headed back to New York to resume that life. A day, maybe two, should do it.

A couple of people looked mildly surprised as he pushed past them and out of the plane, climbing down the metal stairway to the tarmac. Then they appeared to dismiss his rudeness as they cheerfully continued their conversations with those around them.

Rory didn't notice and wouldn't have cared if he had. Maneuvering through the crowded streets of Manhattan at rush hour had robbed him of even the pretense of good manners. He didn't exactly push old ladies out of his path, but just about anything short of that was acceptable.

Once outside, he was pleased to see that the rain had stopped. He had to admit, he had never smelled air so sweet—fresh beyond description, fragrant with the scents of grasses, flowers, trees, and the rich earth herself. The gentle breeze that brushed his face and ruffled his hair stirred his emotions in a way he hadn't expected. The very asphalt beneath his feet seemed to radiate a vibrancy, a life force that he had never felt before.

It was almost like . . .

Like coming home.

Get real, he told himself as he hefted his overnight bag higher onto his shoulder and took off for the small terminal in the distance to collect the rest of his luggage. *Coming home, yeah, right. Travel brochure nonsense.*

Next he'd be seeing the ghosts of his ancient ancestors. A lot of blarney—that's all it was.

Overhead, dark clouds still heavy with rain swept by, breaking apart to allow golden rays of sunlight to stream through. The beams played upon the grassy pastures at the edges of the runways, setting the lush greenery aglow with an emerald flame. A thousand shades of green . . . more travel slogans . . . but oh, so, true.

Ireland was beautiful. Far more beautiful than

Rory had ever imagined it, although both of his parents had talked about the place his entire childhood. Having emigrated to the United States to escape financial hardship, they had never ceased to mourn the loss of their homeland. And young Rory had grown weary of hearing what a "glorious green land" they had left behind. But now, standing here on the airfield, the verdant wind in his face and sweet mother Ireland herself beneath his feet, he had to admit . . .

No, he didn't have to admit anything. This was no time to wax sentimental. If he didn't look out, he'd be crooning songs about a lad named Danny and playing a tin whistle.

Sappy nonsense aside, this was an eccentric, backward country full of poverty and suffering, and the sooner he could return to New York the better.

So there.

Moya had managed to keep her tears under control as the prayers were said at Angus's graveside. She held her emotions in check as the priest sprinkled the holy water on his coffin, as they lowered him below the sod, and as they all tossed wildflowers into the grave.

But when Conn Hallissey played his pipe, her tears mingled freely with the raindrops and streamed down her cheeks. The clear, sweet notes of "A Soldier's Song," Ireland's national anthem, filled the graveyard and touched the hearts of the mourners, just as Angus O'Brien had known it would when he had requested it be played at his burial.

Even Gill Doolin and Tommy O'Sullivan had forgotten about their discomforts and stood with bowed heads and somber faces. The village children hovered nearby, also uncharacteristically quiet, their hands full of wildflowers picked along the route to the graveyard.

Norah Delaney moved closer to Moya and slipped her arm around the younger woman's shoulders. "I know how much you loved him," she said. "And he loved you dearly. No daughter could have been better to him."

"He was a good father to me," Moya replied. " 'Tis unfortunate he had no children of his own."

As soon as Moya uttered the words, she wished she could take them back. It was well-known in Gormloch that Angus and Norah had been smitten with each other when they were teenagers. For years, everyone waited for Angus to pop the question . . . and no one more impatiently than Norah.

But after six years of courting, Norah found herself a ripe old age of twenty-one with no walks down the aisle in sight. So, when Michael Delaney had asked for her hand, she had given it to him, leaving Angus with a broken heart.

" 'Twas his own fault entirely that he had no children," Norah said with a sniff as she brushed her own tears away with the back of her hand. "If Angus died outside the arms of a loving family, he had only himself to thank."

Moya winced at Norah's candor. Norah Delaney might be known for her fine soda bread, her agile knitting fingers, and her down-to-earth practical wisdom but she wasn't known for her tact.

"Angus was content with his lot, such as it was," the old woman continued as they watched the gravediggers shovel the last of the soil into the grave. "He was satisfied to sit on his bum there by the fire, sipping his Guinness and telling his pagan tales."

"It was a good life," Moya interjected. "He was happy."

"He wasn't happy. He was satisfied. There's a difference."

"Satisfied is good."

"Happy is better."

Norah gave her a knowing, sideways glance, obviously aware that Moya was defending her own life as well as that of her deceased friend.

"Angus lived and died, sitting on that stool, reliving past glories," Norah continued. "Be sure you don't live and die the same way, Moya Mahoney. Life should be more than ancient stories."

Moya felt a pain go through her, as though Norah had reached inside her chest and squeezed her heart with a tight fist.

"You don't understand," she protested. "You don't know the joy of being a seanchai."

"Maybe not. But I know the joy of being a woman. Be sure you don't miss it, dear. Don't trade happiness for satisfaction. A hearth fire can only keep you so warm on a long winter night."

Moya walked away, effectively ending the conversation. But as the pipe continued to play one traditional song after another as the gravediggers finished their work, and the mourners left the ancient

cemetery, Moya could still hear Norah's words . . .
and she still felt that inexplicable ache in her heart.

"Where the hell is my limo? I've been waiting for
thirty . . . no"—Rory glanced at his watch—"thirty-
seven minutes and no one can even tell me if it's on
its way. What kind of a place are you running here?"

For emphasis, he thumped his fist on the airport
gift shop counter and the gentle-looking young
woman with cobalt blue eyes and a sweet face jumped
back two feet. "I'm very sorry, sir," she said. "But
this is a souvenir shop you're standin' in, and I know
nothing about a limo. You do mean a big, fancy car,
don't you?"

"Yes, a car." Rory tried to gather his last shred of
patience, but she was the fifth person he had questioned in the airport, and he was getting nowhere
fast. "My secretary called ahead and arranged a private automobile to take me to Killarney. Where is
it?"

"I know nothing of a car arrangement, sir. But I'd
be glad to find out what I can for you. If you'll just
wait a moment, I'll ask about and see if anyone—"

"No, don't bother. I already asked about and about
and everyone else is as clueless as you appear to be.
I'll keep asking. But I'm tired of lugging this suitcase around." He fished in his pocket, produced a
ten-dollar bill and shoved it at her. "Here, watch that
bag for me."

"Of course I'll watch it for you, sir." She glanced
down at the suitcase with wide-eyed innocence. "Exactly what is it going to do?"

He stared at her, unsure if his leg was being yanked a bit or if she was serious. "I don't want it to walk off," he said.

"Here?" She shook her head and clucked her tongue. "You're in Shannon, sir. Ye could leave your belongings out there in the middle of the floor for two weeks and no one would lay a hand on them . . . except perhaps to sweep around them."

"Yeah, well, just watch the bag for me and don't let anything happen to it. It's Louis Vitton."

As Rory left the shop, he thought he heard her murmur something like, "That lad Louis makes fine luggage . . . takes more than a suitcase to make a gentleman."

Ignoring her, he strode back into the terminal's main large room and spotted a big, burly fellow in a blue uniform that was two sizes too small across the belly. "Are you a cop?" Rory asked as he hurried to him. "Because if you are, I have a problem."

The man grinned, showing jagged teeth that appeared to have been rearranged by violent means sometime in the past. "A problem, have you? Well, I'm no garda, but I'll assist you if I can. Tell me what's wrong in your corner of the world."

"I was supposed to have a"—he swallowed the word "limousine" and decided to set his sights much lower—"a car of some sort to take me to Killarney this afternoon. And nobody here seems to know anything about it."

"Ah, why didn't you say so? I happen to know exactly what happened to your car."

Rory waited for three seconds but received only a smirk and a twitch of the fellow's right eyebrow.

"Well? Are you going to keep it to yourself, or are you going to tell me?"

"I am. 'Twas Liam Riley who had intended to give you a ride in his lorry, but—"

"A *lorry*? You mean a truck?"

"Aye. Liam delivers milk, he does, and a truck's what he's drivin' these days, ever since he—"

"Never mind. A truck is fine. Where is he?"

"He's off to Limerick. His wife's youngest sister delivered a baby, so she did, in the wee hours of the night just this last evening. Liam had to take his wife there to help. Then, of course, he had to stay and down a few pints with the lads, celebrate the new arrival and all."

"Of course," Rory replied dryly. "Which leaves me stranded here in the middle of this godfor-saken . . ." His voice faded away to a dull rumble as he cursed Liam Riley and his pints.

"If it's transport you're needin', I can be of service to you." The man visibly swelled with pride, nearly popping the already strained middle button on his uniform shirt.

"Don't tell me you've got a *lorry*, too. What do you deliver? Cow manure?"

As soon as the words had escaped his lips, Rory regretted having said them. He could tell by the hurt and angry glint in the man's eye that his insult had found its mark. And even if he was in a rotten mood, he had no reason to lash out at someone who had just offered to help him.

"Sorry," he said, uttering the word in typical New York fashion—one curt syllable. "It's just that I'm having a lousy day, and I'm late for my uncle's funeral and—"

"Well, why didn't you say so?" The man's face softened. "It's a grievin' man you are. Now that explains your foul temper and your bad manners. But your problems are over, sir. Just board yonder bus, and I'll be drivin' you to Killarney before another hair on your head turns gray. I'm truly sorry for the loss of your uncle. I'm sure he was a fine man."

Rory was taken aback by the bus driver's seeming sincerity, and he felt like an even bigger jerk for having snapped at him. And at everyone in the terminal, for that matter.

"When does the bus leave?" he asked.

"Oh, sooner or later. Once we've a few souls aboard we'll think of takin' off."

Think of taking off? It didn't sound too promising, but—

"I'll get my suitcase," Rory said eagerly, not wanting to be the cause of any delay.

The driver gave him a wide, jagged-toothed smile. "You do that, sir. But take your time, sir. Slow down; you're in Ireland now."

As Rory hurried back to the gift shop, he made a mental note to be kind to the girl behind the counter. She had been nice, and he had been gruff with her. Maybe he'd give her an extra ten.

"There you are, sir," she said, pointing to his suitcase which was, as she had predicted, exactly where he had left it. "Safe as a babe, lyin' beneath the Virgin's picture."

"Ah, yeah. Thanks. Here you go."

He held a bill out to her and was surprised when she didn't take it. Instead, she pressed the money he had previously given her back into his palm.

"You needn't pay a person to do such a small favor," she said, her soft tone gently reproving him. "Kindnesses shouldn't be bought and sold."

Rory didn't know what to say. He felt the blood rising in his face, turning his cheeks hot.

"You're right," he said when he finally found his voice. "I suppose where I'm from, courtesy is bought and sold."

She smiled sweetly. "But you're in Ireland now."

"Yes," he said. "So I've been reminded . . . quite recently, in fact."

Rory was glad he had his own teeth in his head and wasn't wearing dentures. Considering the bone-shattering bumps in the road, false teeth would have long tumbled out of his mouth and into the bus aisle.

A tired young woman with four children who all appeared to be under the age of five chased a merry little boy from the front of the bus to the back, crying out, "Michael, Michael, come to meself, love. It's three-quarters dead I am already and you pushin' me into the grave with all this misbehavin'!"

Rory decided to do her a favor and caught the chubby-cheeked toddler as he raced by his seat at the back of the bus. He held the squirming child until his mother could retrieve him and received a smear of melted chocolate on the front of his shirt for his troubles.

"Thank you, mister," the young woman said as she hefted the boy into her arms and dabbed at his grubby face with a lace-edged kerchief. "He's a good lad, really, just full o' the divil."

"I was just like him at that age," Rory told her. "He'll grow out of it."

The woman sighed. "Aye, but when? When will he become a respectable fellow and not cause his mother so much sufferin'?"

Rory grinned. "When he's about eighty-two."

She laughed wearily. "Ah, somethin' to look forward to. And I thought all was lost."

As she and a squirming Michael returned to their seats at the front of the bus, the vehicle rounded a curve and came to a rather abrupt stop.

Rory fought down his agitation as they waited . . . and waited. Finally, he couldn't contain his impatience any longer. "What's happening up there?" he shouted to the driver. "Why aren't we going?"

"'Tis an old cow in the road," was the driver's somewhat dry reply. "Not to fret. We're sure to be on our way soon."

Rory grumbled a few New York–style curses and drummed his fingers on the seat beside him. He glanced at his watch. Six minutes. Six minutes because of a stupid cow.

"I'd be glad to move her out of your way if you like," he offered in a less than generous tone.

"Naw, that's okay. I wouldn't want to disturb a

passenger," the driver responded. "If she doesn't move along soon, I'll get out and give her a bit of a nudge meself."

"A bit of a nudge, my . . ." Rory caught the eye of the tired young mother, who had turned in her seat and was staring at him. He choked back the rest of his words and was instantly rewarded by having the bus lurch forward and continue its journey.

At this rate, he could have walked to Killarney and arrived sooner than this heap of rusted metal was going to deliver him. He thought longingly of the fast, efficient trains of New York's rapid transit systems and yearned for home.

But he had to admit, staring out the window at the passing countryside, that the view here was a lot better than the black tunnels of the subway. The air smelled cleaner and the people were far kinder. He had to admit he rather liked that lilting brogue, such a contrast to the nasal twang of New York.

And the green. The rolling hillsides were so green they almost hurt the eyes, a verdant patchwork of fields divided by gray stone walls and dotted with mossy woods where wild rhododendrons grew in abandon along with patches of bluebells that clustered among heels of clover in the shade.

The farther south they traveled toward Killarney, the thicker those forests became and the more dramatic the hillsides. That feeling of coming home grew stronger and stronger in Rory, until it was almost a hunger . . . a need he had never even known he had was finally being satisfied.

But then the bus stopped again.

The sweetness of the moment evaporated. Nostalgia was replaced by agitation.

"What's the problem this time?" he shouted to the front of the bus. "Don't tell me there's another old cow in the road?"

He saw the driver glance up and their eyes met in the rearview mirror. The man's mouth pulled into a mischievous smirk. "Noooo," he said coolly, "'tis the same ol' one."

After the burial, Moya had declined a dozen hospitable invitations, asking her to join friends at the pub and others in their homes to share some potables and their sorrows. The twins' mother, Deirdre Kissane, had asked her to come home with their family for a bit of board game playing, one of Moya's favorite activities. Conn Hallissey had insisted that a little music and dancing at the pub would cure her sorrow—or at least take the sharp edge off it. Even Father Shea had invited her to the rectory for a spot of tea and some scones.

Everyone knew how much Angus had meant to her, and none envied her the task of going home to the very place where he had died.

But Moya felt more comfortable in her own house, a modest bed and breakfast establishment, than any other place on earth—except maybe in front of the hearth at Lios na Daoine Sidhe. With only four bedrooms to rent and two bathrooms, her B & B was no great moneymaker, but it was clean and cozy, and Moya was known throughout the area for her soft feather beds and the quality of her baking.

It was in one of those bedrooms that Angus O'Brien had come to stay after his seventy-fourth birthday. He had slipped in the mud at the river's bank while fishing and broken his hip. The village doctor had proclaimed him incapable of fending for himself any longer, and Moya had offered him the room.

At the time, the arrangement had been considered temporary, a few months, until his hip was sufficiently healed. But time passed and months had turned into years. Angus the old bachelor and Moya, who had been orphaned at a young age, had found a family in each other. Even if it was a small family with only two members, it was the difference between eating supper in solitude or having company, in being able to share the day's joys and sorrows with someone who cared.

Now, as darkness arrived and the rain began to fall even heavier than before, pelting against the roof, Moya was alone again . . . without Angus or a single boarder.

But that was the way she wanted it, at least for tonight. With a fire burning brightly on the parlor hearth, her most comfortable easy chair drawn close to its warmth, and a hot toddy fortified with a healthy dose of strong Irish whiskey, she was prepared to experience her grief to the fullest. She would embrace this sadness as freely as the happiness that Fate offered. It was all part of being alive; only those who loved could truly grieve.

When a knock sounded on the front door, she rose from her wingback chair and resentfully trudged to answer it. She really didn't want a boarder tonight, or company of any kind.

And the last person she wanted to see was—

"Gill Doolin, why are you here?" she asked, unsuccessfully trying to hide her irritation.

"Why, I came here to check on you, lass, to see how you're doin'. I know it's not been an easy day for you, and I thought you might like some company."

"No, Gill, it's not company I'm after. To be honest, I was enjoyin' a bit of solitude."

As soon as the words had passed her lips, Moya felt ashamed. Gill was a sorry sight, indeed, standing there, rain pouring off the bill of his hat, his coat soaked through after only a short walk from the pub next door. The only kind thing would be to invite him in.

"Step inside, Gill," she said, opening the door wider. "I'm sorry I snapped at you—been a long day, you know. Now come out of the rain before you drown. But be sure to stand there on the rug. I'll not have you drippin' on my newly waxed floor."

With an eagerness to please that touched her heart, he entered and stood obediently on the oval rag rug just inside the door. "Also, I wanted to offer my condolences," he said, stammering a bit and rolling the rim of his hat between his fingers. "And . . . ah. . . . well . . . I was wondering if . . . ah . . ."

"Yes, what is it, Gill?" she said, fighting the urge to shake the information out of him. "What did you really come over here for? Speak your mind."

"I was wondering if I'd be havin' a job there in

the pub, now that ol' Angus is collectin' his heavenly reward."

"Now, how should I know that?"

"I thought maybe he had said something to you before he died. Maybe he had mentioned whether he was leaving the pub to someone." He stared down at the rug and his feet. "Someone . . . like you."

Moya was surprised how her heart seemed to leap at his words—words she had thought herself, but had never heard spoken aloud. Angus had died without heirs, and she had been his closest friend. He knew how much the pub meant to her. Surely no one loved the place more. Who else would keep the traditional atmosphere the way she would? No one.

But they had never spoken of such things. And Angus had passed on without making his wishes clear.

"I don't know, Gill," she said. "To be honest, I'm still grieving and don't want to think about it tonight."

He looked miserably embarrassed, twisting his hat and shuffling his feet. "No, of course not. I'm sorry, Moya. I should have kept to meself tonight and not bothered you. It's just that with jobs so scarce around here, and me wife dead and gone, and with a son to raise by meself, I was worried that . . ."

She reached out and patted his broad shoulder. "Please don't be embarrassed. You've no reason at all to apologize for asking. I'm just sorry I have no answer for you."

An unsettling sense of apprehension stole over Moya, dampening her already sodden mood. She sighed and shook her head. "We'll have to wait and see what tomorrow brings, Gill. Only time will tell what's to become of Lios na Daoine Sidhe."

Moya wasn't the only one whose mood was soggy. Rory's was, too . . . as well as his head, and his coat, and his feet. And the suitcase he was carrying was getting heavier with every step.

He had taken a lot of steps. In the dark. In the rain. The bus had dropped him on the highway, more than two and a half miles from the village of Gormloch. The road he was hiking was no great shakes, either—dark and full of mud puddles so deep that when he stepped in them, the water slopped over the tops of his shoes.

After traveling for hour upon miserable hour, he was half-frozen and three-quarters starved. He'd had nothing to eat, other than a mangled chocolate bar, offered by the young mother on the bus. His blood sugar was nearly as low as his spirits.

And it was all for nothing. He hadn't yet reached his destination, and his uncle's funeral was over. By now, Angus O'Brien was six feet under.

So much for paying respects to his last paternal relative.

Tomorrow morning, when the rain stopped—if it ever did—he would go out to the cemetery, say a few prayers if he could remember them, put some flowers on the grave, and head back to New York. With any luck he'd be back in Manhattan in time to have dinner at a decent restaurant.

But for now all he wanted was a place with a roof that didn't leak, some dry towels, and a bed that was clean. He'd skip the shower. Considering that he was soaked through to his skin—every single inch of his skin—it seemed redundant.

Damned, stupid, backward, *wet* country.

Thank heavens his people had emigrated! And not a generation too soon!

Moya knew she wasn't ready to go into Angus's room yet, but she couldn't help herself. As soon as Gill had left, she walked down the hallway to the room at the back of the house, Angus's home away from home. His true home had always been Lios na Daoine Sidhe.

The moment she opened the door and walked inside, before she even flipped on the light switch, she smelled the lingering fragrance of his blackberry tobacco. She would always associate that sweet aroma with the seanchai and his ubiquitous pipe.

She flipped on the light and stood, silently absorbing the vibrancy of the room. Filled with the mementos of a long life, the room reflected the personality of its former occupant. The bookshelves were spilling over with books by his favorite authors: William Butler Yeats, James Joyce, and George Bernard Shaw. Yellowed photos of old friends and relatives hung on the walls, along with prints of paintings by Irish artists: James McNeill Whistler and Philip Gray.

In the corner of the room, his small bed was covered with a quilt, handmade by his sister-in-law before her death, bearing an intricate Celtic pattern of spirals and scrolls.

On his nightstand stood a small wooden sculpture, carved in a form from Celtic mythology, the Night Mare. Moya walked over to the statue and allowed her fingers to skim its smooth surface. According to legend, a person saw the Night Mare riding wild through their dreams on the evening before their death. She wondered if Angus had seen that haunted specter the night before his passing—a woman on horseback, her hair streaming behind her, caught in the night wind, an owl perched on her shoulder keeping vigilant watch, and a wolf following close behind at her horse's heels.

Angus had been too sick to speak of dreams, good or bad.

Next to the statue on his nightstand lay a small wooden chest with a parquet inlaid top. Moya steeled herself and slowly opened it. Inside were his blackberry tobacco and briar pipe. She reached for the pipe, but her hand froze when she saw an envelope made of pale blue parchment, there on top of the tobacco pouch.

What was this?

She had cleaned his pipe and replaced it in the box hundreds of times, but she had never seen anything else in here. Angus had always been quite particular about having a place for everything and everything stowed safely and predictably in that place.

Her fingers trembled slightly as she lifted the envelope from the box.

Across it was written in Angus's sprawling hand:

To be opened immediately upon my death

Moya felt the strength go out of her legs and she sat down quickly on the edge of the bed with its Celtic patterned quilt. Carefully she opened the envelope. The odor of the tobacco seemed overwhelming, wafting from the open box, and she could hear the ticking of his mantel clock on his small desk by the window.

She took a folded sheet of paper from inside and slowly spread it across her lap. First she scanned the words written there, anxious to know the letter's message as quickly as possible.

But she couldn't believe what she had just read.

So she read it again, more slowly. And as Angus's words found their way into her mind, time seemed to stop completely.

"No," she whispered. "Oh, Angus, why would you . . . ? How could you . . . ?"

The letter fluttered to the floor at her feet. She leaned forward, placed her elbows on her knees, covered her face, and began to cry.

Rory had thought his long, wet journey was finished when he walked through the door of the pub, but the occupants had sent him on yet another trek to find the elusive dry bed. Fortunately, it was only to the bed and breakfast establishment next door.

The house was Georgian with straight, formal lines, but its gray, stone walls were softened by the vines of wisteria that climbed them, and the golden light streaming through the delicate lace curtains at the windows.

Listening to his wet shoes squeak with every step,

he hurried up the cobblestone path that lay between carefully trimmed hedges to the front door that was painted a cheerful, cornflower blue.

"Finally," he muttered as he set his heavy suitcase on the front step and pounded on the door with the large brass knocker. He flexed his hand, certain that his fingers would never work correctly again. "If I'd had to lug that damned thing another step, I would have left it in the middle of the road, just to see if it would be there two weeks later."

He had to knock twice more before a porch lamp came on, bathing him in soft yellow light. The door opened and—from what he could tell, squinting through the pouring rain—an exceptionally attractive young woman appeared.

At least, he was sure she would have been attractive if her eyes hadn't been full of tears and swollen nearly closed and her nose bright red. But grief-stricken as she seemed to be and as drenched as he was, Rory still had the presence of mind to notice that her silhouette was shapely and her auburn hair glistened like copper in the golden lamplight.

"You poor dear," she exclaimed, throwing the door wide open. "You're drowned entirely! Whatever are you doin' out there in the rain?"

A pretty face, a friendly voice, the interior of a dry home in sight. Things were definitely looking brighter by the moment.

"I've traveled all the way from New York today, to attend my uncle's funeral, but I got here late and—"

"Your uncle, you say?" Her voice sounded a tad less friendly. Her pretty mouth curved downward.

"Yes, my uncle, Angus O'Brien."

Yes, she was growing less cheerful by the moment and the rain was beginning to fall even harder and colder than before. Rory didn't understand.

"And your name is . . . ?" she asked.

Something told him he was blowing this, but he wasn't sure how. Could it be she knew his uncle and didn't like the old guy?

"My name? Oh, it's Rory O'Brien and if you don't mind, I'd like to rent a room from you tonight, because—"

"Rory O'Brien! Couldn't wait until the corpse was cold, could you?"

"Wh . . . what?"

"You greedy devil, remove your mangy arse from my property this instant or I'll set my dogs on you, I will!"

Before Rory could collect his wits to answer her strange accusation, she slammed the door in his face, missing his nose by only an inch. The wind of it nearly knocked him backward.

He could hear her muttering on the other side of the door as she walked away, "Why, the bloody nerve of some people! Don't have the manners the good God gave a mule!"

To add insult to injury, she even turned off the porch lamp, leaving him in the darkness and in the rain.

Again.

Three

Moya had only taken five or six steps away from the door when her conscience assaulted her. *You wouldn't leave a toothless, three-legged hound out in that storm,* she told herself, *let alone an O'Brien.* No matter how she felt about the man outside her door, she at least had to offer him shelter from the elements.

By the time she made it back to the door and opened it, he had walked halfway down her sidewalk toward the street. From the sagging of his shoulders and the weariness of his step, she could see he was just about destroyed entirely.

"O'Brien," she called out. "Rory O'Brien."

He turned to face her, but in the dark she couldn't discern his expression.

"What?" he called out with an abruptness and rude tone seldom heard in county Kerry.

Most of her remorse and compassion evaporated, but she couldn't bring herself to slam the door in anyone's face twice within three minutes. Irish folk were civil, whether Yanks were or not.

"Come in this house this minute," she yelled, like a shrewish mother summoning a wayward child. "You'll be sick as a goat if you trot about in the rain like that. Get yourself inside!"

He hesitated only a second, then hurried up the walk, his step much livelier than before, his formerly hunched back straight. When he met her at the doorway, she was surprised that he was so large. She was a stately lass, herself, but he was taller still, with shoulders so broad they seemed to fill her narrow doorway.

His hair fell in dark, streaming strands across his eyes . . . eyes that were a brilliant shade of cobalt blue seldom found outside Ireland or Scandinavia. He bore little resemblance to the O'Briens Moya had known, but she had seen the picture on Angus's wall of his sister-in-law, and Moya knew that Rory O'Brien was the image of his departed mother.

He pushed past her and dropped his soaked suitcase with a thud on her hardwood floor. Biting her lower lip, she calmly, deliberately picked up the case and moved it to the rug just inside the front door. Then, just as calmly, but firmly, she took his forearm and guided him to stand on the rug beside his suitcase.

Despite his lack of manners and the fact that they weren't getting off to a grand start, Moya was acutely aware of Rory O'Brien: his dark good looks, his impressive size, the masculine scent of his damp, leather coat and an underlying hint of expensive aftershave.

Leading him to the rug, her hand on his forearm, she was far more conscious of the simple contact than seemed reasonable. And she was fairly certain by the glimmer in his eyes that he was equally mindful of her.

"So, what made you decide to let me in?" he said, swiping his hand across his face to remove some of the water.

"I wouldn't leave a dumb beast out in weather like that," she said.

He scowled down at her. "It wasn't so bad," he said, raising his chin a notch. "Just a little rain."

"Aye, well . . . you didn't appear to be making a holiday of it," she said. "I've seen cats fished out of the river after fallin' in who were drier and in a more cheerful mood than you appeared to be outside me door."

He didn't reply, just continued to glare at her . . . and drip water on her rug.

"Whatever the circumstances," she said, " 'tis inside you are now, and I suppose you'll be wantin' a room for the night."

"If it isn't too much trouble," he mumbled.

"Aye, 'tis a bit of a hardship, but I'll bear up."

He stared at her, trying to look tough, but he was shivering badly and his skin was an unhealthy shade of blue-gray.

"Wait right there," she said. "I'll get you some towels and something dry to wear. We'll have you warm and sitting by the fire in no time, Rory O'Brien."

He smiled and she had to admit, when he wasn't

frowning, he was as handsome a lad as she had ever laid eyes on.

"Thank you, Miss Mahoney."

"Me name isn't Ma-*ho*-ney," she said, imitating his accent on the second syllable. " 'Tis *Ma*-honey. And you must say the 'a' very soft, like ah-h-h. Moya Ma-a-honey."

Unconsciously, she had leaned closer to him and found her face only inches from his. Again, she was all too aware of him, of the color of his eyes, of the fullness of his lips and the clean line of his jaw.

Yes, much too aware.

He was Angus O'Brien's nephew, Rory. The worm, the parasite. To the devil with him and all thieving opportunists.

May he roast on the Old Horned One's spit for a thousand years with all his enemies lined up for the privilege of turning him, she thought.

And with that silent but vehement curse, she turned and hurried away to fetch the towels, leaving him standing there, dripping on her rug with an aggravated and confused look on his face.

Moya returned a moment later with an armload of white, fluffy towels and a man's red-and-blue plaid flannel robe. She laid the fresh linens on a piecrust table near the doorway and held the robe out to Rory.

"Crawl out of those wet clothes straightaway," she told him, "and I'll wring them out and hang them up. With any luck at all, they'll be mostly dry come morning."

"Crawl out . . . ? You mean you want me to strip down right here, in the hallway?" he asked indignantly.

"Doesn't seem too burdensome a request," she replied. "You don't appear to be the overly modest type to me. And besides, no one will be watching. I'll be putting on the teapot and those walking down the road won't see you through the window. They've more important things to do, like get home before they're drowned."

His frown gradually turned into a mischievous grin that made him, if possible, even more cursedly appealing. "It doesn't appear that you're the overly modest type yourself, Miss *Ma*-honey," he said. "Ordering a man to get naked in your front hallway isn't very maidenly."

"Maidenly, my arse." She gave a contemptuous sniff. "I've no time for such nonsense. The sight of a man exposin' his . . . ignorance . . . is hardly something that impresses the likes of me. Now, do you want something hot to thaw those frozen bones of yours, or do you want to spend the night standin' there turnin' blue with your teeth chatterin' and your knees knocking against each other?"

He snatched the robe from her hand and began to peel off his jacket. "Thank you," he said with limited enthusiasm. "And where would you like me to put my wet clothes?"

She handed him a plastic garbage bag. "Just deposit them in here and I'll deal with them properly once we have you settled by the fire."

"Settled by the fire . . ." His face softened at the thought. "Ah, that sounds good. Thank you, Moya Mahoney."

Confused by his sudden courtesy, she turned on her heel and strode away toward the kitchen. "No problem, Mr. O'Brien," she called over her shoulder. "Like I said, I would do it for anyone."

"Even a dumb beast," he called back.

"Aye, especially a poor, dumb beast."

Rory couldn't recall when he had been so nonplussed by a female's behavior. By anyone's behavior, for that matter. Half an hour ago she had slammed the door in his face, leaving him in the darkness and the rain. Now he was sitting in a comfortable wingback chair, drawn close to a hearth that glowed with a warm turf fire, dressed in a snug flannel robe with a thick knitted coverlet tucked around his legs and feet.

Ten minutes ago, she had placed a large mug of lamb stew in his hand, and now she was off in the kitchen, rattling about, making him some sort of concoction which she swore would chase away any sign of a pending cold.

No wonder the Irish had a reputation for being temperamental and unpredictable. Especially redheaded ones.

He glanced around the room, which was modestly but tastefully furnished with antiques from the Victorian era. In its day, the house had been a fine one.

To be honest, although he preferred the clean, sharp lines of contemporary furniture, he would have been happy to have owned an apartment on Fifth Avenue in Manhattan so pleasantly decorated.

A Tiffany-style dragonfly lamp glowed atop an oak table, lending the room a cozy glow with its emerald and ruby glass. The door of the large armoire on the opposite side of the room was slightly opened and inside he could see a television set, a VCR, and a stereo. The sofa had a diamond-tucked back and claw feet, but despite its formal style, its cushions looked thick and inviting. An old leather chest with brass strappings served as a coffee table and on it was a bowl of fruit and a stack of books—classics that included American authors as well as Irish in the eclectic selection.

The smell of citrus and spices drifted out to him from the kitchen and he wondered what sort of potion she was brewing. If it was half as good as the stew it would be tasty as well as rejuvenating.

He didn't have to wait long for the answer. She entered the parlor with a copper tray, upon which sat another steaming earthenware mug. Beside the mug was a dainty China cup decorated with red roses and swirling pink and gold ribbons.

"I'm fond of drinking from a pretty cup meself," she said as she set the tray on the leather chest. "But I know you gentlemen prefer a big, manly mug so you can wrap your fingers through the handle."

"Yeah, I'm not much for sticking out my pinkie." He handed her the empty soup mug, took the second one from her, and stared down at its contents as wonderful aromas tickled his nose. "What is this?" he asked.

"An old, tried and true remedy for the chill called whiskey punch. 'Tis fine Irish whiskey, mixed with hot water, a spoonful of sugar, and tiny bit of lemon juice, topped with a slice of an orange that's dotted with cloves. It'll get your blood flowin' sure."

"I'll bet it will." He took a sip and felt an instant fire trace its way from his lips to somewhere deep in his belly. The warmth quickly spread into his arms and legs, then even to his fingertips, tingling as it went.

"Well?" she said as she took her decidedly feminine cup from the tray and sat on the end of the sofa nearest him and the fire. "What do you think?"

"I think I'll be completely wasted in about ten minutes or less," he said. "How much of that fine Irish whiskey did you pour in here?"

"Twice as much as I put in mine," she replied, then sipped from her own cup.

"You're having the same thing? I thought this was just for someone who's been in the cold rain."

She sighed. "I was in the rain meself earlier today. And the chill of it is still with me. I'm afraid it'll take more than a hot toddy to warm me heart this sad evening."

Suddenly, Rory registered the reason for her swollen eyes and red nose. "Ah, you were at the funeral," he said, "my uncle's funeral."

"I was." She looked away, staring into the fire. "Pity you weren't," she added softly.

He heard the disapproval in her voice and bristled at the unspoken criticism. "Hey, it's not like I didn't try to get here in time," he said. "I hopped on a plane as soon as I heard he had passed away, and I've been traveling ever since. The airline connections stunk, the car I had arranged for me didn't show, the bus I took from Shannon stopped every three feet to pick up somebody with fifteen children or because a herd of sheep was blocking its path. I was fit to be tied, but it didn't do any good. The more I complained, the more reasons the driver found to stop or slow down."

Moya said nothing, but brushed her hand over her mouth to hide a small grin.

"I came all the way here just to attend the funeral," he added, "had a hellish experience, and still didn't make it."

She studied him with those intense eyes, which he could now see were a beautiful shade of deep green. Although he had always fancied darkly tanned skin, he found her ivory complexion, dotted with golden freckles, most becoming and intriguing. He only wished he could read the thoughts behind her enigmatic expression.

"So, 'twas only for the funeral you came and nothing more?" she asked carefully.

"Why else would I come?"

She shrugged. "People have many reasons for the things they do. I was only inquiring after yours."

Reasons? Yes, he supposed he did have a few reasons besides just attending the funeral out of respect. More than anything, Rory had wanted to see his uncle's face one more time. The face that was so very like his own father's. Now both faces were gone forever.

He'd been too late . . . again.

Perhaps he had made this ill-fated pilgrimage as some sort of atonement for not having attended his father's funeral. At the time of his dad's death, he had stopped seeing the old man. Since he hadn't communicated with his father in years, Rory had felt it would be hypocritical to attend his wake or funeral. But now, in retrospect, he regretted not going. Somehow he had hoped to even the score by traveling so far to attend his uncle's service.

Or maybe he had wanted to see Ireland, this mystical, magical, emerald island he had heard so much about.

No. Forget that theory, he told himself. Whatever the reasons, surely that wasn't one of them.

"Angus O'Brien was my last living relative," he said simply. "Coming to his funeral seemed like a good idea at the time."

She took another long drink from her cup. "And who was it that told you about Angus passing?" she asked, not meeting his eyes as she stared into the flames of the turf fire.

"Someone named Father Shea called me at my office. I don't know how he knew where to reach me. Angus must have told him sometime before he . . . you know . . . passed away."

"And is that all the good father said to you?" she asked, still looking at the fire. "Just that Angus had gone to meet his Maker?"

"That was the gist of it," he said.

She seemed to have something on her mind but was reluctant to say what. It was driving Rory crazy wondering. He was the straightforward type who would rather be told bluntly what was up rather than waste time and energy on guessing. "Was there anything else he should have told me?"

She set her cup on the tray, and Rory was curious to see that her hand was trembling ever so slightly. What did she have to be nervous about? Surely nothing having to do with him.

"Never mind me," she replied. "I was just wonderin' what he said to you, that's all. How are you feelin'? A bit more like yourself, I trust?"

"Much better," he said with deep sincerity born of pleasant intoxication. "I'm a new man thanks to your hot whiskey punch, Miss Mahoney. I thought I'd never be warm again, but I'm cozy and toasted . . . I mean, toasty."

She chuckled. "I suspect you're right on both counts, Mr. O'Brien. Is there anything else I can get for you?"

"Actually, I was wondering . . . Did my uncle leave anything behind?"

Her eyes grew wider. "Anything behind?"

"Yes. I'd like to take home some memento from him, some small personal thing that he touched every day, that was important to him."

"A small thing, you say." She looked strangely relieved. "You're just after a wee something you could carry with you on the plane?"

"That's right. You know, to remember him by."

She thought for a long time before answering him.

"Your uncle was a sentimental man, Mr. O'Brien, and he had kept many reminders of the people and events in his life. You're welcome to look through his room and choose whatever you like to take home as your memento."

"His room? My uncle lived here in this house . . . with you?"

She raised one eyebrow a notch. "He was one of my permanent boarders, sir. Occupied the downstairs bedroom at the back of the house. I nursed him after he broke his hip, and once he recovered, he chose to stay."

"I can see why. It's a very nice place. Do you manage it for someone?"

"I do. I manage it for meself. I certainly wouldn't work this hard for anyone else."

She gave him a sly smile. "You look surprised, Mr. O'Brien. Surely women in the States make money on their own."

"Yes, but I didn't think that women in Ireland—"

"Yes? Finish your sentence . . . if you dare."

Rory could tell that no matter what he said from this point on, he was already in trouble. Might as well dive in with both feet. "I guess I thought that women in Ireland didn't own property. At least, not most women."

"Is that what you thought, Mr. O'Brien? Well, I guess you have a lot to learn about Ireland and Irish women. From the ancient days, when Ireland was under Brehon law, the old celtic order, a woman was entitled to own property, to divorce her husband if the man was too lazy or too fat to perform his husbandly duties to her, and she could keep half of everything after tellin' him to remove his shiftless backside from her doorway. Irish women have always had plenty o' spark in them, never you mind."

He grinned, enjoying her spirited reply and the gleam in her eye. In that moment, Rory decided he wouldn't want to be on the bad side of Moya Mahoney; but he wouldn't mind being on her good side, either.

"So, you're a lass like those in the olden days," he said teasingly.

"I am," she replied with all seriousness. "And you'll do well to remember that. I've worked hard since I was fifteen years old, did without a lot of things that girls my age enjoyed. I saved my money and bought this house. It was a dreary pile of boards when I got it, but I put it back in fine form, I did. And no man in this village or the next helped me do it. I wielded hammer, saw, and paintbrush all by meself."

"Really?"

She shrugged. "The men didn't make any offers, and I didn't ask for favors."

"So you don't have a husband or a boyfriend stashed in an upstairs bedroom?"

A slight blush colored her cheeks, and she quickly took a sip of her toddy. "I've no husband, nor do I want one. And we Irish girls don't 'stash' a man in an upstairs bedroom, or a downstairs one, either, for that matter, as casually as some American ladies do."

He laughed, feeling the glow of the whiskey and the banter. "I'll remember that."

"See that you do, Mr. O'Brien. We'll be gettin' along far better if you make the effort."

For the next hour, they sat in front of the fire, chatting about life in the village of Gormloch and living in the city of Manhattan. Moya watched every word that came out of her mouth, afraid she would say the wrong thing. She couldn't tell for sure how much he knew about the contents of that letter she had found. And she certainly wasn't going to be the one to tell him.

Well, maybe she was. But she intended to sleep on it that night before deciding.

But "sleeping" on it was the last thing Moya was able to do that night. Suddenly her mattress seemed full of pebbles and thorns. No matter how she lay, she couldn't find a comfortable position. Her flannel nightgown twisted around her like the serpent of Eden and even the slight murmuring of the river in the distance sounded like a freight train coming through her bedroom.

Finally, she threw the quilt aside and got out of bed. Slipping on a chenille robe and a pair of fleece-lined slippers, she walked over to the window, drew the lace curtains aside, and stared outside at the silver-and-black landscape. The rain and the clouds had blown away, leaving a clear sky. The moon was nearly full and its light glistened on the purple mountains in the distance, clearly outlining the crooked peak of Carrantuohill, the highest point of Macgillicuddy's Reeks. To her right lay the river, a ribbon of moonbeams lacing its way between forests and lush meadows.

To her left, in the center of one of those fields, stood a small, perfectly rounded forest with several rings of deep ditches surrounding the copse of trees. Lios na Daoine Sidhe, the ringed fort of the Daoine Sidhe, the fairy people. It was this ancient, sacred site that the pub had been named for. Centuries ago, long before the events of humans were scribed upon paper, the inhabitants of Eire's land had lived in those fortresses, sheltered from the elements by the trees, while the deep trenches protected them from human and animal invaders.

But the modern Irish had chosen not to trespass on those archaic sites, out of respect for their antiquity but also out of fear of retribution from whatever spirits might still inhabit the areas within those ringed boundaries.

Whether they would admit to being superstitious or not, few of Moya's neighbors would have ventured into one of the fairy forts, as they called them, and none of them would have gone there at night. But Moya had gone a few times, and she had felt a presence there, to be sure, but it seemed benign, older than time and wiser than the ages.

"What should I do?" she whispered to any spirits, Christian or pagan, that might be listening. "Should I tell him about the letter, or try to forget I ever found it?"

The same answer echoed around her and through

her—from the fairy fort, from the moonlit heavens above, and from within her own heart.

"All right," she said. "I heard you . . . but I don't have to like what I heard." She thought for a long moment, then added, "And I don't necessarily have to do what's right. I've tried to do the right thing all me life, and where's it got me? Couldn't I just this once . . . ?"

She closed the window and pulled the lace curtains closed. The house had become chilled, in spite of her robe and slippers. She left the wrap on when she slid into bed, hoping to chase away the shivers that were causing her teeth to chatter and her belly to feel queasy.

I shouldn't have gotten up after all, she thought. *I'm more awake than ever and no closer to a decision. And I'll have to be rising in a few hours to make his lordship's breakfast.*

Resentment rose in her as she thought of the man lying in the room down the hall. Resentment, and a few other emotions she couldn't—or didn't want to—name. Why did he have to come here tonight? Why did he have to change from a rude, obnoxious fellow pounding on her door to a rather pleasant companion sitting by the fire with his dark hair curling around his face, watching her with those blue eyes that seemed to read her every thought?

She rolled onto her left side, but the moonlight was too bright, shining in her eyes. So she rolled onto her right. And there was her desk and in its top drawer was the letter.

She rolled onto her back and cursed the nightgown that was threatening to strangle her again.

And those pebbles in her mattress had turned to boulders.

Four

Moya was standing at the kitchen counter, slicing soda bread, when a soft knock sounded on the back door. She glanced over at the bangers and rashers, just beginning to sizzle nicely in the skillet on the stove, then she hurried to answer it.

"Good morning to you, love," Moya said as she opened the door and ushered Shauna Kissane and her burden inside—a basket of fresh eggs from her grandmother Norah's hen house. "Just set that on the table and collect your coins from the biscuit jar."

Every morning the ritual was the same. Before going to school, little Shauna would deliver eggs to Moya's kitchen and share a cup of tea, a scone or biscuit, and some "girl talk" with Moya.

Sometimes Moya wondered if the child received enough attention at home. The girl's mother seemed to spend most of her time watching television shows or reading magazines about the scandalous conduct of movie stars in the United States or the royal family of Britain. Considering how sweet the child was, Moya couldn't imagine not spending time with her, had she been her own.

Since Shauna had begun delivering eggs for her grandmother about a year ago, their friendship had grown over each morning's strong cup of tea. Watching the girl dunk her chocolate-dipped biscuit into the tea and savor each bite, Moya thought, What a pleasure it would be someday to have a daughter of her own.

But there was that one small matter . . . no husband for Moya, no father for the baby.

So, for the present, she had to be content to borrow Shauna.

"Ye had a Yank here last night, aye?" Shauna said as she munched on her morning snack and Moya sliced vine-ripened tomatoes in half. "He came into the pub last night, askin' where he might get out o' the rain. Ma told him to come here."

Moya turned to see the girl's chocolate-smeared face broaden in a smile. "So?" she asked playfully. "Make your point if you have one."

"Don't have a point." The girl shrugged. "Just saying."

"You always have a point to make, Shauna Kissane, every time you open that mouth of yours."

"Unless I'm openin' it to shove a biscuit inside."

Moya laughed and shook her head. "You'll put me in the poorhouse, sure, eatin' those biscuits like they were goin' outta style."

Glancing down at the half empty tin, the girl

blushed and giggled. "Have I eaten too many, truly? Have I made ye poor?"

"Not at all. Though the bakers at Cadbury will be hard put to keep up, and you'll soon be too plump to come and go through the back door, narrow as it is."

"He's a handsome one, don't ye think?" Shauna pretended to be fascinated by the swirls of chocolate on an orange-flavored delicacy.

Moya removed the bangers and rashers from the skillet and then carefully placed three eggs and the halved tomatoes into the pan, cut side down. "Whoever could you be speaking of? Young Kevin Doolin, perhaps."

Shauna blushed much deeper. "No! Not Kevin. He's not handsome, not even a bit, but a smelly, ill-mannered boy, and I can't bear him at all, at all. 'Tis the Yank I'm speakin' of."

"Now, I don't think Kevin smells bad at all, and he combs his hair quite nicely."

"I hadn't noticed. But I did observe how very tall that Yank was and—"

"And Kevin was givin' you the twinkle of his eye at the wake. I heard him ask if you'd like to dance and—"

"And I was thinkin' how fine it was that a handsome lad like himself, the Yank, that is, was comin' here to stay at your house, and you not married."

"Stop that, Shauna Kissane. I want no part of any Yank, handsome or not, married or not. And besides, that one is rude—he's from New York, you know— and he wasn't particularly attractive when he arrived last evening. He looked less like a fine prince and more like a drowned rat."

"Well, I thought he was handsome, indeed, and so did the other ladies and girls when they laid eyes upon him. We talked of nothin' else after he'd left, saying how Lady Luck had smiled upon Moya Mahoney to have such as him under her roof."

Moya stopped what she was doing and scowled at the girl. A twinge of irritation that felt a lot like jealousy passed through her, but she mentally swept it away. Why should she care if the village ladies were admiring Rory O'Brien? What was it to her? What was *he* to her? A boarder, like any other. Well, not exactly like any other, but. . . . "Gossips, that's what you all are," she told the girl. "And you know Father Shea says that's a sin."

Shauna snickered. " 'Tis no sin to be tellin' the truth as you see it. And if you weren't blind as a rock, ye'd see how fine a lad he is, that rude Yank from New York."

Moya snorted as she took a warmed plate from the oven and placed the food she had prepared on it. "Yes, well, I hope he's up and about, because he asked for his breakfast at half eight and it's ready for him. Why don't you run out into the parlor and see if he's stirring?"

Shauna looked at the remaining biscuits wistfully. "Why don't *you* go out and look?" she said.

"Because I'm not the one smitten with him and pining for just a glimpse of his handsome face."

"Who wants to see my handsome face?" said a deep voice and they both turned to see Rory standing in the doorway that separated the kitchen from the dining room. His hair was boyishly tousled, he was wearing his uncle's old plaid robe, and his feet were bare. The smirk on his face made him look ten years younger than the soggy, ill-tempered fellow who had knocked on Moya's door last evening.

"Well, it certainly isn't me whose eyes are sore, strainin' for a look at you," Moya said, giving the embarrassed seven-year-old Shauna a grin.

Rory laughed and sat down at the table across from Shauna. "Then there's at least one female in Gormloch with good taste in men," he said, reaching over and tweaking one of her dark chestnut curls.

"And fine taste in Cadbury biscuits, too," Moya added. "There were four tins of them sitting there on the table when she began this morning and look . . . she's destroyed three and a half of them already and the last one isn't long for the world."

"I have not!" Shauna objected. "There was only this one tin and—"

"I know, I know," Moya said, laughing. "Can't you tell when someone's coddin' you, child? Here, let me warm that tea of yours, and Mr. O'Brien, if you'll move along to the dining room, I'll serve you breakfast."

"Can't I eat it here?" he asked. "I'd rather share the company of this lady of discriminating tastes than eat in there alone."

Moya was a bit surprised. She always served her guests in the more formal, much nicer dining room. The kitchen was for intimate friends and family, and in all the years she had operated the bed and breakfast, she had never had anyone make that request.

She had to admit: she rather liked his attitude and understood it. She, too, preferred to eat in here with company than in the other room alone.

Surely, she had eaten too many meals alone already. And with Angus departed, she was destined to eat many more solo.

"Have it wherever suits you," she said as she carried the plate full of steaming food to him and set it on the table under his nose. "As long as you eat every bite, you'll get no argument from me."

"What is all this?" he asked, studying the contents of his plate. "I thought I was having a Continental breakfast. I just have coffee and a bagel at home."

"What's a bagel?" Shauna asked.

"A lovely dog with large eyes, long ears, and a keen nose," Moya replied. "Eat your biscuits and drink your tea before you're late for school."

"There's no school today," Shauna corrected her. "'Tis Saturday."

"And a bagel isn't a dog," Rory added. "That's a beagle. A bagel is—"

"I know the difference!" Moya shoved a plate heaped with sliced soda bread in front of him. "For heaven's sake, doesn't anyone at this table know when his leg's bein' yanked a bit? Eat, the both of you. If you don't, you'll soon grow weak with hunger. You'll faint dead away on the streets, and everyone will see you and say, 'That Moya Mahoney starves her guests, she does.' And I'll have no business at all."

Rory nudged Shauna. "Is she yanking our leg again?"

"No, indeed, she's entirely serious. Moya is always afraid someone might go hungry in her presence. 'Tisn't allowed at all."

He growled and looked back at the meat and eggs on his plate. "I can feel my arteries hardening, just looking at it. I don't usually eat meat except at dinner."

"Well, don't be expecting much of an evening meal in this village," Moya told him as she poured him an enormous mug of coffee. "You're looking at your finest opportunity of the day. In Ireland we say, 'Food is golden in the morning, silver at noon, and lead at night.' You'll do well to wrap your teeth around a cheese and tomato sandwich after dark."

"I'll be on my way back to New York by then," he said smugly, "where I can buy a gourmet meal at three in the morning if I like."

"How grand for you," Moya replied. "I'm sure New York will be enormously pleased to receive you."

For just a moment, a sad look crossed his eyes and Moya regretted her sarcasm. She knew the look; it was loneliness. She knew it all too well. She wagered there would be no one special to welcome Rory O'Brien when he stepped off the plane in New York. She wondered which pain was more acute, being alone in a city of millions of people who didn't know you or care about you, or having no one special in a village where everyone considered themselves your friend.

"Is New York City grand?" Shauna asked, her eyes bright with childish intrigue. "Are there truly buildings there so high you can't see the top?"

"There are many tall buildings in the city," he replied. "I work on the sixty-fourth floor of one of them. But you can see the tops of all of them unless, of course, it's cloudy and the tops get lost in the fog. Sometimes I look out my window and realize I'm in the clouds myself."

Shauna gasped. "Imagine such a thing! Just like the lad in the story, Jack, who climbed the beanstalk all the way to the sky! Isn't that amazing, Moya?"

Moya grunted, pulled out a chair, and sat next to Shauna. "Um, yes, I suppose New York City is quite grand. But I prefer the peace and quiet of our part of the world."

Rory gave her a long, searching look. "Have you ever been there?" he asked, his tone more gentle than hers.

"No," she admitted reluctantly.

"Then how can you be sure which you prefer?"

"Look about you," she said. "Do you have lush green fields that have been fed the blood of Irish heroes throughout the centuries? Can you see the castle ruins of your ancestors from your back window, or a fairy fort where people lived at the dawn of time?"

"No," he said. "But I live in a city full of skyscrapers that were largely built by Irish immigrants, and if I get a yen for antiquities, I can go to the Museum of Natural History and see Egyptian mummy treasure and dinosaur bones."

Moya stared back at him, her mouth slightly opened, momentarily taken aback.

"I believe he's got ye there," Shauna whispered, loudly enough for all to hear.

"Oh, hush and eat your biscuits."

"And why," Rory asked Moya, "do you keep calling those things she's eating biscuits? Biscuits are round, puffy, bread-type things that southerners eat with butter and sorghum molasses. Those are cookies."

"Now that depends which side of the Atlantic you're standing upon when you're eating them, doesn't it?" Moya pointed at his plate. "Your bangers and rashers are growin' cold."

"You mean my bacon and sausage?"

Shauna sighed, stood, and shook her head sadly. "'Tis no use, at all," she said.

"What's no use?" Moya asked.

"Do you remember what I told you before? What all the ladies were saying in the pub last night about . . . you know?"

"Oh, aye." Moya glanced over at Rory, trying not to think of how boyishly cute his mussed hair was or how nicely his broad shoulders filled out Angus's robe. "I remember you sayin' they had reached a consensus on a certain matter."

"Well, it doesn't matter at all," Shauna said. "Because, even if it's true, 'tis plain the two of you hate each other entirely."

After nabbing two more biscuits and shoving them into her pocket, the seven-year-old raised her pert nose a couple of notches and marched out the back door, leaving Moya and Rory in a heavy silence.

Finally Rory spoke. "What was that about? What consensus did the women of the village reach?"

"Nothing that would be of interest to you," Moya said. "Just village gossip. Ply Shauna with tea and her tongue loosens."

"And what's this about us hating each other? I don't hate you. Do you hate me?"

From across the table she studied his face, noting the sparkle in his blue eyes. He was teasing; she was sure of that. And she wouldn't allow him to win this little verbal sparring match.

"Hate?" she said. "No, I'd say hate is too strong a word. So is revulsion. Mild dislike. That's it. Bordering on indifference."

It was his turn to look nonplussed. "Oh," he said. "That's good. Thanks. I guess."

Her arms full of clean linens, Moya turned a corner in the hallway and nearly ran headlong into Rory . . . and the towel he had wrapped around his waist . . . and nothing else.

"Almost every time I lay eyes on you, you're wet through and through," she said, trying not to notice how incredible he looked in nothing but a bath towel and water beads on his otherwise bare body. She didn't want to think about how his hair curled even tighter when wet and hung boyishly down his forehead and into his eyes. His clear blue eyes.

No, she didn't want to think about them, either.

She had already decided to hate—no, thoroughly dislike—this man.

He seemed to sense her discomfort and to be enjoying the fact that she was blushing. "Sorry," he said, "but I couldn't find the robe you loaned me last night. Did you put it away somewhere?"

"Ah, yes. I thought you had finished with it, so I returned it to your uncle's room where it belongs."

"My uncle's . . ." A look of sadness crossed his face. "Oh, I didn't realize it was Uncle Angus's robe."

"I would have mentioned it last evening, but I didn't know how you'd feel about wearin' it, and it was all I had to offer you . . . other than my pink chenille one or a black peignoir."

As soon as she mentioned the latter, she was sorry. His eyes lit up with typical male interest. "Now, *I* wouldn't be interested in wearing that," he said, "but *you—*"

"Never mind me or my peignoir. Would you like me to fetch you the robe back again?"

"No, that's all right. But as soon as I'm dressed, I would like to ask you for another favor."

"Which is?"

"The use of your telephone. I need to confirm my departure flight this evening and arrange for some transportation to Shannon. I don't want to find myself having to ride that decrepit bus again."

"Certainly, you may. I'll give you some phone numbers of lads here in the village who have no job at the moment and would be glad to give you a lift."

"I'll pay them well for their time," he said, running his hands down his arms to remove some of the water, then wiping his palms on the towel that was damp and clinging to his hips and thighs in a way that made the blood rush even faster to Moya's cheeks.

"You needn't pay for their time. That they'll gladly give you. Buy them a tank of petrol and a pint and they'll be more than happy."

"I don't ask anyone to do anything for me without paying for it."

She studied him a long moment, then shook her head sadly. "I'm sorry to hear you say such a thing. Aren't there people on God's green earth who love you enough to help you without holdin' out their open hand?"

"Of course there are," he said. But he didn't look as sure as his words. "I just don't ask them."

"Well, you should start askin'. It does a person good to ask for help once in a while."

"Why?"

"If nothing else, it keeps us humble. We must never forget that we need other people and they need us. No one is so strong they can walk down life's road without another to lean on from time to time when the way's rough."

Rory shrugged his still damp shoulders and said with a cocky smile, "Well, *I* pay my own way though life. If you shell out the cash, you can have whatever you want, exactly the way you want it."

"Unless you don't have cash, and then you must decide to want it the way you have it." She shifted her burden of linen that was beginning to make her arms ache. Besides, she had seen and heard quite enough of Mr. Rory Half Naked O'Brien and his pompous opinions.

"There's one other thing I'd like to ask of you," he said, "besides the phone calls, which, of course, I'll pay for."

She smiled wryly. "Of course. What is it?"

"Before I leave, I'd like to see my uncle's bedroom, you know, to choose some sort of memento."

Moya had forgotten about his request the night before and was surprised at how the thought of letting him into Angus's room bothered her. Somehow, she had thought of the bedroom as a private sanctuary that had belonged to Angus and now to her, and her alone. But she supposed, if a dead man's relative wanted to see his room, what could you say?

"Meet me out here in the hallway in ten minutes," she said. "And I'll show you what Angus O'Brien left behind."

"Is this where he died?" Rory asked with a candor that Moya found both unsettling and comforting. This man might not be the most sensitive soul on earth, but you would always know where you stood with him, unlike some of the village folk who were kind to your face and then spoke ill of you when your back was turned.

"Aye, this is where he passed on," she said as they both stood in the middle of Angus's room and looked around at the relics of a man's life and experiences.

"Was it bad?" Rory asked. "Was he in a lot of pain?"

"No, thank the heavens." She glanced over at the

bed, at the pillow that still bore the indentation of his head. She hadn't had the heart to fluff it. "As dyin' goes, it was gentle enough."

"Good." Rory walked over to the small desk and lifted first one object, then another, studying the old teak and ebony fountain pen, the faceted Waterford crystal paperweight, a yellowed photograph in a silver frame—two boys, arms around each other's shoulders. The boys looked exactly alike.

"My dad and Angus were twins," he said softly, staring at the picture.

"I know," Moya replied. "Angus told me all about him. They had been very close . . . before your parents emigrated to the States."

"He told you *all* about him? Did Angus tell you that a couple of years ago, he traveled all the way to New York to see his twin brother, but my father couldn't be found. I visited with my uncle for a couple of days, showed him the city, then drove him back to the airport. My father was out pub-hopping and didn't show up until a week after my uncle went home."

Moya could hear the pain and bitterness behind his words and she understood. Angus had told her a little about his brother's problem with the drink. She had heard about the abrupt changes in his personality, from a kind and loving man to one who was angry and unreasonable, from an industrious longshoreman to a shiftless drunk who spent his days and nights holding down a bar stool. Moya had heard about Rory's mother, who had once been a carefree beauty, but had lost her youth and her health, trying to provide for her son with the meager earnings of a seamstress.

But Moya wasn't going to add to Rory O'Brien's pain by revealing all she knew about his family's problems.

"Angus spoke of your father often," she said carefully. "And of your mother, and of you. Mostly, he talked of how much he loved you and wished you lived nearer to him."

She walked over to the wall opposite the bed and pointed to one of the many pictures that hung there in wood and silver frames of all shapes and sizes. The photo was of a pretty, dark-haired girl, about sixteen years old, standing between two dashing lads who looked like bookends.

All three were dressed in fifties fashion, the girl in a simple shirt dress with a full skirt and a close-fit waist that showed off her hourglass figure. On her feet were black-and-white saddle shoes. The boys were both in short-sleeved sports shirts with loose slacks and brightly polished wingtips. They were standing on a bridge that crossed the river just outside the village.

The bridge was still standing about a mile down the road . . . looking exactly as it did in the picture.

But all three people were now gone.

"My mom liked Angus, too," Rory said as he joined her to look at the picture. "When she gave Da grief about his drinking, he used to tell her she should have married Angus instead. He wasn't as fond of his pints as my father. But then, most weren't."

Moya reached up and took the picture down from

the wall. "Would you like to take this with you?"
she said. "I think Angus would have wanted you to
have it. *I* want you to have it."

He hesitated a moment, then took it from her and
held it against his chest. She wondered if he held it
that way to embrace it, or so that he wouldn't have
to see it.

"There's something else I think you should have."
She walked over to the bed and pointed to the quilt.
"Your mother made this and—"

"I know," he said. "I watched her make it. She
used to sew all day and half the night in sweatshops
in the garment district of Manhattan. Then she'd
come home and sew for us."

Rory walked over to the bed and touched the quilt,
tracing the interlocking swirls that formed the intricate pattern. "I was ten years old when Uncle Angus
first came for a visit from Ireland. It was a really
big deal, having a family member as a guest. We
didn't have any relatives in New York, and my mother
and father were really excited to see someone from
'home.' He stayed with us for a month, sat at our
kitchen table and told us stories, smoked his pipe,
and shared old times with my folks. My mom gave
him this quilt when he left. She said, " 'Tis just a
wee somethin' to remember us by.' "

Overcome with emotion, he sat down on the bed
and continued to study the tiny stitches. " 'A wee
somethin', she called it. She had worked on it for
months."

Moya walked over to him and placed a comforting hand on his shoulder. "And it worked well, it

did. He remembered you—all of you—until the very day he died." The words caught in her throat as she thought of the letter that had been in the wooden box with his pipe and tobacco. The letter was now in the bottom of her lingerie drawer . . . where she had intended to leave it.

At least, she had intended to until that very moment.

Seeing Rory O'Brien genuinely grieving the loss of his last living relative was all the prompting her heart needed to do the right thing.

"I think you should take the quilt, as well," she told him. "And anything else from this room that you want. I'll ship it along to you after you've left for New York."

"Thank you," he said. "That's very kind of you. I've met a lot of kind people here in a short time. My mother was a very gentle, loving person. I'm beginning to see where she got it from. I hadn't expected to like you Irish as much as I do. You're good people."

The guilt rose in Moya's throat like a big lump of sod that would strangle her. "There's somethin' else I must show you," she told him. "Somethin' that belonged to your uncle."

"Oh, this is enough," he said. "All I wanted was just something simple to remember him by. The quilt seems most appropriate."

"No," she said. "'Tisn't enough. You're to have all your uncle intended you to have. Come . . . follow me. There's somethin' most important you must see."

Five

Even at ten o'clock in the morning, Lios na Daoine Sidhe had no shortage of patrons. The newspapers had arrived, and there were more than enough hot topics to stimulate companionable conversation as well as the occasional violent debate. One knot of villagers sat in the rear corner of the room, heads close together, as they discussed the latest on the troubles in the North. At the bar, Tommy O'Sullivan and Conn Hallissey had exhausted every topic relating to Irish politics and had moved on, arguing whether the gun control bill being introduced to the United States Senate would pass.

Tommy's nine children were running in the front door and out the back, bringing a pack of hounds with them, tracking mud all over the floor. No one seemed to mind the mess or the noise. One of the dogs decided to linger and slipped beneath his master's stool, where he promptly began to nap.

Gill Doolin stood behind the bar, as he had for years, pulling pints as though the pub's owner hadn't been buried the day before. He and the others paused in their various activities and conversations to greet Moya when she walked inside.

She wasn't surprised to see Gill manning the bar, even though the pub's owner was fresh in his grave. Gill was one of those rare, fortunate individuals who actually enjoyed his work. She didn't recall when he had ever missed a day, even for sickness. Angus had counted on him to keep the pub running smoothly, and his trust had been well invested.

"This is it," she told Rory proudly as she ushered him inside and waved her arm with flourish, as though introducing royalty. "This is Lios na Daoine Sidhe, which in Irish means Ringed Fort of the Fairy People, named for the ancient fairy fort that is located on the pub's land, closer to the river. This building has stood as it is, on this very spot, for the past three hundred years. When your own country was signing its Declaration of Independence from England, this pub was serving food and drink to the locals and offering hospitality to weary travelers. It's provided shelter and refreshment of body and spirit for generation after generation, and, as you can see, it's none the worse for wear."

Rory glanced around at the rough-hewn tables and benches, the thatched ceiling, the stone walls, and the oil lamps that flickered in primitive, iron sconces on the walls. "I've seen barns that were more modern," he said, "and comfortable."

Moya gave him a look that could have melted the

Rock of Cashel. "There's more to life than just what's modern or comfortable," she said. "This pub has history. A grand and glorious lot of it. Why, Daniel O'-Connell himself sat at that very table in that very corner and drank a pint and scribbled out his notes for one of those mighty speeches he gave at his monster political rallies."

"Daniel who?" Rory said. "O'Connor?"

Moya was mortified, but only for a moment. He was teasing . . . surely. "O'*Connell*" she said, "and don't be pretendin' you don't know he was called the Great Liberator, the finest Irish statesman of all time in many folks' opinion. I'm sure you heard your parents speak of the grand Daniel O'Connell champion of Irish freedom against the oppressive British."

"Oh, yeah. I guess they might have mentioned him." Rory looked bored to death, as though he couldn't care less about the pub's pedigree or its former, famous visitors.

Moya felt her anxiety level rising. Considering why she had brought him here, she wished he would show a bit of enthusiasm for the place. Of course, she couldn't expect him to love Lios na Daoine Sidhe the way she did, but he could at least display a modicum of interest—to be polite, if for no other reason.

"Your uncle sat there by the fireplace," she said, pointing to the hearth and the blazing turf, "and told stories to the village children by the hour. The adults listened, too, truth be told. We all loved to listen to him."

"My parents said that Angus always could spin a

good yarn," Rory said as he walked over to the bar and took a seat on one of the stools.

"He didn't *'spin yarns'*," she said, plopping down on the seat next to his. "Angus was a seanchai, a bard, a keeper of the ancient tales. If he had been alive a thousand years ago, he would have sat at the table with kings, worn royal colors, and shared the best cuts of meat and the best ales with them. He would have advised them on everything from warfare to their relationships with their wives, and they would have followed his counsel."

Rory gave her a little grin that irritated her; he wasn't taking her, or his uncle, or the traditions of this place seriously. This certainly wasn't the reaction she had been expecting, and she felt her temper and indignation rising by the second. What had happened to the sentimental lad in Angus's bedroom? Maybe he only felt nostalgic about people and things he had known personally.

Sadly, it was apparent that this pub and its history meant nothing to him.

"What will ye have, sir?" Gill asked Rory as he set a cup of hot tea in front of Moya.

"I don't want anything," Rory said. "I don't drink before six."

"Neither do I," Gill replied. "Six in the morning, that is. It's sound asleep I am at that hour. Will ye have a bit of tea, then, like me friend Moya here?"

"No, thanks. I've downed more tea in the past twelve hours than the rest of my life combined," he said. "But I'd like some coffee, if you have a fresh pot."

"I do, indeed. Coming straightaway."

Moya grinned to herself. The only reason Gill would have brewed coffee was for the occasional Irish coffee, complete with whiskey and heavy cream. The "fresh pot" had probably been brewed yesterday before the funeral.

"So, what is it you wanted to show me?" Rory asked, looking around with obviously feigned curiosity. "What is it that belonged to Angus that I'd want to see here?"

Moya wanted to grab the nearest newspaper, preferably a thick one, roll it up, and bash it over his head. But she refrained. "Y'er not the sharpest pike in the battle, are you?" she muttered under her breath. Then she said, "The pub. The pub belonged to himself. 'Twas his home—lived right upstairs, he did, where Gill and his son are livin' now, until he broke his hip and moved in with me. And besides Lios na Daoine Sidhe, he owned all the property it sits upon. More than fifty acres of fine land, including the fairy fort itself."

"Oh, really. So, Uncle Angus owned a piece of the ol' sod . . . fifty acres, a rundown pub, and a leprechaun fort. That's nice."

"Nice?" She shook her head. He certainly wasn't making this easy for her with his blasé attitude. " 'Tis far more than *nice*. A freshly baked scone on a misty mornin', now that's nice. Not a piece of history itself, like this place. This is grand."

Rory looked around him doubtfully. "No. The Plaza is grand. This is a shabby, decrepit building that should be bulldozed before it falls in on some-body."

It took every ounce of restraint that Moya could muster not to slap him so hard his ears would ring like church bells pealing in a belfry. How dare he! Of all the rude, insensitive, conceited fools she had met, this Rory O'Brien had to be one of the worst.

And it didn't matter if he had bright blue eyes and broad shoulders. It didn't matter if he had appeared to have a heart and to be a gentle, sentimental soul there in the bedroom, looking at the photos and touching his mother's handiwork.

He was an obnoxious Yank—a New Yorker, and everybody knew they were the worst kind of Yank. And Moya was convinced that he was the worst of the worst.

"You're not makin' this easy for me," she said, glaring at him. "Not easy at all, at all."

"Not making what easy?" He took a sip of the coffee that Gill had served him and made a wry grimace. "Why did you bring me in here? To poison me?"

"No, though that is a fine idea. I brought you here because I've an announcement I must make, to you, and to the entire village. And while this"—she waved her hand, indicating everyone present—"isn't everybody in Gormloch, it's a fair sampling. The news will travel fast, to be sure."

"What are you talking about?" he asked, pushing the offending cup of coffee across the bar and away from him.

"Just you wait," she said. "It will all be clear in a moment."

She stood and turned away from the bar to face the room. "Forgive me," she said in a loud voice, "for interruptin' your fine conversations, just when I'm sure y'er all about to solve the political problems of the world. But I've somethin' to say to you. Actually, I've somethin' to *read* to you."

She reached in her jeans pocket and took out Angus's letter, which she had retrieved from the bottom of her lingerie drawer just before bringing Rory to the pub. Her legs felt a little shaky as she walked to the center of the room and began to unfold the papers.

"Are you all right, love?" Conn Hallissey asked her. "Ye look a bit weak in the knees and yer face is a mite pale."

"Sure," she said. "Thank you for asking. What a true gentleman you are, Conn." She gave Rory a look over her shoulder that told him, all too plainly, that her opinion of him was far less generous.

"What is it ye've got there, lass?" Gill asked as he wiped his hands on his apron and came out from behind the bar. "Is it a letter of some sort?"

"'Tis. A letter from Angus," she said, holding the pages up before her as though she were the town crier about to make a proclamation. "'Tis his final written words . . . a last will and testament, if you please. While it wouldn't be considered a proper will because it wasn't witnessed or signed by anyone else, it states quite clearly what his wishes were, concerning his property."

Gill hurried across the room to Moya, his face eager and worried. "Well, don't keep us in suspense, love. What does it say?"

Drawing a deep breath of resignation, Moya glanced at Rory and saw that she had his full attention, as well as everyone else's. She began to read:

"To all my friends and loved ones, I wish to express my gratitude to each and every one of you all for a lifetime of joyful memories. I would like to thank you individually, but writing is difficult for me at this late date. It is taking me days just to pen this letter. So I'll put it where Moya will be sure to find it and ask her to read it to you in Lios na Daoine Sidhe.

"I don't have much in material goods for a man who has lived as long as I have. Nor do I have children to pass along what little I do own. But you were all my children in many ways, and my parents, brothers and sisters, so I was never lonely.

"I would like my library to be divided among you, each taking turns choosing a book, from the eldest of you to the youngest, and over again, until all are gone. I hope they give you half the pleasure they did to me.

"I will entrust Moya with the task of giving away whatever personal items anyone would want. Gill, you're welcome to that Hawaiian shirt of mine that you admired so much, and Tommy, my slippers are better than yours. Take them and throw those disgraceful abominations of your own in the fire straightaway.

"I would ask that someone among you contact my

brother's son, Rory O'Brien, in New York City and inform him that I am leaving Lios na Daoine Sidhe and the property where it stands in his hands to do with as he chooses. He is a very successful gentleman of commerce, and I trust he will know what is best.

"And finally, to Moya Mahoney, the daughter of my heart, I leave my most precious gift—the stories, the heritage that is hers and all sons and daughters of Eire. Traditionally, a seanchai passed his knowledge and his station to his children, the art of poetry to daughters, the gift of storytelling to sons. But I have no sons and no gift for poetry. So, I leave the bard's cloak to you, Moya. I know you will wear it with grace, and my soul's deepest wish that you would know the joy of being a seanchai, a lifetime of stories passed on to the next generation.

"My love and best wishes to you all. I'll be waiting to greet you when you cross to the other side. Your friend, Angus O'Brien."

The villagers were still and silent as Moya refolded the pages and tucked them into her pocket. She fought back the tears, unsure of her own mixed emotions. As when she had first read the letter, she was deeply touched by the last paragraph, by the bestowing of the metaphoric bard's mantle, and Angus's expressions of paternal affection for her.

But to hand Lios na Daoine Sidhe over to a stranger, a foreigner who had no feeling for the place at all, no appreciation of its unique character and value to those who loved it. Why?

She still couldn't believe it, and she was sure she would never understand it.

"Well," she heard Gill grumble under his breath, "that's surely a bite on the arse."

"Sorry, Moya," Conn whispered as he rose from his bench, walked over to her, and put his arms around her in a bear hug. "Never could figure ol' Angus. He was a bit daft in some ways."

"No, he wasn't," she said, pushing Conn away— not because she was so offended by the reference to Angus's weird ways, but because she was afraid that his display of affection might cause her to burst into tears. "Angus was just . . . different . . . that's all. He was very wise—gifted, in fact. I'm sure he had his reasons."

She steeled herself and turned to Rory, who hadn't spoken, but sat, frozen, on his stool at the bar, a stunned look on his face.

"Well, it appears you're to be congratulated, Mr. O'Brien," she said. "It seems you're the not-so-proud owner of a ramshackle pub and the piece of ol' Ireland that she sits upon."

He sat quietly, eyes locked with hers for a long moment, then he glanced around the room at the less-than-friendly faces watching his every move. "Gee . . . thanks . . . I guess," he said glumly.

Moya walked over to him and held out her hand. Reluctantly, he shook it. She was surprised to find his palm cool and damp. His face had lost a bit of its tan and had taken on a slightly ashen appearance.

"I'd offer to buy you a pint," she said, "but I distinctly heard you say you don't drink until after six, and by then you'll be on your way back to New York." She gave him a sarcastic smirk. "Unless, of course, you'll be movin' in upstairs straightaway."

"I'll be heading back to New York as I had planned," he said, "in spite of this new . . . development."

Gill slipped behind the bar again and was trying his best to appear casual when he asked, "What do you think you'll be doin' with the place now that you're its rightful owner?"

Rory looked at Moya and a chill ran through her as she recalled his "bulldozer" comment. He wouldn't. He couldn't. She wouldn't let him. Already visions were forming in her imagination: herself lying prone in the road, blocking the bulldozer's path, her wrist handcuffed to the front door, Rory dragging her out of the pub by the hair and news photographers from Killarney snapping pictures of the abuse.

"I just found out about my, ah, good fortune," he said slowly as though he were carefully weighing his words. "I'm not sure what I'll do about it yet. But I see no reason why things shouldn't continue as they are. You can run the place in my absence, Mr. . . . ah . . ."

"Doolin. Gill Doolin." Gill thrust his big hand out and grasped Rory's. The forced smile on his face made Moya sick at heart. Gill would do anything to keep the job and a roof over his son's head. And she tried not to blame him; jobs and roofs were scarce in their community.

For the past seven years, Gill had been courting a young widow from Tralee, but, hadn't proposed marriage because he couldn't afford to support a wife. He had to hang on to what little financial security he had in this world, even if it meant being friendly to the enemy. It was a shame to see a person sell their honesty for a paycheck, but Moya had seen many do it for the ones they loved.

"I'd be glad to take care o' the place for as long as ye'd like me to, sir," he said. "Since old Angus broke his hip, 'twas mostly me runnin' it anyway. I'll keep the pub lookin' good and I'll send along the small profits to wherever ye say."

Rory gave a dismissive wave of his hand. "We'll worry about all that later. I'll be in contact. For right now, I'll ask only one thing from you, Mr. Doolin."

"Yes, sir," Gill replied eagerly. Too eagerly, Moya thought. "Anything you want, sir."

"Learn how to make a decent cup of coffee. That stuff is absolutely vile."

Gill blushed and nodded vigorously. "I'll do that, sir. I'll read up on the subject and—"

"Fine. That's fine." Rory turned to the others. "In a couple of hours, I'm going to need a ride to Shannon Airport. I'd like to hire one of you to take me. Of course, I'll pay you well for your trouble."

No one spoke. They just sat there and stared at him blankly.

"I assume you don't have regular employment," he said, "or you wouldn't be sitting in a pub, drinking and shooting the breeze, on a weekday morning."

Stony silence.

"Come on. Doesn't anyone here want to make a buck? For cryin' out loud, don't you people—"

"Excuse me, Mr. O'Brien," Conn said, rising from his bench and taking a few steps toward Rory. His face was grim. "We 'people' would be glad to give you transport to Shannon, any of us who owns a vehicle. I myself would be glad to do the deed. But 'twill be a favor, from me to you, one man to another. I won't be your servant, sir, and you needn't pay me for my trouble. 'Twill be no trouble at all."

Rory seemed to shrink, right there on his stool, and Moya enjoyed his discomfort. Mr. High and Mighty needed to be put in his place and she was happy to see Conn, the village's humble giant, be the one to put him there.

To her surprise, and everyone else's in the room, Rory rose, walked over to Conn, and held out his hand. "I apologize," he said. "I'm not used to this kind of generosity, and I'm making an ass of myself trying to get used to it. Will you forgive my rudeness—all of you?"

The shocked villagers looked at one another, their mouths open, then, one by one, they nodded and mumbled their acceptance.

"We'll forgive ye, sir," Conn said, accepting his hand and shaking it firmly. "'Tis hard, learnin' the ways of a people not your own. We'll have patience with you, if you'll be patient with us."

Rory laughed. "I'm from New York. Patience isn't exactly my strong suit. But I'll work on it."

Conn nodded. "That's all we ask of any man—

his best effort. Now, will ye be wantin' that ride to Shannon?"

"I will. I mean, I do. Thank you."

"Then I'll collect you at half one."

"Half one?"

"One-thirty," Moya translated. "He'll bring the car 'round my place to pick you up then."

"Oh, I see. That'll be fine." He turned to Moya. "There's just one more thing I want to do before I leave."

"Pay your bill at my guest house?" she said with a half-smile.

"Okay, two more things. I also want to visit my uncle's grave before I go. Will you take me there?"

For some reason, which had to do with the letter in her pocket, Moya felt sick inside, and the last thing she wanted to do was go back out to that grave . . . especially to take Rory O'Brien there.

But what could she do? She could hardly refuse him such a request.

"Let's go," she said. "I have no car meself, but it's a short walk from here."

As they were leaving the pub, Rory took one last look around the inside and shook his head. "I can't believe it," he said. "I never saw this one coming."

"Neither did I," Moya muttered under her breath. "Who would've thought?"

Six

"*I don't like* graveyards. I never have," Rory said as Moya led him through the huge, iron gates of the cemetery behind St. Bridget's Church. The sky was as gray and gloomy as Rory's expression. For a recently informed heir, he wasn't in a particularly festive mood. "I don't have a single good memory of a graveyard," he said. "But, I don't suppose anyone else does, either."

"Actually, I do," Moya replied. The gates protested with an eerie screeching sound as she forced them open. "I rather like this place. Sometimes when I'm weary or upset, I come here to take a nap for myself."

Rory stopped walking abruptly and turned to face her. "You *are* kidding, right? I mean, that's just too weird."

"What is weird about it? A graveyard is the most peaceful place on earth. Where else can you go that no one will give you an argument on politics, religion, or the price of petrol?"

Rory quirked one eyebrow, and although she didn't want to, she couldn't help smiling a little. "Now I know you're pulling my leg."

"Aye, I am . . . about the argument part. Irish folk will argue even from beyond the grave. Sometimes my parents and grandparents give me a strict talkin' to when I visit. They tell me when they believe I'm bein' foolish or headin' down the wrong path."

He shook his head and laughed at her. "Moya Mahoney, you're one leaf shy of a shamrock. Are all Irish as crazy as you?"

"We prefer to think of ourselves as colorful," she replied. "There's more to life than what you can see and touch and explain with science, Rory O'Brien. Some of us are quite aware of that other world; we're spiritually attuned, if you like. We accept the things we feel and know instinctively—whether they can be defined or not. Just because something is inexplicable doesn't mean it doesn't exist."

Rory simply stared at her, as though she had suddenly grown a second head. "Are you serious? You expect me to believe that you commune with your dead relatives out here?"

"I'm not some sort of necromancer, if that's what you mean," she said. "I don't conduct seances, bury dead black cats by the light of a full moon, or any other such hocus-pocus out here among the gravestones. But I find that in the peace and quiet of the place, I'm aware of those who have gone on before. And I feel they're nearby, watching over me."

Rory glanced down at the small bouquet of wild-flowers Moya had given him for the visit. He was holding the stems so tightly, they were beginning to wilt. "You're giving me the creeps," he said. "I told you, I don't like graveyards."

"Let's see if we can't change your mind." She pointed to the only grave that wasn't covered with grass. "That's Angus's restin' place over there. He's laid next to a whole herd of O'Briens, most of them as stubborn as yourself. That's one of the family crypts, right there. See the name 'O'Brien' big and proud carved over the doorway? Go see if you can raise one of your ancestors. Not from the dead. Just enough to have a bit of a conversation."

She turned and began to go back down the path the way they had come. "I'm going to leave you now and trot along home. That way you'll have some time to commune with your kinsmen in private. Come back when you've finished. You know the road."

With that, she walked away, leaving him standing there with his wilted bouquet, his departed relatives, and his graveyard shivers.

Before she was even halfway home, Moya realized that she hadn't left Rory O'Brien there in the cemetery just to teach him a lesson about the spiritual side of life. No, she had wanted to be rid of him. At least, she had wanted to be rid of the conflicting feelings she experienced in his presence.

She couldn't remember when she had met a person so rude, so abrupt. And yet, although his words sometimes offended her, she had to admire his honesty and candor. While she might not always like what he said, she liked the fact that he spoke his mind.

A person always knew where they stood with someone like Rory O'Brien. You weren't likely to hear that he had said something dreadful about you behind your back. If he had something derogatory to say, he'd say it to your face.

She also liked his toughness, which translated into a raw masculinity. Rory wasn't soft, but he did have a gentle side. She had seen it that morning in the way he had interacted with Shauna. Any man who liked children couldn't be *all* bad.

And she respected him for the way he had apologized to Conn for his insensitive remarks. His remorse had been genuine, showing a humility that belied his boisterous manner.

For a Yank—especially for a New Yorker—he wasn't half bad. If he hadn't just inherited Lios na Daoine Sidhe, she might have almost liked him.

But he had. And what was worse, he didn't even appreciate it. He thought it should be bulldozed into the earth.

That made him the enemy.

And how could she like someone she felt so obliged to loathe?

Rory waited until she was down the road and well out of sight before he walked over to Angus's grave, knelt, and carefully laid the limp bouquet on the ground beside the others. He remained on one knee for several minutes, whispering prayers he hadn't spoken for years, but would never forget. The nuns at the parochial school had seen to that.

He recalled his uncle's face, so like his father's, his voice deep, masculine, and dramatic as he had sat at the small table in Rory's parents' kitchen in New York and told stories of Ireland, of this very village and its people. His voice and the smell of pipe smoke . . . those were Rory's favorite memories of his father's only brother. Then meeting him as a man, showing him the city. He wouldn't exchange those memories, few though they were, for anything.

And now he had the pictures, too, thanks to Moya Mahoney. Strange woman that she was, he had to admit he liked her—the glint in her eyes, her temper softened with kindness.

Kneeling there on Angus's grave, he recalled what she had said about "conversing" with her dead parents. He wondered what had happened to them. Moya had the air of a person alone in the world; Rory was all too familiar with the feeling and spotted it in others a mile away. People alone had protective shells around them, shells that were only illusions of protection. If anything, their thin barrier made them all the more vulnerable. The fear of loss caused them to reject the very thing they needed most, human companionship and affection, leaving them more alone than before.

He rose and glanced down the road again to make certain she was well out of sight before he walked over to the crypt that bore his family name above its door. If he was going to "commune" with his ancestors, he wasn't going to let her catch him doing it.

Good grief, he thought as he approached the small square building made of mortared gray stone, *the next thing you know I'll be chasing leprechauns and looking for the ends of rainbows. This country is full of weirdos, and a whacked-out state of mind seems to be contagious.*

But he had to admit that he did get a sort of a half tingle down his back when he saw his name carved in stone on a structure that looked positively ancient. The crypt's walls were half covered with moss and vines of ivy crept up and over the door, forming a graceful arch. The roof was covered with slate tiles—and more moss and ivy vines. He also had to admit, it looked peaceful, a good place for a gentle, eternal sleep.

"So, who's in there?" he asked, keeping his voice low in case anyone happened to be walking by and would think him as crazy as Moya Mahoney. "Exactly who are you dead guys lying in there? Are you my father's cousin's grandma's aunts and uncles?"

Realizing how stupid he sounded, he shook his head and wondered at Moya's influence on him. Somewhere deep inside, he had almost expected some sort of reply from inside the crypt.

Of course, he would have been scared witless if any had been forthcoming but the phenomenon wouldn't have been entirely unexpected. In a country as superstitious—some might call it mystical— as this, anything seemed possible.

He laughed at himself and tried to shrug off the

feeling that he was being watched. "Harumph," he said. "Nothing like tracing your roots back to the ol' sod to get a guy weirded out."

He left the crypt and strolled among the grave markers, admiring the stonework on some of them in spite of himself. One in particular caught his attention. Instead of stone, like the others, it was made of wrought iron, a Celtic-style cross with ornate knotwork which resembled the one his mother had sewn into Angus's quilt.

The name and date inscribed at the cross's stone base caught his eye.

Rory Colm O'Brien

1915–1977

The shock of seeing his own name there in stone was quickly followed by the emotional impact of realizing that this was his grandfather's grave. The grandfather he had heard stories about from both his parents and Uncle Angus, but had never known.

"Me da was a blacksmith," Rory's father had told him more than once. "The finest smith in the whole of county Kerry. Made the iron gates on the cemetery where he himself is buried, there behind the church. And he did it the old-fashioned way, not with fancy, modern machines, but by the sweat of his brow and the muscles of his arms and back. A man of strong constitution and character. You should be proud to be his grandson, lad. Proud, indeed."

Rory hadn't recalled that conversation for at least

twenty years. And now, here he was, standing on the ground above his grandfather's grave. And he had just walked through those very gates, not realizing that they had been skillfully crafted by his own family.

His interest piqued, he hurried back to the cemetery's gates and looked at them with new eyes. They were, truly, the work of a great artist. Like the grave marker, they contained the scrolling designs of ancient, Celtic art, signifying the immortality of the soul. Forever turning, forever changing, infinite in the continuation of its life cycles.

Rory couldn't imagine how many hours had been invested in those two gates, the strength, discipline, and the skill necessary to bring such beautiful creations into the world.

And his own grandfather had done it.

Rory couldn't help being proud.

He walked up to one of the gates and slowly, reverently, laid his hand on it. To his surprise, the metal didn't feel dead and cold, like iron was supposed to feel. He could sense a vibrancy in it, as though it somehow held life energy . . . the life energy of its creator. Rory thought of his grandfather, standing before that hot forge oven, sweat pouring from his skin as he forced the iron to yield to his will. This very metal that Rory was now touching had glowed as the hammer descended on it, sparks flying, the ring of metal on metal filling the air.

"Welcome home, Grandson."

Rory let go of the gate as though it had shocked him and stepped back several paces.

The words had been as clear as if they had been shouted in his ear. But they hadn't. They had been whispered to his soul. And Rory had heard them as plainly and as loudly as anything he had ever heard before.

Was he going crazy? A *gate* had talked to him? How ridiculous was that?

But Rory couldn't bring himself to ridicule the conviction that was spreading through his mind at that moment. The experience was too sacred to be mocked.

As he walked away from the cemetery and down the path toward Moya's home, his knees weak and his mouth dry, Rory knew he would never understand what had just happened to him.

And he knew he would never be the same.

"'Twas kind of you to offer Mr. O'Brien a ride to Shannon," Moya told Conn as she poured him yet another cup of tea and rewarmed her own. They had been sitting in Moya's kitchen, chatting and having a bit of refreshment as they waited for Rory to return from the cemetery.

A shy, sweet smile crossed Conn's face, a face that was browned and deeply lined from many days in the sun, cutting bricks of turf from the earth. He cleared his throat and toyed nervously with the handle of his cup. "Well, I had to cancel my midnight rendezvous with the queen of England, herself, but I thought you might appreciate it if I gave the lad a lift away from here."

When she didn't reply right away, he added, "Ye

were after gettin' him on his way, weren't ye? I didn't think ye were happy havin' him underfoot."

Moya nodded, understanding. "Ah, I see. Your only motive was for me to be rid of him."

"Exactly. 'Twas all done for you, love."

"Then I suppose I owe you a scone to go with that tea."

His smiled broadened, showing several missing teeth. Conn had been quite a fierce fighter in his youth. But now, in his late forties, he had calmed down a bit and his interests had turned more toward the romantic. Toward Moya, to be exact. And while she was flattered by the attention and affection of a kind man like Conn, she wasn't inclined in his direction.

Daily he tried to change her mind.

"One of these days soon," he said, "you and me must take a trip to Shannon ourselves. Then maybe on over to the Cliffs of Moher. 'Tis a lovely spot, so they say, on the days when the strong winds don't sweep ye off yer feet. We could take some dinner in a basket and make an evening of it."

"Mmm, that's nice, Conn. But I have a hard time gettin' away, you know, with my guests and all. Maybe you should ask Siobhan, now that she's not keeping company with James anymore."

"I don't have an eye for Siobhan," he said, his lower lip protruding in a pout that looked strange on his rugged face. "I was hoping for *your* company, not Siobhan's. She's a short, stout lass, and I like the tall ones meself. Like yerself."

"Yes, well, like I said, Conn, I have so much to

do around here. In fact, I should be baking this very minute instead of talking with you. If you'll run along to the pub, I'll send Mr. O'Brien on to you when he's ready to leave."

The lip stuck out even farther. "I suppose yer hopin' to have some private time with himself, to say good-bye and all."

Moya laughed and shook her head. "No, Conn. I don't need private time with Mr. Rory O'Brien. All I'm likely to tell him is, 'Good-bye and don't let the door slap your arse on your way out.'"

Conn beamed again. "Then ye don't like him, truly? I thought maybe ye did."

"That's what you get for thinkin', Conn. I suggest you refrain from that activity as often as possible, seein' where it leads. Away with you now; I've work to do and you makin' a nuisance o' yourself."

Satisfied, Conn sauntered out the back door, nabbing a scone off the platter as he left.

Moya leaned back against the sink and stood quietly for a moment, trying to sort out her own feelings. Within the hour, Rory O'Brien would be heading back to New York, leaving almost as soon as he had arrived. And with him he was taking her peace of mind.

With all her heart she wished that he would just return to New York and forget he had ever visited Ireland, forget Gormloch, forget Lios na Daoine Sidhe, forget all of them.

No, that isn't true, she reminded herself. At least one part of her . . . a rather large part, she would have to admit, didn't want him to forget. She would have actually been quite sad if she had thought she would never see Rory O'Brien again.

But she couldn't bear to think what he might do if he stayed. What changes he might bring to her world.

No. It wasn't worth the risk. She wanted him to go. She did.

She heard the front door open and close and her pulse quickened. He was back. She could already recognize his step, heavy but quick, much quicker than those of the villagers. He was still on New York time, not Ireland time.

When he walked into the kitchen, she could have sworn that his face was a bit pale, and he was perspiring, although it was a cool, spring day.

"How was your stay at the cemetery?" she asked, eyeing him closely as he walked past her and over to the refrigerator.

"Fine," he replied, looking inside. "I need a cold glass of water."

"No problem," she said, taking a crystal tumbler from the cupboard. "Have a seat there at the table and I'll fetch one for you. You look a bit done in from your walk."

"I'm okay," he grumbled, but he took her advice and sat down—hard—on a chair at the table.

She took a pitcher of water from the refrigerator, poured him a glassful, and set it in front of him. "Did you have a fine time, exploring the graveyard?"

"It was all right," he said. "What's to explore? Just a lot of gravestones and grass."

"Mmmm, you're a hard man to impress, Rory

O'Brien. 'Twas your own grandfa'r made those fine gates . . . the ones in front."

"I know."

"Your father spoke of him, did he?"

"Yeah."

"Well, I'm sure he must have been proud of his da, fine smith that he was. Those gates are quite grand, really. I'd be really proud if I were—"

"Yeah, yeah, they're all right. Where's that guy that's supposed to drive me to Shannon? I suppose he'll flake out on me like the other driver did and not even show up. Then I'm going to be stranded again and have to ride that damned bus. I hate inefficiency, and from what I've seen so far, this is one inefficient country."

Moya scowled at him and propped her hands on her hips. "Mr. Hallissey was waiting here patiently for you when I returned from our walk, and he lingered awhile, sippin' tea, until I told him to go on back to the pub. I said you'd come get him when you were ready to go."

"Oh. Good." He took a long drink of the water, ignoring the fact that she was glowering at him.

"Well, are you?" she snapped.

"Am I what?"

"Ready to be goin'?"

He grinned. "You sound like you're ready for me to leave."

She set the pitcher down hard on the table, within his reach, then turned her back on him and walked over to the sink, where she began scrubbing vegetables. "What a clever lad you are, thinkin' I'm after gettin' rid o' you. Figured that out all by yourself, did you?"

"Ah, yeah. Not being blind, deaf, and dumber than dirt, I picked up on it right away." He stood and walked over to stand behind her. Leaning close to her, he lowered his voice and said, "Exactly why is it that you don't like me, Moya Mahoney?"

When she turned to face him, she realized they were nearly nose to nose. His blue eyes filled her vision and she felt her knees go soft beneath her. She backed up against the sink as best she could, but he was still close enough for her to feel his warm breath on her cheek.

"I can think of a dozen reasons why you might not like me," he continued in that hushed, conspiratorial tone that she found strangely pleasant and upsetting at the same time. "Maybe it's because I'm a smart mouth, because I'm not as nice as most of these polite Irish lads that you're used to, or maybe you just don't like Yanks, New Yorkers in particular."

She took a deep breath and tried not to notice that his lips were quite full for a man's, the only softness in an otherwise rugged face, and they were oh, so close. Only inches from hers. She could smell the faint scent of his aftershave and a provocative fragrance that was all his own.

When he placed one hand on either side of her and leaned on the countertop, effectively pinning her inside his arms, she thought she was going to stop breathing altogether.

"I've nothing against Yanks," she said, barely able

to force out the words. She, too, sounded as though she had been running a marathon. "But I'd say the other reasons for not liking you are good ones. You do have a way of—"

He leaned still closer, his eyes on her lips. He was smiling, obviously enjoying her embarrassment. "Yes?" he said. "I have a way of . . . ?"

"Of . . . of saying the wrong thing . . . at the wrong time . . . and . . ."

"And do I make you uncomfortable, Moya Mahoney?"

She nodded. Vigorously. "Aye, you do. You make everyone within hearing uncomfortable."

"Do I make Conn Hallissey and Gill Doolin uncomfortable . . . the way I do you, Moya?"

He leaned even closer until his mouth was only a breath away from hers, his body so near she could feel his heat. But he was grinning, mocking her, as if it were only a game they were playing, with him in control of every move.

"Perhaps 'tis another reason entirely," she said, deciding to counter his strategy. "Maybe I resent the fact that you've inherited something which is a precious jewel but you have no appreciation for it. Maybe I feel as though Angus O'Brien cast his pearl to a swine, and I sorely wish he hadn't done so."

He couldn't have moved away any faster if she had slapped his face. And as he backed away from her, Moya cursed herself. Since when did she speak so bitterly—and to someone who was family to a dear, departed friend?

"Mr. O'Brien, I beg your forgiveness," she said. "That was a terribly unkind thing to say."

She saw the hurt in his eyes, then watched as he pulled a shield down over his feelings. His face went blank, his eyes cold. "Don't worry about it, Ms. Mahoney. I've had a lot worse said to me, though never by anyone quite so pretty. And not by someone who, I'd wager, is usually kind and soft-spoken. I must have really messed up with you. I'm sorry."

Tears flooded her eyes, adding to her shame. She stared down at the floor and twisted her hands in her apron. "You haven't been so very dreadful, Mr. O'Brien. I suppose I'm just overwrought, what with losing Angus and then . . ."

"Losing the pub?"

She glanced up at him, surprised.

He gave her an understanding smile. "Do you think I didn't figure that one out? I'm a clever lad; you said so yourself. Angus had no heirs other than me. You nursed him in his sickness, provided a loving home for him until he died. It would only be right that he'd leave the pub to you. Do you have any idea why he didn't?"

The tears that had filled her eyes came spilling down her cheeks, and she wished she could die rather than stand there in her humiliation.

"No. I haven't a clue," she said with a sniff. "But I feel like a foolish, selfish child, wantin' what wasn't mine. What I did for Angus, I did out of love. He owed me nothin' at all. The pub was his to do with as he chose."

He reached up and brushed her tears away with

his fingertips in a gesture that went straight to her
heart and caused still more drops to fall. "You aren't
a child, foolish, or stupid, Moya. You have every
right to feel the way you do."

Moya closed her eyes and stood quietly as he continued to stroke her cheek softly. His touch felt so
good, soothing and healing. Then she felt his lips
against her forehead. He gave her a kiss, just below
her hairline . . . a kiss that lasted a few seconds longer
than just a friendly kiss. It was long enough for her
to savor the warmth of his lips against her skin, to
think of other, more intimate kisses, and then it was
over.

Moya wondered at the depth of the disappointment she felt when he didn't continue. The simple
kiss had been sweet, a balm to her wounded heart,
but she wanted more. She *needed* much more. His
gesture had stirred desires that were far from pla-
tonic.

But those needs wouldn't be answered, at least,
not now.

Instead, he pulled away and walked toward the
door. "I'm going to go walk around this property that
I've been given. I want to see at least some of it before I leave. What are the boundaries?"

She gathered her senses and tried to speak normally, as though her blood hadn't left her head entirely and pooled in more personal, intimate spots.
"Ah . . . the stone wall on the east and the west, the
road to the north, and the river to the south."

"Thanks. I'll be back in half an hour or so."

"Wait! Before you go—"

He paused, his hand on the doorknob. "Yes?"

"There's something I must give you."

His eyes lit expectantly. "And what's that?"

She reached into the refrigerator and pulled out a loaf of bread. Pinching off a small piece, she said, "You're goin' to be crossin' hungry grass. You must have a bit o' bread in your pocket."

"What are you talking about? Hungry grass?"

She walked over to him and pressed the scrap of bread into his hand. "You'll be crossing fields where people died during the terrible potato famine—the Great Hunger, we call it. Folks died of starvation there in those pastures, their mouths stained green from eatin' the grass. You must carry a bit of bread in your pocket when you walk on that grass, out of respect for them and their sufferings."

Rory closed his hand around the bread and held it, saying nothing. For once, there were no comments about superstitions or ridiculous fantasies. He nodded solemnly and put the bread into his shirt pocket. "Thank you, Moya Mahoney," he said. Then he left, shutting the door softly behind him.

Seven

As Moya stripped the sheets off the bed where Rory O'Brien had just slept, she could smell the same enticing scent of aftershave and man that had caused her such delicious discomfort in the kitchen. It instantly evoked the sensation of his fingertips on her cheek, the whisper of his breath as he leaned close to her, and the look of gentle concern in his eyes.

Perhaps all wasn't lost after all. He might be a fellow who made offhand, rash remarks, but he didn't seem like a bad sort, really. He could be rather nice, she decided, when he wasn't acting the part of a donkey's hind leg.

And he *did* smell nice.

She heard someone coming up the stairs, and again she recognized his brisk, no-nonsense stride. Rolling the sheets into a bundle, she stuffed them into a portable hamper, then began to spread the fresh linens on the bed.

When Rory first entered the room, she didn't look up at him, though she could feel his eyes on her. The last thing she wanted was to betray what she had been thinking a minute ago about his pleasant scent . . . or that he might be a reasonable decent human being.

He stood quietly until she finished tucking in the sheet and glanced his way. "It's a nice piece of property," he said.

"Yes, 'tis," she agreed, pleased that he had finally said something positive about his inheritance. "The river is lovely, peaceful, don't you think?"

"Oh, yeah, I guess so. I noticed what looks like it used to be a small airstrip on the east side."

"Aye, 'twas before my time, but I've heard that some planes came and went there during World War Two. There's not much use for it now."

"Hmm." He looked thoughtful. "And most of the acreage on the road side of the property is level and cleared."

"That's true. 'Tis. Except for the fairy fort with its trees and the trenches around it."

"The what? Oh, yeah. I noticed that. But it's no big deal. Wouldn't present a problem."

Moya bristled. "No big deal? I beg to differ with you, Mr. O'Brien. 'Tis a big deal indeed! That fort is—"

He held up one hand in mock surrender. "I know, I know . . . it's a precious archaeological site filled with benevolent spirits who—"

"Not necessarily benevolent, sir. I wouldn't count

on their good nature, if you're going to be so disrespectful when referring to them and their habitation."

He stared at her, his mouth open, then he laughed and shook his head. "You really believe in that crap, don't you, Moya? I can't believe you people are so superstitious in this day and age. I mean, you have communication with the outside world, television, radio, movies. Why are you so backward and out of step with the rest of civilization?"

More than anything Moya wanted to hurl the pillow she was holding at him, but a pillow fight seemed so juvenile. And she had no guns in the house, so. . . .

"Backward, are we?" she shouted. "Uncivilized? Who's the one without a civilized bone in his body in this room right now? 'Tis yourself, Mr. O'Brien. At least we have the courtesy not to say such unkind things to others. Superstitious barbarians that we are, we know better than to criticize another person's country when we're standing on his soil.

"Take me, for instance," she continued, "I've resisted the terrible urge to tell you what a loathsome creature you are. Why, I've met goats with better manners than yourself and mules who were more cooperative and accommodating to others. Pigs who were—"

"All right, all right, I catch your drift," he said, backing away from her with both hands up, palms out, in front of his face. "Thank you for restraining yourself, Miss Mahoney, for being so civil and not telling me what you really think of me."

He was smiling at her. She couldn't believe it. She had just insulted him dreadfully, said things to him that she couldn't imagine saying to any other person, and he wasn't even angry. If anything, he was amused.

There was simply no understanding this strange Yank.

"You aren't furious with me for sayin' that?" She dropped the pillow she was holding onto the bed and took a step closer to him.

"Why should I get mad at you? You were just saying what you think in that colorful Irish way you have. Everybody's entitled to their opinion. And apparently you think I'm not quite as refined as the average goat, mule, or pig."

She stared at him, completely nonplussed. Then she began to laugh. "There's no understandin' you, Rory O'Brien. If I spoke to any man in this village the way I just talked to you, he'd never utter another word to me for all our livin' days."

"Then he's a fool. I wouldn't miss an opportunity to spar with you, Miss Mahoney, for all the Guinness in Ireland."

"Do you like Guinness?"

"Hate it."

"I thought so."

"But I like you."

His smile was mischievous, but sincere. Moya felt the same unsettling sensation of heat spreading through her body that she had felt in the kitchen when he had pinned her between his arms.

"You don't even know me, Mr. O'Brien."

"I know you better than you think. I was raised a street kid, and on the streets you learn to tell a good person from a bad one very quickly. In my neighborhood, sizing someone up in an instant was a basic survival technique. And my gut instinct tells me you're a fine woman, Moya Mahoney. A bit testy. Easily offended. But you're exceptionally bright, strong-willed, and determined, and you have a kind heart."

"Strong-willed, you say? Stubbornness and kindness don't usually go together in a person's makeup."

"I didn't say stubborn. Stubbornness is standing by your opinion without giving honest consideration as to whether you're right or wrong. That's foolishness. But there's nothing wrong with being strong-willed. Only the strong can truly be kind."

"What do you mean?"

"When a weak person is kind, it isn't true kindness because it's coming from fear. But when a strong person is kind and cooperative, submitting his will to another, it's a true gift. He's putting the other person's welfare before his own, because he chooses to, not because he's afraid not to."

She considered his words carefully, then said, "You *do* have a gift for reading people, Mr. O'Brien."

"Not bad for a mule with the manners of a goat, eh?"

She blushed. "I'm truly sorry I said that, sir. I'd be in your debt if, as a gentleman, you'd never refer to it again."

He threw back his head and laughed heartily. "We've already decided that I'm not a gentleman. And I'll never let you live that one down. I intend to refer to it frequently for years to come. If for no other reason, to see you blush. You're really very pretty with your cheeks all pink like that."

Moya wasn't sure what made her more uncomfortable, his compliment or the suggestion that he and she might remain on speaking terms for years to come. Both pleased her—and made her want to run out of the room all the way to Tipperary.

"Besides tormenting me, exactly what are your plans, Mr. O'Brien?"

"Well, first I have to think of a way to get you to use my first name, instead of calling me 'Mr.' all the time. Then I'm going to go back to New York and consider my options where this property is concerned."

A chill went through her. Whether of premonition or paranoia, she couldn't tell.

"What's wrong, Moya? You look worried."

"I am. The pub and the land it's sittin' on means a lot to this community—to me. It worries me that its fate rests in the hands of a stranger."

He took a couple of slow steps toward her, his eyes glowing with a light that made her uneasy about his intentions.

"Well," he said in a low voice that gave her an involuntary shiver, "there's something we can do about that."

Her heart began to pound as he took another step and stood in front of her, only inches away . . . much too close for comfort. It occurred to Moya that Rory O'Brien was forever making her uneasy. She always seemed a bit off balance in his presence.

"What?" she asked cautiously. "What exactly did you have in mind?"

As in the kitchen earlier, his nearness flooded her senses and made her weak all over. His face was so near, his eyes on her lips.

"We . . ." he said, ". . . could make sure that I'm not a stranger anymore."

He reached for her, his big, strong hands sliding around her waist as he pulled her to him. Bending his head to hers, he waited a few seconds, as though giving her the opportunity to resist.

But resisting was the last thing on Moya Mahoney's mind.

Her own hands found their way to his shoulders, and she moved closer, lifting her face to receive his kiss.

When their mouths touched, his lips were warm and firm, just brushing hers, until he teased a small, frustrated groan from her. Her hands moved upward from his shoulders to the back of his head, and she buried her fingers in his hair, holding his head as she forced him to kiss her fully.

He laughed, a throaty, bass chuckle as he responded by deepening the kiss and pulling her body tightly against his. Moya reveled in the hardness of him pressing against her own soft curves, the delicious contrast of male and female as she arched into his embrace.

His lips took hers with just the right mixture of passion tempered with gentleness. He lingered until she was almost completely breathless. When he finally pulled away, she had to cling to him to keep her balance. She felt as though every drop of blood had flowed out of her head and limbs and into the center of her body.

"So, she's bright and strong," he said, still holding her tightly pressed against him, "and lovely and kind . . . and she kisses like an angel—with a bit of the devil just below the surface. That's what I call an all-around great girl."

"And you," she breathed, "are what I call an astute and clever lad to have noticed all those things."

He placed a quick kiss on the tip of her nose. "I may have the manners of miscellaneous barnyard animals, but I know a good woman when I see one . . . and certainly when I kiss one."

His grip around her tightened and he buried his face in her hair. "Have faith in me, Moya. Believe that I'll do the right thing, for the pub, for you, for your community. Angus trusted me; he said so in his letter. Can't you?"

She pulled back so that she could see into his eyes. The sincerity shining there touched her heart. "I will," she said. "I'll trust you to do the best thing for all. But promise me you'll give it your most serious consideration. 'Tis important, to all of us."

"I don't care that much about 'all of us,' but I do care about you. And I want to stay in contact with you, by telephone and letter when I'm in New York. I want to see you when I come back here to settle things, once I've decided what I'm doing with the property."

"Of course you'll see me, if you come back," she said. " 'Tis a tiny village. Everyone sees everyone every day. All you have to do is look out your window to see half the population at any given moment."

"You know what I mean. I want to see you as in spend time with you. Talking like we were last night over a hot toddy. Going for walks, like the one we took today out to the cemetery. And, of course, becoming less of a stranger to you."

His mouth found hers again, and this time his kiss was less gentle. His lips took hers as though he were trying to draw enough from her to last until he could return for more.

She finally pulled away, gasping for breath. "You'll always be a bit strange to me, Rory O'Brien," she said. "But I think I could enjoy gettin' used to your idiosyncrasies."

He smiled, satisfied. Then he released her, walked across the room, and picked up his suitcase. "I'll be back, Moya *Ma*honey. Will you have a bed for me here at your fine establishment?"

"And breakfast, too."

"But no dinner?"

She smiled. "No dinner."

His mischievous smirk returned. "Who needs an entree? How about just going straight to dessert?"

Thoughts of sharing "dessert" with Rory O'Brien flooded her thoughts . . . and set other, more intimate parts of her body to tingling. The decadent fantasies that played across her mind had nothing to do with queen cakes or apple tarts.

But, delicious scenarios aside, this New York Yank was moving much too fast for an Irish female who had decided long ago to be ruled by reason, not imagination. No matter how sweet her dreams might be.

"I've only one thing to say to you, Rory O'Brien . . ."

"And that is?"

"Slow down. You're in Ireland now. And we do things a wee bit differently here."

He scowled. "I've noticed."

"Give us a chance. You might discover that you like us. A busy, harried New Yorker like yourself might even find that he enjoys 'slow.'"

He laughed and shook his head. "Ah, Moya, you're a pisser."

"I beg your pardon?"

"That's a compliment, New York style, believe me." A slow smile curled the edges of her mouth. "And yes, I think I might enjoy some lessons in 'slow' from an Irish lass like yourself. In fact, I'll be looking forward to that. I'll see you soon."

"Safe home," she said, already questioning her own cautious nature. In her experience, "safe" seemed to always translate into "alone."

In less than a New York minute . . . he was gone.

Moya wasn't the only one questioning her own decisions. By the time Rory had left her house and marched to the pub, he was in a foul mood, anticipating his lonely return home. He was going to miss that irritating redhead . . . far more than he cared to admit, even to himself.

He entered the pub and dropped his suitcase on the floor with a thud that disrupted the pleasant murmur of conversations among the patrons. Glancing around, he spied Conn Hallissey, who was sitting at a booth in the rear, chatting with several friends.

"If you're going to be driving me to Shannon, I'd appreciate it if you didn't spend the morning in the local pub getting soused," Rory said to him, far more abruptly than he had intended.

A flush of anger colored Conn's already ruddy face. He slowly stood to his full and impressive height and glared at Rory, nose to nose. "I was enjoyin' a cola, along with some political debate, Mr. O'Brien, as I always do when I'm drinkin' with friends."

"Aye," Tommy O'Sullivan piped up. "Conn's a teetotaler, he is. No alcoholic beverages ever pass those virgin lips, to be sure."

"And himself is quite proud of that fact," added Gill Doolin as he collected empty glasses and bottles from the table and replaced them with filled ones. "I wouldn't trod on his toes, were I you, Mr. O'Brien. Conn takes his sobriety very seriously."

"Aye," added Tommy, "he's likely to pounce on ye and do ye serious damage if he thinks yer callin' him a drunkard. Now meself . . . I take pride in bein' a champion pint drinker. Each man must seek fame in his own way."

The other men nodded seriously, agreeing all around.

Rory felt his temper rising, but the grimace on Conn's face kept him from saying anything else that might be construed as an insult. The last thing he wanted was to have to hike to Shannon . . . with a black eye and skinned knuckles.

"I'm glad to hear you're sober, Mr. Hallissey," he said. "I meant no disrespect, but I'm—"

"Didn't ye, now?" Conn's angry look was fading, to be replaced by something that was more like a quiet sadness. Rory preferred his anger. "I thought, perhaps, you were suggesting that all Irishmen are worthless, lazy drunkards. But ye say ye meant no disrespect, so that must not be what ye were sayin' 'cause sure, that would be most impolite—even for a New York fella."

Rory quirked one eyebrow. "Did I hear you right? Did you just imply that all New Yorkers are rude?"

Conn grinned. "Not at all. I've met one or two who didn't insult someone every time they opened their mouth, a couple of them who didn't deserve to be shot at sunrise. But I'd say a civil New Yorker is as rare a jewel as a teetotalin' Irishman."

Rory laughed. "Touché. And it appears there's no shortage of bigots on either side of the Atlantic."

The men at the table chuckled and nodded. "Aye," Tommy agreed, "bigotry thrives in all corners of the world, sad to say. But without it, we'd have to stop lookin' at others' faults and concentrate on our own shortcomings."

"And then where'd we be?" Gill asked.

"In the pubs, drinkin' to dull the pain of all that self-examination," Tommy replied, hoisting his fresh ale. "So, here's to a full glass. *Slainte.*"

"*Slainte. Slainte. Slainte.*" The toast went around the table, glasses lifted.

"Are you after leavin' us now, Mr. O'Brien?" Conn asked.

"I am," Rory replied. He glanced around one last time, evaluating his new inheritance. An Irish pub. Left to him—a guy who had spent much of his formative years looking for his father in just such establishments, swearing he would never waste his life sitting in such a place.

Fate certainly had a sense of humor. And apparently it was black, sardonic, Irish humor.

Moya knocked on Norah Delaney's massive front door and listened as Norah's tiny Yorkshire terrier inside barked furiously, announcing her arrival. Moya shifted the bag she was carrying to her other hand as she waited for Norah. It took a while for Norah to answer, longer than it had last year or the year before. The huge, rambling house was a challenge for an elderly woman to get around in. But Moya hoped she was as spry as Norah when she reached that mature age. Norah was a living example of how a nimble mind preserved agility in the body.

And no one got anything over on Norah Delaney.

The door opened an inch, and Moya saw an eye peering out through the space. "Ah, Moya," Norah exclaimed as she threw the door wide open, "ye should have rung me up before ye called on me. If I had known ye were comin', I'd have caged this fierce beast of mine. Don't let his small size lull ye into a false security. Surely, ye could lose a leg or an arm to this flesh-eatin' monster."

Moya resisted the urge to snicker; Norah took her dog's ferocity much too seriously, probably due to a lack of drama in Norah's day-to-day existence. Like his mistress, the terrier's growl was much worse than his bite. He had lost several of his teeth over the years, and arthritis had slowed him considerably. He could hardly hobble from his feed dish to his bed to the yard. A person would have had no problem outrunning him and avoiding getting gummed to death.

"Ah, I'll take me chances," Moya said, looking down at yellow, bared fangs showing in the shaggy, white face. "He acts like a tough guy, but he's really a sweet, soft lad under all that snarling."

"Eh, don't count on it. Come on inside . . . if ye dare."

"I have something important to give you, so I'll risk it."

"To give me?" The old woman's face lit up as she eyed the paper bag in Moya's hand. "Is it some sort of gift?"

"It is, indeed."

"Then come directly inside. I'll not let Wolfe Tone here chew upon ye."

"You're too kind, Norah. Too kind."

"I know. 'Tis true." She reached for Moya's sleeve and gave it a tug. "Hurry in now, and give me the present straightaway."

The moment Moya stepped across the threshold, the bristling ball of fury became a docile sweetheart with wagging tail and lolling tongue. She shifted the bag she was carrying to the other hand, reached down and scratched the dog behind his right ear. He closed his eyes and whimpered with delight.

"Oh, yes, you're a big, fearsome creature, aren't you, Wolfe," she said as he leaned against her hand.

"Your mistress has trained you to go straight for the Achilles' tendon."

"Come on in, lass, and have a seat for yerself," Norah said, shoving her toward the opulently furnished parlor. French provincial furniture, Waterford chandeliers, Persian rugs and artifacts from the Delaneys' many journeys to the most exotic parts of the world testified to the fact that Norah had found the adventure she was craving when she'd married Mr. Delaney.

This house and its property, which extended nearly to the foot of the great mountain Carrantuohill, was far more than one woman needed, but Norah had paid a great price for her wealth and adventure. She had given up Angus O'Brien, her poet lover.

Moya wondered if she was still happy with her choice. Pushing Moya toward a satin brocade loveseat, Norah dropped into her own easy chair and stuck out her hands. "What is it ye have there in yer bag, Moya?" she said. "What are ye givin' to me, and it not even being me birthday?"

"Truth be told, Norah, 'tisn't from meself. 'Tis from Angus O'Brien, given to you from beyond the grave."

"No! It can't be true."

"'Tis. In the very last letter he wrote on this earth, he mentioned you and asked that this be yours. So, I brought it 'round to place it in your hands, precious gift that it is."

Moya opened the paper bag and took out the small wooden chest. She placed it into Norah's outstretched hands.

"Oh, my, his very own snuffbox," she said, stroking the ornately inlaid top. "I've seen him reach into it a thousand times a thousand to fill his pipe."

"I think it was his favorite thing on earth, that box," Moya said. "I'd say you were still his favorite girl, right up until the end."

"No. That's two lies rolled into one, Moya. Angus's favorite thing on earth was his pub. And you were his favorite girl. But I'd say I ran a close second, or he wouldn't have left this for me."

Moya hesitated, weighing whether or not to ask a question that she had puzzled over for years. She decided that if there was to be a proper time, this would be it.

"Norah, if you don't mind me askin', and if it's not too personal, are you glad that you married Mr. Delaney instead of Angus?"

"Angus never asked. Pure and simple. He hinted. He made half promises by the light of the moon. But hints and promises unfulfilled don't put a ring on a girl's finger. Plus, Angus wanted to live the rest of his life here in this village. His idea of a fine time was a jaunt into Killarney. I wanted more than that.

"And Angus was a bit daft, as all poets are. He had his head in the clouds and not on earth. Poets like himself don't provide a roof over a woman's head. Michael Delaney, may he rest in peace, offered me security and great adventures, and I was gettin' too old to be waitin' for Angus to come 'round."

"I'm sure Angus loved you. Why do you think he didn't get around to askin'?"

"He had great and mighty dreams, that Angus.

Every day another plan, another scheme. One day he would be a famous novelist, the next a powerful politician, maybe a singer who would perform on demand for the crowned heads of Europe. Ah, what a pain in the arse was that man. So busy dreamin' so much and doin' so little. Michael didn't dream—he just did."

Moya sighed, a little sorry she had asked. She hated to hear such unkind words about her departed friend . . . even if they did have the ring of truth.

"But Angus was a charmin' fella."

"Aye, but charm doesn't pay the rent or put food on the table. And Michael Delaney was good at both. I learned young, Moya, not to listen to a man's words, but to watch what he does. And Angus O'Brien was a talker, not a doer."

"But he loved you."

"Aye, and love won't pay the rent, either. There's no truer way to show affection than to go to work every day and help a woman raise a family. Hard work, that's what shows the real character of a man."

Moya decided that she was, indeed, sorry she had asked. This wasn't what she wanted to hear about her old friend the day after he was put into the ground.

But Norah seemed to sense her discomfort. She reached over and patted Moya on the knee.

"But I am proud and happy that Angus left me this bit of himself. I'll always cherish it, and I'll let it be known that when I pass on, it'll be comin' back to you."

"Thank you, Norah. That's most kind of you. I

should be goin' now. I'll not have any boarders in my house tonight if I'm not there to receive them."

"How is business then, Moya?"

"Slow, Norah. They're not exactly cuttin' the queue outside my door to be the first in."

"These are hard times." Norah clucked and shook her head as they walked to the front door. "Hard times, indeed. I don't know how this village is goin' to survive."

"The way we always have, Norah."

"Barely."

"Aye, barely."

Less than five minutes later, Moya was gone, and Norah was looking inside the tobacco box. For what, she wasn't sure. But Angus had always been rather secretive of that box, protective of it, and now that it was truly her own, she wanted to see if there was some particular reason why.

Inside was the usual—a bag of blackberry tobacco, scenting the box with its sweet, wild fragrance. Next to it was a small box of matches from a pub in Killarney, and, of course, Angus's briar pipe. The pipe was stained dark from smoke and the oils of Angus's fingers as he had held it, year after year.

In spite of what she had told Moya, Norah couldn't help feeling a twinge of regret for the love lost between herself and the man who had smoked that pipe. Angus had been her first love, and she would always hold a special place for him in her heart.

Over the years, she had thought of him far more than she would have admitted to anyone, including herself. Seeing him daily in the village had been difficult at times, when her own hardworking husband had been absent for long stretches and she had been lonely.

But she had never spoken of her feelings to Angus—out of devotion to her husband and because she wasn't sure how Angus felt. He had probably long forgotten those moonlit strolls through the apple orchards and how delicious it had been to sample forbidden fruits there beneath the flowered boughs.

Sometimes, when she had passed him on the streets, she wondered if he remembered as vividly as she did. Nothing in his eyes ever suggested that he did.

But he had left her this box.

He must have had some feelings for her, some pleasant recollections that kept him warm on a lonely winter evening, even as her memories comforted her.

She touched the bottom of the box and felt it tilt slightly beneath her finger. There was something under it. She lifted the rectangle of wood and found it was a false bottom. Beneath it was a bundle of letters, all written on pale blue linen stationery, which she recognized as Angus's business paper. Many times she had seen him posting letters from the pub on that paper. And here was a stack of blue letters, each with her name written in his long, flowing hand on the outside.

With trembling fingers she opened the first one and saw that it was dated three years ago, shortly before her husband's death. It was a love letter, telling her in florid, unabashed terms the depth of his love, the heat of his passion for her.

And also telling her that, having ruined his chances with her, he would never burden her by confessing his feelings openly.

Tears ran down Norah's face as she opened the next letter, dated several months before that. The sentiments expressed in that one were just like the first she had read. He did remember. He recalled even more than she did as, there on paper, he detailed their first night together.

A warm flood of emotions swept through Norah Delaney as she read one letter after another, testaments of his devotion to her that were written over a period of fifty years. Fifty years of reliving on paper what had been and recording the regrets for what had never been.

"Ah, Angus," she said as she held one of the letters to her lips and kissed it, "ye were a pain in the arse. I'll not take that back, because 'twas true. But, truth be told, I never quite got over ye. And I'm so happy to see ye carried a torch for me, too."

She was about to put the letters back in the box when she saw one more envelope, a white one, still left in the box. But it didn't have her name on it. Instead, Angus had written, *To Be Opened on the One Year Anniversary of My Death and Not Before.*

"Now, Angus," she said, running her finger over the well-sealed edge of the envelope, "ye knew me better than to give me such a thing as this. If ye'd not wanted me to take a look at the contents of this letter, ye'd have given it to the good Father Shea.

He's the closest we have to a saint in this village. And it would take a saint not to sneak just a small peek."

She glanced up at the heavens. "So, if yer upset, ye've only yer own bad judgement to blame."

A few minutes later, Norah was standing over a teakettle that was steaming on the stove top. She was holding the envelope's seal over the steam and coaxing it open an inch at a time.

Wolfe Tone sat at her feet, whimpering because he had passed his suppertime with an empty dish.

"Go away, ye flea-bitten terror," she told him. "Can't ye see I'm in the midst of a delicate operation?"

Finally, she had it open. She turned off the flame under the kettle, walked over to the kitchen table, and sat down.

As she read, a gentle smile spread across her face. "Ah, Angus O'Brien," she whispered. "Maybe ye weren't such a fool after all."

Then she read it one more time just for good measure. And resealed the envelope.

Eight

Rory was enormously grateful that the return trip to Shannon was faster and less eventful than the first. Like the bus driver, Conn stopped frequently for flocks of sheep to cross in front of the car. Occasionally they found themselves behind what Conn called a "caravan," a colorfully painted gypsy wagon, drawn by a horse and driven by a tourist couple who were experiencing an alternative style honeymoon.

"They think it's gonna be grand," Conn said as they passed one of the disgruntled-looking pairs, "and they say it is for the first ten kilometers. Then when the horse wants to stop and nibble the grass on the side of the road and they've no clue how to motivate him to move ahead, they change their tune right quick. And those seats can wear yer arse flat in no time at all."

"That's not my idea of an enjoyable honeymoon,"

Rory said, mentally clocking the horse at about one mile per twenty-four hours.

Conn gave him a sly, sideways glance. "So, it's a married man, ye are?"

"Who, me?" Rory laughed. "No. Not even close. And you?"

"Naw. There's only one woman for me, and I haven't the money for a ring to put on her finger. A lot of us fellas are in that very position. Havin' full hearts but empty pockets. Times are bad now in our corner o' the world."

"I thought Ireland was experiencing an economic boom right now."

Conn turned a corner and pulled the car sharply to the side of the road to avoid hitting a sudden flock of chickens. Rory hung onto his seat, still trying to adjust mentally to the fact that they were driving on the left side of the street. The roads weren't much wider than the car and Conn was whizzing around the tight curves, apparently with little regard as to who might be coming from the opposite direction.

Rory wasn't particularly fond of flying. But this time he was going to be happy to board a plane, as though he had received a reprieve from death.

"Aye, the country as a whole is doin' well," Conn agreed. "But Lady Prosperity hasn't found her way to Gormloch yet, or the villages around us. Killarney does well because o' the tourists, but the rest of us could do with a bit of commerce. 'Tis hard on a man's spirit, having no work to do."

Rory nodded. "That's true. When I was a kid in New York, my father was out of work a lot. But that was his own doing. He chose to drink rather than look for a job. But there were a lot of people in our neighborhood who walked the streets, morning to night, looking for an honest way to make a buck and not finding it. It was very hard on them and their families."

Rory decided not to add how his best friend's father had suffered such despair that he had thrown himself off the 59th Street bridge. Or that several men in their building had died early deaths, brought on by the stress of poverty.

"And what is it ye do for a livin'?"

"I'm into computers."

"Ahhh, computers. Now there's a complicated business."

"It can be. But mostly, it's just all in a day's work."

"And do you make a heap of money doin' it?"

Rory laughed, enjoying the man's candor—Irish style. "Never enough. Never, never enough."

Conn chuckled, too. "'Tis the way of the world, no matter where yer standin'."

"True."

Since the beginning of the trip, Rory had wondered how and with whom, he could casually bring up the subject of Moya Mahoney. He wanted to pump Conn for information, but he didn't want word getting back to Moya that he had been asking about her.

He had just opened his mouth, ready to plunge in, when Conn broached the subject for him.

"So, what did ye think of Miss Moya Mahoney?"

Rory could hear more than idle curiosity in Conn's voice, so he decided to play it safe. "She's all right,

I guess. A nice enough woman. A bit opinionated and touchy about some things."

Conn raked his fingers through his mop of blond hair and a muscle twitched in his cheek. "Moya's a fine woman. The best. She's been through a lot, that lass, and come through shinin'."

"What do you mean?"

"Life's been unkind to her so far. When she was just a wee girl, about seven, I think, her ma died from a bad heart. Then a couple of years later her da was killed in a farming accident. She was sent to her grandmother's house, and the old lady made it clear she didn't want the burden of a child. When Moya was a teenager, the grandmother died—of pure meanness, I'd say—and she was on her own."

Rory felt a painful twinge of empathy. Apparently, his and Moya Mahoney's lives had traveled similar, rocky paths. "Moya didn't have friends or family other than the crabby old grandmother to help her?" he asked.

"She didn't have any other family. But your uncle, Angus O'Brien, gave her a job there in the pub, cleanin' and the like. She did odd jobs about the area, everything she could find to do: cookin', cleanin', watchin' after people's children, doin' laundry. Worked desperately hard, she did, made a bit 'o money here and a bit there. She spent hardly any. Then, some years back, the woman who lived next door to the pub passed away and the house was for sale. Moya bought the place with all the money she'd saved, fixed it up in fine form, and opened a guest house. She's done well for herself ever since."

"You're proud of her," Rory observed. "And you think a lot of her. She wouldn't happen to be the woman you'd like to give a ring to, would she?"

Conn grinned. "She might be. I could do worse than Moya Mahoney. Any man could do worse than a well-balanced lass like herself."

"Well-balanced?"

"Aye. She's a fine figure of a woman, if ye hadn't noticed."

Rory decided not to admit he had noticed. He also didn't deem it wise to mention this morning's passionate kiss which he could still feel on his lips.

"She's attractive enough, I guess," he said, glancing out the side window to avoid any eye contact with Conn, "if you like them tall and 'well-balanced.'"

But Conn didn't buy it. He became instantly attentive. "Aye, well, most lads like a long, cool drink of a woman like Moya. I'm sure ye must have noticed all that fine red hair of hers and those green eyes."

"Ah, yeah. I sorta noticed."

"Mmm . . ."

They traveled on in silence for several minutes. The mountains and forests were giving way to gentle, sloping hills lined with ancient stone fences and country lanes dotted with dainty, yellow primrose blossoms. A soft mist of rain began to fall.

"Does Moya know?" Rory asked at last.

"Know what?"

"How you feel about her."

Conn smiled so sweetly, so sadly, that Rory felt

a bit sorry for him. The big man looked like a lovesick teenager. "I don't believe she does," he said. "I've kept it to meself until now. I'm not sure why I told you."

Rory could easily guess. Conn had detected the chemistry between him and Moya and he was staking out his territory . . . or trying to.

Rory thought of the sweetness of Moya's kiss, that finely balanced figure and the lovely red hair that Conn had mentioned.

He felt sorry for Conn, but not that sorry. In love and war, it was every man for himself.

But, since he hadn't yet reached the airport in Shannon, he wasn't going to challenge Conn for Moya's affection just yet.

He would be coming back to Ireland. He was sure of that. And there would be plenty of time to battle Conn Hallissey for Moya Mahoney. That is if he still wanted her when he returned.

Rory thought about how Moya had molded herself into his embrace, yielding so sweetly to him.

Yes, he was pretty sure he would still want her.

Truly, there was nothing like a lively, Kerry jig to chase away a blue, misty mood, Moya decided as she sat on the small, makeshift stage at the back of the great room of Lios na Daoine Sidhe and pounded out a heart-throbbing rhythm on her bodhran. The round, flat drum had registered the pulse of the Irish people for centuries. And, like the generations of drummers before her, Moya played with a double-ended stick, her lightning agility matched by the flying feet of the dancers and the nimble fingers of the other musicians.

The large room, located at the back of the pub, was opened for special occasions, when it would be filled with the local citizenry, celebrating some aspect of life. It didn't require much in the way of a holiday. Almost any observance would serve.

Tonight, it was the Spring Dance Festival, where boys and girls of all ages competed for medals, distinguishing them as champions in the art of Irish dancing.

With their arms held stiffly at their sides, the performers showed little movement above the waist. Lips curled into shy smiles and curls bobbed vigorously, but otherwise, all the movement was reserved for the lower half of the body.

Feet flew at breathtaking speed, furiously pounding the intricate patterns that had been handed down through the generations. Legs pistoning, toes tapping, knees bobbing, all to the beat of the Celtic spirits.

Sean Kissane and his twin sister Shauna had already performed and done well, though Moya had seen Shauna dance better. Her young friend had sneaked a few too many sideways glances at Kevin Doolin and lost her concentration.

Now she sat, pouting in the corner of the room, as two other girls performed their victory dances, having already received their coveted medals. Two hours earlier, she had been so proud of herself, modeling her new green velvet dress with its beautiful patterns in the jewel tones of a brilliant stained glass window. But now she slouched, skirt crunched beneath her, sleeves pushed up to her elbow, the picture of dejection.

Kevin Doolin was helping his father by tidying up the empty glasses and emptying ashtrays. He didn't seem to have noticed whether she had won or lost—which, no doubt, accounted as much for Shauna's bad mood as her having lost the competition.

Sean had done better, having earned second prize. He strutted around in his elegant dancing costume, a formal black jacket, white shirt and tie, a plaid kilt, knee stockings, and brightly polished shoes, like a Riverdance star. His medal was pinned to his jacket lapel, along with several others. Sean was becoming quite famous for his furious flying feet—and it was going straight to his head.

Kevin walked by him, whispered something in his ear, and Sean balled up his fists as though ready to punch him. Moya laughed to herself, speculating on what the insult might have been. Kevin's father, Gill, had no extra money for dancing lessons. And that which could not be afforded must be held in utmost contempt.

As they were nearing the end of the song, Moya increased the tempo, making it a battle of musicians versus dancers in who could continue without tripping over their own feet—or their own fingers. It was a tie and all finished with a crescendo that set the room to cheering and clapping.

Gill Doolin stepped to the microphone and gave the winners one more acknowledgment. Then he thanked all for coming and wished them a safe journey home.

Moya lingered, chatting with the fiddler, the piper, and the children who had danced. Deirdre Kissane stood with her twins, congratulating the proud and victorious Sean, ignoring the pouting Shauna.

"Well, I think you both did brilliantly," Moya said, as she toyed with one of Shauna's thick braids. "That medal looks grand, shining on your chest there, Sean, and your sister is a vision of loveliness in her new dress."

"'Twould look better still with a medal upon it," Shauna said, her lower lip quivering.

"Naw, 'twould be gildin' the lily," Moya replied. "Perfection needs no improvement."

Deirdre Kissane seemed tired and less patient. "Sometimes ye win, and sometimes ye don't, and I'll not have any snifflin' about it," she told her daughter. "You stick in that lip before a bird perches on it and get your things together, we're headin' home."

"The evenin's still young, and 'tisn't a school night," Shauna complained. "We want to hear a story before we go. I want to hear about Grania, the queen of the pirates. Moya, will you tell us that one? Will you, please?"

Moya looked at Deirdre. She could see the tired mother was weighing the benefits of having the children at home and in bed against the pleasures of an hour at home alone with her husband and free child-sitting.

"You and Frank can run along now if you like,"

she told her. "I'd be glad to walk the children home after the storytellin's done."

"No longer than an hour," Deirdre said, trying not to look too pleased.

"A cup of Gill's fine hot chocolate and a story, and they'll be home."

Deirdre glanced across the room at her big, handsome husband who was packing his fiddle into its case. "Two cups of chocolate and two stories would be all right enough. After all, 'tisn't a school night."

Sean perked up. "Two stories! Then I want to hear a story of Brian Boru and how the coronation stone cried out when he was crowned the true High King of Ireland."

"Come along then," Moya said, taking their hands. "Let's help Kevin tidy up so that he can listen, too. And we'll ask Gill to stir up some of his grandest chocolate."

When the chores were finished and they and the other village children sat around the fire in a companionable circle, mugs of hot chocolate in their hands and the anticipation of a good story thick in the air, Moya counted her blessings.

She might not have children of her own. Not yet, anyway. She might have lost her own family at an early age. But until the day she had a husband and wee ones of her own sitting at her feet, this village was her family. She would share its children, its dances and celebrations, its wakes and funerals.

There was enough joy and sorrow within that small community to keep a soul filled. And Moya with a soul that was filled to overflowing counted herself very lucky.

Within the walls of Lios na Daoine Sidhe she had all she needed.

Except, perhaps, a man of her own. Someone who kissed as good and smelled as fine as Mr. Rory O'Brien from New York.

But with better manners.

Moya postponed the moment when she would have to return the children to their homes as long as possible, not only for the little ones or their weary parents, but also for herself. Without Angus or Rory O'Brien in her house, she knew she would feel the old devil of loneliness haunting her night hours.

Having spent many, many solitary hours as a child, Moya didn't mind being alone so much in the daylight hours. But, for the same reason, she minded being the only one in a house once the sun had set. An evening meal alone, no one to wish a good night, knowing that not a soul was sleeping under her roof except herself: those were the prices she paid for being a single lady.

Sometimes she thought that was why she operated a bed and breakfast guest house. At least, during the summer months, when the tourists were thick in the Killarney area, she had other people within in her walls. It was company, of a sort, even if the visitors were strangers.

So, it was late when she escorted the gaggle of children down the streets and to their homes, to parents who seemed somehow refreshed and happy to see them.

"Safe home and around the fairy forts, Moya," Deirdre Kissane shouted from her front door as the twins scrambled inside.

"Aye, and a good, long rest for yourself," Moya replied, waving to the children.

They were all delivered now. Time to go home.

Reluctantly, she turned and headed back toward her own house, extending the evening walk by strolling and savoring the fresh, damp smells of night.

Crickets chirped and frogs croaked in the nearby ditches that were filled with water from yesterday's deluge. A crow cawed in the gnarled branches of the old oak tree that stood in front of the post office that also served as the village's grocery store and pharmacy.

As she passed her neighbors' houses, Moya could smell the smoke from their turf fires, drifting out of their chimneys. From open windows, she could hear the sounds of radios and televisions, along with the occasional nighttime prayer being uttered by children on their knees beside their beds.

Gormloch was a fine place to live, she thought. A fine place to be born, to raise a family, to die and be carried to your final resting place by loved ones. Except for the lack of money, which sometimes caused grief and hardship, it was almost ideal, like no other place on earth that she had ever heard tell of.

Where else could a woman walk down a road, alone, at midnight and have no fear? She and everyone else in the village knew that if you got into any class of trouble, all you had to do was let out a yell and the lads would come running to your aid.

They counted on that. They counted on each other. And they were hardly ever let down.

Moya had nearly reached her house when she heard footsteps behind her. She turned and saw Conn Hallissey hurrying up the road in her direction. She knew it was him from his blond hair that shone in the moonlight and the size of him. Then there was the fact that he walked a bit like an overgrown ox. But Moya was kind, and she tried not to think of that.

"Evenin', Conn," she called to him. "Is the devil himself on your tail, or have you a fire to go to?"

"I'm just tryin' to catch up to you, lass," he said, breathless. "I thought ye might be needin' an escort home."

She smiled and pointed to her front porch, which wasn't far away. "It seems I've located me house all by meself, but I thank you nonetheless."

He caught up to her and stood, huffing and puffing, his breath making small, silver clouds in the crisp night air. "How are ye this fine spring evenin', Moya, darlin'?"

She gave him a playful grin. "And aren't you bein' the cheeky one, callin' me your darlin'. I'm no man's darlin', not even Conn Hallissey's."

" 'Tis a shame," he said as he grabbed her hand and placed it in the crook of his arm. "But, whether you're me darlin' or just me friend, yer in sore need of an escort to yer door."

"And is that all you were hopin' for, Conn? Just to lead me to my door and say 'good-bye'?"

"A man can always hope for more, but a smart one will take what he gets and be happy for it."

They stepped up on her porch, and she retrieved her hand from his arm. Unable to bear his look of disappointment, she stood on tiptoe to place a kiss on his cheek. His frown dissolved into a wide smile.

"Are you a happy man, Conn Hallissey?"

"I am."

She thought how she and Rory O'Brien had kissed and wondered if Conn would be so pleased if he had seen them. She didn't have to think long, knowing the answer to that one.

"I'm happy, so I am," Conn repeated. "Not delirious with joy, mind you, but content."

She decided to ignore the not-so-subtle hint to be invited inside. "Ah, good. If you're happy and content, so am I. Did you get Mr. O'Brien delivered to Shannon?"

"I did."

"And did he catch his plane?"

"He did. And I'll not be missin' that one."

Moya glanced at her front door and thought of the empty house. The house where she and Rory had shared a hot toddy, some companionable conversation, and a kiss that she would never forget if she lived to be as old as the Stone of Fal.

When she pulled her mind back to the present, she saw that Conn was studying her, a worried look on his broad face.

"But it seems, maybe you will be—missin' that fella, that is," he said.

"A bit, maybe," she said, unwilling to lie to him. There was really no chance for Conn, and while she found his attentions flattering, she didn't want to give him false hopes.

"Well, I don't think he'll be missin' you. Didn't speak very highly of ye, he didn't. When I said what a fine and attractive woman you are, he acted as though he had hardly noticed."

Just for a second she felt a pang of disappointment. Then she looked deeper into Conn's eyes and knew that he wasn't telling her the truth. At least, not the whole of it.

But she understood the reason behind his falsehoods and she couldn't bring herself to embarrass him by exposing him.

"Thank you for escorting me home, Conn. You're a fine lad, no matter what anyone in this village says about you."

She left him standing on the porch, looking puzzled and slightly miffed. She giggled as she closed the door behind her. While she might not want to embarrass him entirely, she wouldn't let him get away with that nonsense altogether.

And it was nonsense, wasn't it?

Surely Rory O'Brien had been as impressed with her as she had been with him.

Hadn't he?

She thought of his hands, big and warm, stealing around her waist, pulling her against him. She recalled his lips on hers, firm and demanding. She remembered the gleam of pure desire in his eyes when they had finished their kiss.

Yes, Rory O'Brien had been equally impressed with her as she had been with him.

At least, she certainly hoped so.

Nine

Rory O'Brien looked around his boardroom table and realized that his staff thought he had dumped his sanity somewhere in a Killarney lake. And he couldn't blame them.

"Do you want my honest opinion?" asked Mark Giordano, his vice president.

"Of course," Rory assured him. "I want everyone's input. That's why I called this meeting."

"Okay, I think this is out of character for you, Rory," Mark admitted. "You're usually the one reminding us not to take on high-risk ventures. Medium-risk, maybe, but this company isn't the patron saint of lost causes."

"It's hardly a lost cause," Rory argued, slapping the report binder he had been holding down on the table in front of him. "There's a very real possibility of it succeeding. A computer hardware assembly plant in that part of county Kerry is a very good idea. The community of Gormloch is small, but there are plenty of neighboring villages and towns to draw employees from, and—"

"Rory, I know you want this," his general manager, Herman Irving cautiously interjected. "But the area is too remote. Transportation would be a problem, both receiving raw materials and shipping finished product."

"It isn't all that rural," Rory argued. "The country isn't exactly in the dark ages, you know. I was surprised myself at how advanced it is. And there's already an airstrip right there on the property. Shipping's a breeze."

Herman looked doubtful, but he registered no further objections.

"Do we have the surplus to invest right now?" Mark asked Darla Wodehouse, the head of accounting.

Darla gave Rory a quick, dubious look. "Well, yes, we're in good shape right now, but I don't know if—"

"There you go," Rory interjected. "We can afford it. Let's jump on it. It's a golden opportunity."

"Golden? It's a barely *okay* opportunity," Mark said quietly but firmly. "Rory, you can't sit there and look us in the eye and tell us this is a good idea. If one of us came to you with something like this, you'd send us to the company shrink. Why do you really want to open a plant, even a small one, in that area, when you know it probably won't succeed?"

"In the first place, I *don't* know that it won't succeed. I believe I can make it work."

"But why bother, Rory?" Darla asked, staring down at her copy of the report. "Why choose an up-hill battle when there are so many more suitable places to open a plant? Your reason can't be just because you inherited the property. The land isn't so valuable that it has to be used. Sell it to someone there in the village, or keep it for sentimental reasons if you want and build a summer cottage there. But a plant? Don't use the property for that. Buy a parcel somewhere more suitable."

"You're right; the land isn't particularly valuable within itself," Rory said, feeling very uncomfortable, as he often did when he was in the middle of an argument and had the feeling he was wrong. "I don't feel compelled to use it purely for business purposes."

"Then why?" Herman asked. "Why a plant there?"

"Computer companies have been expanding into Ireland and doing very well," Rory argued. "For years, the Irish economy has been shifting from agricultural to industrial and it's a graceful and efficient transformation. We can be a part of that."

He took a deep breath and decided to lay his full hand of cards out for all to see. "Also, that area needs the plant. Unemployment is a real problem there and we can provide a solution. It will have a positive impact on a lot of lives, the lives of good people. I think it's worth doing."

He looked around the table, studying the faces of some of the most talented people in the business. He knew their abilities because he had hand chosen each of them.

He knew why they were objecting. They were

right—if anyone else had presented the idea, he would have shot it down before it could fly. They were in business to make money, not provide employment for a bunch of Irishmen. Sure, they were proud of their contributions to various societies, but like any other enterprise, the bottom line was profit.

So, Rory didn't really expect them to feel the same way he did. They hadn't been to Gormloch. They hadn't been touched by the people there the way he had.

"If you all feel strongly against this plant," he said, "if you don't believe we can do it, I won't ask you to participate. I'll open the plant myself, outside the company, using personal funds. And I won't ask any of you to contribute your time or expertise to its building or its operation."

The room was silent for a long time, with only the hum of the air-conditioning to fill the heavy void. The board members simply stared at one another across the table and shifted uneasily in their seats.

Rory stood, picked up his binder, and tucked it under his arm. "I'm going to go get a cup of coffee," he said. "I'll be back in ten minutes. You can let me know then what you decide."

He grinned. "And, no, I don't have the room bugged, so you can speak plainly in my absence. Just don't plan any 'interventions.' If the men in white suits come to take me away, Fredl has orders to fire you all."

Eleven minutes later, Rory returned. As he walked back into the room, he was surprised to feel his own pulse pounding in his temples. He was puzzled about his own reaction—the fact that this issue was so important to him.

He could have done the steamroller routine and told them that they were going to open the plant whether the board agreed or not. But he didn't like to work that way. What was the point of paying these people the big bucks to advise him if he wasn't going to take their advice?

Setting his cup of Starbucks on the table, he took his seat and said, "Well, what did you kids do while I was gone? Have you planted a bomb under my chair?"

Mark Giordano passed a hand over the bald spot on the top of his head. It was shining; he was perspiring. Mark didn't like to lock horns with Rory, but he would if he thought Rory was wrong.

"We talked it over, boss," he said. "If you're going to fall on your face in the mud, we figured we should be there, facedown, beside you, blowing bubbles."

"Gee, thanks," Rory said with subdued enthusiasm. "With such a positive attitude, how can we fail?"

Darla stood and picked up her papers and calculator. "Give me twenty-four hours," she said. "I'll probably be able to predict at least twenty different ways."

"'Tis a lonely wash that hasn't a man's shirt in it," Norah said as she watched Moya take the sheets from the clothesline, fold them, and place the linens in a wicker basket at her feet. "How long has it been since that nice Mr. O'Brien contacted you?"

"I received only one wee card from him since he left, two weeks ago, and 'twasn't the romantic sort. So don't start with me, Norah," she said, tossing a handful of clothespins into a cloth bag that hung from a wire rack on the line. "My laundry is big enough without worrying about some lad's shirts, or underdrawers, for that matter. I do well to get my own washed and dried."

"So, buy yourself a clothes dryer. It's high time."

Moya shook her head and reached for a fluffy bath towel. She buried her face in its softness and breathed in the sweetness of outdoors. "No," she said. "There's no softener from a bottle that can make towels smell like this or feel so good against your cheek."

"Eh, washed is washed and dry is dry. It makes no difference to anyone but you."

Moya looked up at the sky and saw the dark clouds that had threatened earlier, approaching rapidly, driven by a brisk wind from off the Atlantic. "Right now, Norah," she said, "I'd be far more pleased to have your assistance at getting these items off the line than to be receiving your opinions. No offense intended."

"None taken. But I'm too old to be bothered with such things. You're doin' fine on your own. Besides, 'tisn't goin' to rain for a while."

"How can you be certain? It looks likely to me."

"Me left shoulder isn't achin', and it always aches mightily when the rain's about. You've got an hour, probably more."

Moya couldn't help smiling. Although the old

woman was an irritating busybody, Moya enjoyed her company.

As she worked her way down the line and Norah watched, cheerfully idle, Moya saw Gill Doolin rushing down the street toward her house.

"Well, look at him," Norah said. "He's movin' like he's got a briar upon his breeches."

"Or some news," Moya said with a twinge of anxiety. "He's frownin', and Gill seldom frowns unless he's bearin' bad news."

"I'd frown, too, if I had a belly as large as Gill's. He's sampled far too much of Angus's stout over the years. All that Guinness journeyed to his middle and took up permanent residence there."

"Norah, please. Gill's a good friend, a fine lad. His heart's even bigger than his waistline. And he does look like trouble has knocked upon his door. Gill!" she called, "back here, behind the house."

"Moya, you'll never guess who rang me up!"

"Rory O'Brien," she said, speaking the first words that came to her mind.

Gill's face fell as though he were disappointed to have his surprise guessed so easily. "Well, not exactly the man himself, but his secretary, a German lady with a fierce way about her."

"What did she tell you?" Norah asked, stepping between them. "Exactly what did she say?"

"She wanted me to know that Mr. O'Brien will be arriving tomorrow evening and she wants me to have my accounts at the pub well settled and the books up to date for his inspection."

"Hmm," Moya said, twisting one of the clothes-

pins between her fingers. "Did she say what he in-
tends to do with the property?"

"She didn't say, but whatever it is, he seems to
feel he needs to be here himself to accomplish it."

"Settling the books, huh?" Norah mused. "That
has a note of finality to it; that's what I say."

"Then don't say it," Moya snapped. "The last thing
we need are words of doom coming out of your
mouth and into the universe. Don't you know, you
can speak evil into being, bringing bad fortune that
wasn't even on its way until you summoned it?"

"It doesn't matter what I say," Norah returned with
a sniff. "That Rory O'Brien has a mind of his own,
he does. And he'll do what suits himself no matter
what I think or speak. I'm sure his decision is already made, or he wouldn't be headed back this way."

"I wish you had questioned his secretary," Moya
told Gill. "You should have squeezed her a bit for
more news."

"She wasn't the squeezin' type. Scared me, she
did, over the telephone. She reminded me of some
of those nuns in the schools who used to slap my
hands with a ruler. All she said was 'get ready, he's
comin.' And she didn't invite more conversation than
that."

"I wonder if he'll be in need of a room for the
night." Moya could feel the color rising in her cheeks,
and she could also feel Norah's watchful hawk eyes
trained on her, registering her changing complexion.

"He will, indeed," Gill said, nodding vigorously.
"I forgot to mention it. That fearsome secretary said
I was to tell you that Mr. O'Brien will be stayin'

with you several nights. She doesn't know exactly how many yet, but she told me to reserve your best room for him indefinitely."

Indefinitely? What would happen if he stayed several days? When he had roomed with her only one night, they had gone from being total strangers one day to kissing like lust-besotted spaniels there in the bedroom the next. This could present a problem, indeed.

So, if the situation was potentially so desperate, why could she feel her face spreading in a mischievous grin . . . which was also not lost on Norah Delaney?

"Well, now, see how yer news paints a smile upon her face," Norah said, giving Gill a gouge in the ribs with her elbow. "For a woman who finds the man detestable, she surely perked up at the thought of a visit from him, don't you think, Gill?"

"She's not lookin' too sad. There's no need to put her on a suicide watch tonight."

"You're both havin' me on, and don't think I won't remember it. I'll laugh last, you'll see." And with that Moya gathered up her laundry and huffed away to the house with it, trying to look indignant. But the blasted smile wouldn't stay gone from her face, so it wasn't easy.

Rory was coming back. He was coming back *tomorrow*.

And Moya could think of a thousand things she had to do around the house—and to herself—to get ready for him.

It was only until later that afternoon, after she had

cleaned the sitting room, conditioned her hair, tweezed her eyebrows, and given herself a manicure, that she began to wonder . . . what about Lios na Daoine Sidhe?

She also began to wonder when her priorities had been turned upside down.

Ten

When the rented car pulled up in front of Moya's house mid-afternoon the next day, it was raining— again. Moya watched him from between the slightly parted sitting-room curtains as he pulled two suit-cases from the boot and hurried up the walkway to her front door.

She had the overwhelming urge to run to the door and throw herself into his arms. Somehow she was pretty sure he wouldn't push her away.

But she also wanted to leave him to stand outside in the rain for the rest of the afternoon, to punish him for whatever he might have planned for the pub. Of course, she didn't know what those plans were, but she was fairly certain she wouldn't like them.

She compromised by sauntering to the door while he pounded furiously. It was good for his soul, she decided, to learn a bit of patience. And if she had to be the one to teach him, so be it.

By the time she finally opened the door, he was fairly damp and, as before, the wetness suited him, giving him that soggy, bedraggled, schoolboy look with his black curls hanging down into his blue eyes.

"Tell me, Rory O'Brien," she said, her arms crossed over her chest as she looked him up and down, "do you have a near-drownin' experience every time you travel or only when you're comin' to see me?"

He pushed by her, hurrying into the shelter of the foyer. "*You* tell *me,* Moya—does it ever stop raining on this friggin' island?"

"We have many a sunny day," she replied. "But I ordered rain today, just for yourself. You seemed to enjoy it so much last time you took a holiday here."

Wet hair and all, he smiled at her, his eyes bright with excitement—the same excitement she had felt since she had heard he was returning.

"I couldn't stop thinking about you," he said, stepping closer to her. "I tried, but I couldn't."

She was taken aback by the suddenness of his admission. No "Hello, and how have you been?" or "What's been happening in your corner of the world?"

She was surprised, but infinitely pleased as well.

"Me, too," she said, her voice soft and a bit shaky as he moved closer still.

He dropped his suitcases on the floor and reached for her, his hands going around her waist and pulling her to him.

"Well . . . ," he said, his voice low and intimate, "I didn't exactly think of you every single minute.

Only when I saw a woman with beautiful red hair, or heard anything about Ireland, or saw a storm cloud in the sky, or got this strange, overpowering urge to eat a big, cholesterol-ridden breakfast . . . or any time I felt the need to kiss somebody, or . . ." He pulled her into his arms and, once again, she was overcome with the feel, the scent, the heat of him. "Okay," he murmured, "maybe I did think about you all the time."

Lightly, he brushed his lips across hers, teasing— a sweet torture. "Did you think about me all the time, Moya?" he whispered.

She grinned and shook her head. "No, hardly at all. I've been dreadfully busy and—"

He cut off her words—and her breath—with a hard, long kiss. When he finally pulled away, he said, "I don't believe you, Moya."

"'Tis the truth I'm speakin'. You only came to mind . . . oh, when someone complained about the breakfast I served them, or when a rude guest dripped water on me floor, or—"

"And how often was that, Moya?" he asked, his hands stealing up her back and pressing her to him until her breasts were tight against his chest.

She sighed. "It *has* rained a lot, truth be told. So, there's been a great heap o' drippin'. Like to drove me to distraction, it did. All the drippin', the moppin'—"

"The rememberin'?"

"Aye, that too."

He chuckled. "Umm, I can imagine."

"You can?"

"Oh, yes. I have a very creative imagination. And since I kissed you in Angus's room two weeks ago, I've imagined a 'great heap,' as you call it."

A flurry of erotic images played across her mind, visions that she, too, had conjured during the long, lonely nights. She blushed just to think that he might have been fantasizing anything so explicit.

She could feel her face growing hot, but a second later, she didn't care. Because he was kissing her again, just like he had upstairs. It was a long, firm, hungry kiss that left her aroused, but weak all over.

Her own hands roamed across his shoulders and chest, feeling the rain drops on the supple leather of his jacket and the solidity of his muscular body beneath it. When his cheek brushed hers, she felt the rasp of beard stubble on her skin and enjoyed the rough maleness of it.

His cheeks were damp, his skin cool from the rain, but his lips were warm as he kissed her again . . . then again. And the feel of his mouth on hers was so much better than any of those midnight fantasies she had entertained. She couldn't believe how much she had missed him, or how good, how right, it felt to be back in his arms.

His tongue played lightly across her upper lip, then her lower, teasing and coaxing her to open and allow him inside. She moaned, answering his parrying with her own, savoring the taste of him, the feel of him as she melted into him. With her breasts pressed against his chest, she could feel the hard, fast thudding of his heart, that matched her own racing pulse.

When they finally pulled apart, she realized that the front of her blouse was wet from the contact. The lace of her camisole showed clearly through the thin, damp cotton.

"Hey," she said, "thanks to you, we both look like rats who've gone swimmin' in the river."

He laughed. "I have an idea. You could go get another one of those garbage bags and we could both toss all our clothes in it . . . right here in the hallway, like I did before."

She raised one eyebrow. "I'm sure you'd like that, Mr. Rory O'Brien."

"I'd make sure *you* liked it, too. Promise."

"I'm sure you would. But if we're to live under the same roof for some time, we'd best behave. Surely we can't be doin' this kissin' and squeezin' nonsense every few seconds."

He grabbed her again. "No. Absolutely not." He gave her another kiss. "We'll have to show some self-discipline." And another. "I mean, we just met and it would be foolish for us to—"

She stood on her tiptoes and with her fingers buried in his curls, cut him off mid-sentence as she forced his head down to hers one more time. He didn't need much coaxing.

"We must start practicing that self-discipline," she said in a breathy, quivering voice, "and we should begin this very minute."

"Exactly why is that?"

"Because I'm a good Irish girl, not some maiden of ill repute, like maybe you're used to there in New York."

He threw back his head and roared with laughter, but managed to keep his grip on her. "Maidens of ill repute. You make it sound like I pick up my dates on Forty-second Street."

"Is that where the—"

"Yes, that's where the ladies of the evening hang out, among other places. But I'll have you know I'm a man of discriminating taste. And I'm finding that I have an appetite for good Irish girls with copper curls and eyes the color of emeralds. Which reminds me that I need to unpack. I brought you a little present."

"Of course, you must unpack and freshen up a bit. You're probably as weary as a worm in a henhouse, and I waylaid you in the hallway before you could even—"

"I don't mind. You can . . . way . . . lay me anytime you like."

She gave him a playful swat on the shoulder and turned to lead him upstairs. "I gave you the same room as you had before, if that's all right," she said. "You said you slept well in that bed."

"Pretty well, considering that you were right down the hall."

As he followed her up the stairs she had the distinct feeling he was watching her rear end. And while the thought pleased her in a warm, shivery sort of way, she had the discomforting sense that everything was moving much too quickly.

Like every other Irish girl, she had been warned about American men who would play loose with a woman's affections. Here was the very proof, and her not wise enough to resist the temptation.

If she wound up playing the fool in this game, she would have only herself to blame.

And then there was Lios na Daoine Sidhe.

"Gill told me that you wanted him to get his books in order," she ventured as she escorted him into his room. "He said you've made your decision about what you're intendin' to do with the pub."

Rory placed one suitcase on the floor and another on an easy chair that was comfortably placed in the corner beneath a reading lamp and next to a bookcase full of classics.

"Yes, after careful consideration, I have reached a decision," he said with a self-satisfied smile. "And I think it's one that serves everyone's interests in the long run. Most importantly, I think you'll like it."

He sounded so sure, so convincing. For a moment, she allowed herself to dare to hope that all might turn out well in the end. Maybe trusting this fellow wasn't such a bad idea after all. Maybe Angus had been wise to leave it in his hands.

Rory opened his suitcase and began to rummage through its contents. "Aha! Here it is!" Proudly, he produced a small box, a white, velvety box that could only hold jewelry. He walked back to her and laid it in her hand.

"I hope you like my plan, which I'm going to tell everyone, including you, about tonight. I told Gill to invite all the villagers to an eight o'clock meeting at the pub to discuss it. And I hope you like what's in

the box because the salesgirl assured me that you
would."

"Rory, you shouldn't have. I mean, we scarcely
know one another and it just isn't proper that you
should . . ."

She couldn't finish the statement because she had
opened the box and was staring at the most beautiful pair of earrings she had ever seen. The stones
were emerald cut and the same deep green as that
gem. But they sparkled much more and caught the
light with more brilliance than any emerald Moya
had ever seen. The stones dangled from delicate fil-
igree clasps that were shaped like tiny leaves of ivy.

"The lady who sold them to me called them tour-
malines. I described the color of your eyes to her
and she said these would look good on you. And the
settings are made of yellow gold and rose gold. She
said the rose would go nicely with your red hair.
Let's see them on you."

"No, Rory, really, I can't."

"You better. I carried those things all the way here
from Fifth Avenue, and I'm not taking them back.
So you'd better wear them."

She wanted them. She wanted them so much she
ached from wanting. Because they were beautiful,
because they *would* look wonderful on her, because
she had never owned anything so pretty . . . and
mostly because he had described the color of her
eyes and hair to a saleslady, because he had brought
them all the way to her from Fifth Avenue. And because his eyes were shining like those of a little boy

who was giving his first girlfriend something very special he had made for her.

She couldn't say no.

"Turn around to that mirror there, and put them on," he said, nudging her. "I'd offer to do it myself if it were a necklace or a ring, but with pierced earrings, I—"

"That's all right. I'll do it myself."

She lifted them gently from the box and turned them this way and that, allowing the sunlight that came through the window to twinkle across the facets. "Oh, Rory, how am I going to explain these to the nosy bodies in the village?"

"If they ask, tell them it's none of their business."

"Then they'd make sure it was their business. This village is far too small for a person to have any business that's just their own."

He grinned down at her. "Are you worried what the 'busybodies' are going to say about you?"

"Yes," she admitted, "but not enough to refuse these lovely baubles."

He reached over and held her hair up at the nape of her neck as she fit the jewels into her ears. She felt like a princess getting ready to attend a royal ball.

"Wow!" he said when she had finished. "I'll have to go back to that shop and tell the lady how great my girl looks in those."

She turned and gave him a quick peck on the cheek. "I'm not a girl, Rory O'Brien . . . haven't been for years. And, although these are grand, indeed, 'twould take more than a pair of earrings to make me yours . . . or any other man's, for that matter."

He smiled, reached up, and gently tweaked one of the earrings, making it swing and brush against a tiny, erogenous spot on her neck, just below her ear. "Then I'll definitely have to go back to that shop," he said.

This is happening too fast, Moya, she told herself. *You've plenty of time to make a fool of yourself over a man. You needn't accomplish it all so quickly.*

But the earrings were lovely. And Rory O'Brien was lovely, standing there, smiling at her with those blue eyes full of what seemed to be some sort of affection.

It was simply more than a lass could bear.

"What pretty earrings, Moya! I spied them a-twinklin' all the way across the room, I did," Norah said as she hurried across the assembly room in the back of the pub that was now full of excited villagers. "Wherever did ye come by those?"

The gleam in Norah's eye and the bounce in her step told Moya that the old lady already knew exactly where she had "come by" them. But if she confirmed Norah's suspicions, the news would be wall to wall in thirty-two seconds. And Moya wasn't ready to announce to the entire village that she had received an expensive present from a gentleman she hardly knew.

"I've had them a while now," she said with a quick glance toward Father Shea, who was speaking to Gill and Tommy in the opposite corner. It wasn't the blackest lie she had ever told, even if the "while" was only a few hours. But she was also sure the good father wouldn't approve of her playing loose with the truth.

"I don't recall seein' those upon yer ears," Norah said. "In fact, I'm certain I haven't laid eyes upon them before tonight."

"Then maybe you should have those eyes of yours checked by Dr. O'Halloran in Killarney. 'Tis goin' blind, you are."

There. That should quiet her for a moment, Moya thought. Norah was too vain to wear glasses, though she had needed them for more than forty years now.

"I'm not goin' blind," she snapped. "I see a lot. I see things that no one else in the village sees."

"Aye, and you chat about all you see," Moya mumbled under her breath.

"And I'm not deaf, either," Norah replied, "so watch what yer mutterin' there. I hear every syllable. And the stiffness in me shoulder isn't so great I can't slap someone who needs it."

Moya grinned, but she decided not to push it. Norah wasn't making an idle threat. She had grown up in a world where adults enforced their authority with words, palms, sticks, brooms, whatever was handy. And they made no apology for their brand of discipline. It was effective at keeping the younger generations in line, and that was all that mattered.

At that moment, Rory entered the room, and Moya could see why it had taken him an extra half hour to get ready for the meeting. Every unruly hair on his head was neatly combed, and he looked absolutely dashing in a double-breasted, charcoal gray suit that accented his already perfect physique. Moya felt a surge of pride that she deemed completely inappropriate. Why should she be proud of him? He wasn't anything to her, was he? A pair of earrings, a few breathtaking kisses, an offhanded reference to her being his girl—that hardly established any sort of connection between them that would give her the right to take pride in him.

But she was. Logical or not.

She liked the way he moved among the crowd, completely at ease with himself, friendly, as he greeted each villager individually, giving them a few seconds of his undivided attention. And when he walked away, they were beaming, as though they, too, felt a pride at being somehow associated with him.

Rory O'Brien wasn't like any man she had ever known. And she found his unique personality intoxicating.

"Was it himself who gave those to ye?" Norah asked, nudging Moya with her elbow. "They look like New York baubles to me."

"Him?" Moya's eyes widened with false innocence.

"Aye, no other lad around here would be transportin' jewels from the States."

"Why, Norah. I hardly know him."

Norah grinned. "Ye know him well enough. Earrings and kissin', too. 'Tis goin' well, I'd say."

Moya gasped. "How did you . . . ?"

Laughing, Norah replied, "I didn't know, not for

certain. But judgin' from the rosiness in yer cheeks, I know now. And that he's a fine kisser, too. A girl doesn't get that red thinkin' of it if he's no good at it."

"I've had just about enough of this conversation," Moya said, trying to feel haughty—but all she could summon was embarrassment. "I'm going to go get a seat for myself before this meeting begins. I'm tired, and you're the cause of it."

"I'd like to take the credit," Norah called after her as she walked away, "but more likely it was all that activity we were discussin' beforehand. It can be exhaustin', when done properly."

Moya escaped to the other side of the room, where Gill and Kevin were unfolding metal chairs and arranging them in rows. But no sooner had she claimed one of the seats than Shauna Kissane bounded over to her and landed on the chair next to hers. "What grand earrings those are!" the girl exclaimed, reaching up to touch one. "Did that handsome Mr. O'Brien give them to ye? Is he after makin' ye his girl now? Are the two of ye in lo-o-ove?"

"Eh, away with you, girl," Moya said. "In love, is it? You've been watchin' too much television. Why don't you trot along and help Kevin set up those chairs?"

"Naw, 'tis boy's work."

"Work is work. 'Tis neither lads' nor lasses'."

"I'd rather sit here and be a bother to you."

"And you do it well. You're more like your grandmother every day."

Shauna grinned. "I'll take that as a compliment."

"Don't. I didn't mean it to be one."

Thumping one of the earrings to make it dangle, the child laughed. "Yer most fond of me, and of my grandmother, and ye know it. Now, tell me aaall about the Yank. Did he give ye a big kiss along with the earrings?"

"It won't be a kiss someone's gettin' around here, but a swat on the bum, if they don't stop makin' such a nuisance o' themselves. Go collect your brother and the both of you help Kevin straight-away!"

Moya sighed as she watched the girl do as she told her. There were advantages to age and the ac-companying patina of authority. She could control at least one generation of that incorrigible family.

"Lads and lasses, if ye would sit yerselves," Gill announced in his booming voice. "We have a gen-tleman with us this evening—Mr. Rory O'Brien from New York City, nephew to our recently departed friend and neighbor Angus O'Brien—and he has somethin' he must say to us. Gather 'round now. Time's bein' wasted."

Chattering with anticipation, the citizens of Gorm-loch took their seats, and Rory walked to the front of the group and raised his right hand like a traffic officer. "Good evening, ladies and gentlemen. As you've no doubt heard by now, my uncle, Angus O'Brien, willed his property here in your village to me. That includes this building and the property it stands on from here to the river."

They all nodded in unison and most clapped,

though a few grumbles could be heard among the applause.

"When I returned to New York, I met with the board members of my company, Nova Tech, and we discussed how the land could be put to good use."

Moya's ire rose, and she couldn't contain herself. " 'Tis already bein' used in a worthy manner," she said. "The same manner as it's been for the past two hundred years."

She could tell Rory was irritated with her interruption of his speech, by the aggravated look on his face, but his voice was calm and measured when he replied, "A decrepit pub and pastures of grass for sheep and cow grazing? I'd say two hundred years of that is plenty. It's time to make some changes for the better."

"And just what changes do ye have in mind?" Norah asked. "Are ye goin' to build us one of those fine shoppin' malls, like ye have in the States?"

Several of the women giggled and some men registered potential complaints.

"No, I'm sorry, but I don't think a mall would thrive in an area where the unemployment is so high. And speaking of unemployment, that brings me to my point."

He motioned to Kevin, who came forward, proudly bearing a long cardboard cylinder, which he handed to Rory. From inside the container, Rory took a long, rolled piece of paper. "If you would hold one end of this for me," he told the boy.

With the same aplomb as a town crier unrolling

a royal decree written on the palace's parchment, Kevin held up his end of the paper.

Rory continued to unwind the scroll until all could see. It was some sort of blueprint—a drawing with technical-looking symbols, squares, circles, measurements, and descriptions all over it.

"These," he said proudly, "are the blueprints for the new plant that Nova Tech is going to build, right here."

The crowd gasped. "Here in Gormloch?" someone shouted.

"Right here where we're standing at this minute," Rory replied. "We'll begin small at first and expand as needed. But, even in the beginning, from the day we begin construction, we'll be employing between seventy-five and a hundred people. Nova Tech manufactures hardware for the computer business and—"

"I know nothin' o' computers," Tommy Sulllivan shouted.

"Me either," Conn Hallissey added. "Nor do most of us."

"That's not a problem. We will bring a team from New York to conduct training classes. You'll learn all you need to know from us. We prefer it that way. Our company's salaries are somewhat higher than the industry standard, and we also offer generous benefits. I don't have to tell you how much revenue that will bring into your community or how it will raise the standard of living in this area."

The room exploded in a flurry of conversation, drowning out any more of Rory's speech. Only Moya sat, silent and stunned.

Here? she thought. *On this very spot? Surely he must not have meant that literally!*

That would mean . . .

She flashed back on the words he had spoken when she had first brought him into Lios na Daoine Sidhe. What had he said? Something about the place needing to be bulldozed?

"Wait a minute!" she exclaimed, jumping to her feet. "Wait just a bloody minute!"

Several mothers cringed at her cursing, and normally Moya would have apologized, but this time she hardly noticed.

The room fell silent with everyone, including Rory, staring at her.

"What is this?" she asked, looking from one to the other of her neighbors. "Didn't you hear what he said? He said he's going to build his establishment right here, where we're standing this minute. That means the pub will be destroyed."

"Is that what yer intendin' to do?" Gill asked Rory. "Will ye be tearin' the ol' place down?"

"Yes, but—"

Before Rory could finish his statement, a dozen men's voices drowned him out with objections.

"We can't be havin' that, now can we!" Tommy yelled. "Where would we get a pint to appease the thirst?"

"You could do with a bit less appeasing," Tommy's wife said, grabbing his shirttail and yanking him down onto his chair. "And the rest of the men in this town could benefit from a steady paycheck."

"But . . . ," sputtered Gill Doolin, "what of the

table where Daniel O'Connell himself sat and drank a pint and wrote his speech? We can't be havin' that destroyed. 'Twould be sacrilege, surely."

"I've already thought of all that," Rory said. He pointed to a spot on the lower left corner of the map. "Right here, near the western boundary of the property, right on the road, will be the new pub. A much more modern establishment with Mr. Gill Doolin in charge of that one as well. And if you like, Gill, we can put Daniel O'Connell's table right in the middle of the room and a brass plaque right in the center of the table itself, commemorating his visit."

Gill beamed. "A new pub? With sinks that don't leak and an extra lavatory?"

"Two, if you like."

"But, sir . . ." Shauna raised her hand high. "It must have a great room, like this, for the dance competitions and village meetings."

"It will." Again he pointed to the map. "See that spot right there? That's a large stage with lights and a fine sound system—perfect for your dances."

"We don't need a sound system," Moya protested. "Our musicians do fine without one. And we don't need a new pub, either. This one has served us well all these years. I say it stays!"

A few of the villagers voiced their agreement with her, but more of them stayed silent, siding instead with Rory, embracing the idea of new jobs and a modern pub.

Moya felt as though her whole life was slipping out from under her, as though there had been a great earthquake and the ground had moved beneath her feet.

It was a natural disaster named Rory O'Brien.

Suddenly the earrings in her ear lobes began to burn, along with her flaming cheeks and her fiery temper. How dare he! Come to her village, would he, turn everyone's heads around, attack what she loved, and change everything?

"Who do you think you are, Rory O'Brien?" she shouted in a voice so harsh she hardly recognized it as her own. "What makes you think we want you to waltz into our village and tear our lives apart? Do you imagine that's what Angus had in mind when he placed his property in your hands, for your safe-keeping? I can assure you, it isn't."

"Now Moya," Tommy said, rising to his feet and walking over to her. "Don't offend Mr. O'Brien here. He's talkin' of doin' a fine thing for this village. If you insult him, he might change his mind."

"Then I'll insult him!" She shook off the hand Tommy laid on her arm, and continued her tirade. "I'll call him the jackass fool he is, the callous boar, the stubborn goat, the—"

"Ah," Rory said, dismissing her with a wave of his hand, "here we go again with Noah's ark. I'm sorry you don't like the plan, Moya," he added most sincerely. "I thought you would want the best for your community."

"I *do* want the best!" she returned. "But we already have the best. We don't need *your* idea of what's best for us."

"Speak for yerself, Moya," Conn said. "You have

gainful employment. Many of the rest of us don't and would like the chance this offers."

"You're crazy," Moya left her seat and pushed past those who were standing against the walls, making her way for the door. "I can't expect more from Mr. O'Brien. He's a Yank, and a New Yorker besides. But the rest of you should know better. I guarantee you, this is not what Angus wanted. Not even close! And I won't allow it! I won't!" She turned back to Rory and shook her finger at him. "And you won't remove one stone of this place. Not one stone, I promise you."

But as she stormed out the door, through the main room of the pub and out into the night, Moya realized if Rory O'Brien wanted to do this, and if most of the village was behind him, there wasn't a thing under God's broad heaven she could do about it. Except cry for what was lost.

Eleven

Rory caught up to Moya before she could get more than a few steps out the door. She would have had to break into a full run to get away from him, and that was a greater sacrifice of her dignity than she was willing to make.

But she did walk briskly, eyes straight ahead, ignoring his shouted demands that she stop and talk with him.

When they reached to her walkway, he shot ahead of her and stood blocking her front door. He crossed his arms over his chest, a dark frown on his face.

"You're going to talk to me, Moya Mahoney. We're going to discuss this like two rational adults or I'm going to—"

"To the devil with you, O'Brien. And may you roast there forever and a day, without a drop o' Guinness to quench your eternal thirst."

He chuckled. Her temper rose. "I don't like Guinness, remember?" he said. "So that curse doesn't have much bite."

"May your teeth rot, your hair fall out, may you be afflicted with the leprosy, the dropping palsy, the creepin' lice, and a desperate case of constipation . . . and may the worms take your eyes."

He considered her words carefully, thoughtfully, then nodded solemnly. "Well said. Now *that one* bites." Switching into a bad impression of an Irish brogue, he added, "'tis mighty impressed, I am."

"'Tis mighty dead you'll be if you don't step aside and allow me to pass."

He did as she asked, and she pushed the door open. "You're not welcome in me house any longer, Rory O'Brien," she said. "Stand by—I'll be tossin' your suitcases to you from the upstairs window."

She went inside and tried to slam the door behind her, but he was too quick. He darted in and followed her as she stomped up the stairs.

"Let's talk, Moya. Let's work this out."

"The only thing goin' out is you and your belongin's."

"That's a bit harsh, don't you think? The least you could do is hear me out."

She stopped abruptly halfway up the stairs and whirled around to face him. "I listened to you, every word you spoke back there in the pub. Your stand seems clear enough. I have only one more question for you."

"And what's that?"

"I want to know: What class of an idiot are you,

Rory O'Brien? You should be sent straight to the asylum, comin' up with a foolish plan such as that!"

"Well, obviously, Moya, *I* thought it was a good plan, or I wouldn't have presented it to the village."

"If you think that scheme of yours is a wise one, you haven't the sense the good Lord gave a goose."

"Ah, here we go with the barnyard animals again. Could you win an argument without some zoological reference?"

"Am I winnin' this one? I hadn't noticed."

Suddenly Rory looked sad. "If we have a big fight about this and lose our friendship, no one is going to win."

Moya could feel tears spring to her eyes, burning her lids. She blinked them away, hoping he hadn't seen them. "Is that what we have, Rory, a friendship? Do we have as much as that?"

"I thought we did. A short-lived one, maybe, but the beginnings of a very nice one. I don't want this to come between us."

Moya stepped down one stair to be closer to him. His eyes seemed to have turned three shades darker. "If you tear down that pub," she said with deadly deliberation, "a building that I love, that is as much my home as this one, I'll never forgive you for it. And I won't be your friend if you have no more respect for my feelings than that."

"How about the people in this village? They're your friends. Don't you love them? They want this plant; they need it."

"They've done fine without it all these years."

"Not that fine. Look around you. There are children wearing shoes with holes in them, houses that need paint and new roofs, rusted cars that barely run on the roads. And the men while away their lives in that pub you love so much because they have no meaningful work to do. How can you think everything is just fine? Wake up and take a hard look around you, Moya, and tell me again that everything is just hunky-dory and that this village doesn't need that plant."

She shook her head. "No, you don't understand. Lios na Daoine Sidhe is the hub of social contact in this village. We celebrate life's happiest events there in the pub, and when sorrow comes, we console each other there, too."

"And you'll continue to do that in the new pub."

"But it won't be the same."

He reached out, took her hand, and squeezed it gently. "Life changes, Moya," he said. "Places and people change. They're supposed to. It's a good thing. It's called growth, progress."

"Not in my world. And if you're going to come into my world and try to change things, then I don't want you in it."

She turned and continued up the stairs. He followed her as she walked down the hallway toward the room where he was staying. "Are you really going to throw me and my suitcases out the window?" he asked. "You're the only bed and breakfast in the village. I'll have to spend the night in the ditch, and I'll tell everyone that passes how you evicted me. By morning everyone from here to Killarney will know that Moya Mahoney denied hospitality to a weary traveler."

"Bollocks."

When she reached the door to his room, she hesitated, considering her options. Yes, she could throw him out. She certainly wanted to. But, on the other hand, if he were here, under her roof, she might still have some control over him, she might still win him over to her point of view and convince him to spare Lios na Daoine Sidhe. It might be worth keeping him around for the hope of influencing him.

"Are you gonna throw me out, Moya?" he said in a teasing, little boy tone that softened her anger, whether she wanted it to or not. "Are you, huh? Huh?"

"I want to."

"I know. But wanting and doing are two different things. You aren't really going to throw away a friend just because you and he have opposite views on an issue, are you?'

She sighed. "Na, I suppose not. At least not yet."

"Thank you."

He gave her a smile that made her want to slap him—or possibly kiss him. Her emotions were so raw and confused, she couldn't be sure which.

"But you must disappear into your room," she said, "close the door and stay there for the rest of your time here. I don't want to see your face, or hear your voice, or be aware of you at all, at all. Do you understand me, Rory O'Brien?"

"Hmmm," he mused. "My mother used to tell me the same thing. You Irish women are all alike."

Moya walked down the hall to her own room, went inside, and slammed the door as hard as she could.

Then she threw herself across her bed and sobbed.

"Is Moya still not speakin' to ye, then?" Gill Doolin asked Rory as he followed him and the surveyor along the roadside edge of the property. Rory had brought in the surveyor from Limerick, and he was pleased with the man's progress so far.

But that was the only thing he was pleased about.

He paused and leaned on the wooden fence that separated the pub's land from the lane. "She hasn't said a word to me. Not one word. For three days now, I've gotten out of bed and found my breakfast on the table in the dining room, but no Moya. I take a shower and when I come out dressed, the dishes have disappeared, and still no sign of her. I go out, do some business here on the property and when I return, my bed is made and my room straight. But I haven't seen her since the night I made the announcement."

"Aye, well, Moya doesn't like what isn't familiar to her. And Lios na Daoine Sidhe is most familiar to her. She holds it very dear."

"Why? It's just a building." Rory wiped the sweat off his forehead with his sleeve and realized how tired he was from traipsing all over the property all morning.

And his fatigue might have had something to do with three nights of tossing and turning.

"Lios na Daoine Sidhe was the first real home

Moya ever had," Gill said, "and Angus the first family. Her own family died when she was just a wee one."

"Yes, I know. Conn told me about it when he took me to Shannon last time."

"And her grandmother was a cold, bitter woman, didn't want a little lass to tend."

"And she died, too?"

"Aye, unexpectedly like. Moya has had more than her share of changes in life, and most of them weren't for the better. And I think she's feelin' poorly about the pub because of losin' Angus so recently. None of us like it when things we love are taken from us and we have no power to stop their leavin'."

"So, do you think I'm wrong, building this plant, tearing down the pub?"

Gill thought carefully before answering. "No. I think it's a fine thing. We can't reach out for something better without lettin' go of what was before. 'Tis the lettin' go part that's hard for Moya. But she'll get over it."

Neither man spoke for a while as Rory considered what Gill had just said. Gill Doolin might not seem to be the brightest person Rory had ever met, but he did possess a certain down-to-earth wisdom that Rory respected.

Gill looked up at the nearly cloudless sky. " 'Tis a fine, warm day today. If you've no more need of me, I think I'll move some of those turf bricks from the field into the shed."

"Sure. But I want to hook up with you later. I need your input on the layout for the new pub."

Gill beamed. "Ye've got it, sir. I'd be glad to help any way I can." Then he added, "Don't sprout a head full of gray hairs over Moya. She's a strong lass. She'll see the light sooner or later."

As Gill walked away, Rory thought of the pair of earrings that were lying on the dresser in his room. She had placed them there the day after their argument. He had sneaked into her room and placed them on her pillow, but the following day, they were back on his dresser. For three days, the earrings had gone back and forth, and he wondered if they would be there when he returned to his room this afternoon. Somehow, he knew they would be. Miss Moya Mahoney was a strong lass, all right. Downright stubborn, in fact.

Maybe Gill was right. Perhaps Moya Mahoney would see the light sooner or later. But would they ever be friends again? Once he had hoped they would become lovers . . . now he would just settle for not being her most bitter enemy.

Moya knew that when Father Shea couldn't be found in the church or the rectory, he was probably tending his garden. The priest had only one obsession outside the church, and it was his flowers. In the late spring, his rhododendrons, foxgloves, violets, orchids, and woodbine were the talk of the village.

She found him on his hands and knees in the shade of an arbutus tree, picking weeds from a patch of bluebells. He had exchanged his priestly cassock for a pair of baggy dungarees, but he still wore his collar. Father Shea was a devoted shepherd to his flock and was always on duty, even when he gardened.

"Good mornin' to you, Father," she said. "How are your flowers standin' today?"

He grunted and brushed the dirt from his hands. "Not as well as me weeds, to be sure. For every one I pull, there's two takin' their place the next time I look. 'Tis losin' the battle, I am, Moya. The briars and brambles are the victors, sure."

"Sounds like you need another soldier in the field," she said, dropping to her knees beside him. "If I help you pull your weeds, may I bend your ear a bit?"

He gave her a sweet smile that eased the wrinkles in his worn face. Father Shea was no more than sixty-five years old, but he had heard many confessions in his life, and they had aged him. His hair, once bright red, was white, his fingers were a bit stiff in the mornings, and his back was bent from the burden of his parishioners' sins . . . and too much weeding.

But his spirit remained supple, his mind youthful. And Moya went to him for advice as often as she did for absolution.

"Ye needn't help me garden," he said. "I'll listen whether ye get yer hands in the soil or not. If it pleases ye, we can go to the church or my office."

"No, thank you, Father. This isn't official. 'Tisn't a priest I'm in need of, but a sensible, objective friend."

He chuckled. "Well, I don't know if I can fit such qualifications as sensible and objective, but I'll do me best. What is it that's troublin' yer soul, Moya?"

She began to pull at the weeds that were growing thick among the bluebells, threatening the delicate flowers with their dainty blossoms. "'Tis this business with Mr. O'Brien and him intendin' to tear down the ol' pub," she said.

Father Shea nodded. "I thought as much. Yer opinions on that matter were stated most clearly the other evenin' at the assembly. It appears the two of you are of very different minds on the matter."

"We are. As far as the North Pole is from the South. He says 'tis a boon to the community, somethin' we're in desperate need of."

"And you, Moya?"

"I think it's a sacrilege."

"Mmm . . . I see."

He resumed his gardening, a thoughtful frown creasing his forehead beneath his shock of white hair.

"And what do you think, Father?"

"Well," he said carefully, "I don't think 'tis exactly a sacrilege."

"I'm sorry, Father. I didn't mean that literally."

"I do believe ye did, child. I think that place is sacred to ye. And there's no wrong in that. But ye must understand that not everyone feels the same as yerself."

Moya forgot the weeds and sat down hard on the grass. "Father, you know the people of this town better than anyone, how they feel, what they think. If you were to take an unofficial count, would you say most are for the new plant or against it?"

He didn't even have to stop and think. "For it. No doubt."

Her heart sank. "Really?"

"Aye, Moya. I know ye don't want to be hearin' it, but 'tis true. A few feel the way ye do, a couple of the older fellas who enjoy drinkin' there and can't imagine havin' a pint anywhere else. But the rest want the plant, the work, and the money it would bring. It would mean a lot of things to many people: better food and more of it, finer clothes than the rags they're wearin', roofs that don't leak, petrol for their cars, better schoolin' for some and health care for others."

Moya was beginning to wish she had never sought out the priest. Traditional fellow that he was, she had somehow thought he would side with her. But hearing all this just made the stone in her heart all the heavier.

"But what about the history of the place?" she argued. "All the fine stories that have been told within those stone walls?"

"The stories were around thousands of years before the pub was ever built, Moya, and the tales will be told long after the two of us have turned to dust in our graves."

Tears flooded her eyes, as they did so frequently these days. The fear, the anger, the hurt just seemed to turn to hot liquid and spill down her face.

"You're only saying that because you don't really care about the stories of ancient Ireland, Father. You consider them pagan tales about dark times before the dawn of Christianity, and you don't approve of—"

"Moya! 'Tisn't so and ye know it. I understand

that yer in pain, but ye mustn't stretch the truth to prove yer point. The old stories would have been lost to the world centuries ago, had not devoted, hard-workin' priests written them down by candlelight, goin' blind from the task, just to preserve those tales, pagan or not."

Moya blushed from shame. "I'm sorry, Father. 'Tis true. I beg your forgiveness."

"Then forgiven ye are, child." He reached over and patted her hand with his own dirty, rough one. "I'm sorry, too. Ye came to yer priest for comfort, and he's sendin' ye away with a heart that's heavier than before. I wish I could say somethin' to relieve yer pain."

She stood, anxious to get away before the tears began to fall even faster.

" 'Tis all right, Father. I asked for your opinion and you gave it to me. I can't ask for more. Thank you, Father."

"I'll say a prayer for ye, Moya. Two if ye like," he called after her as she hurried across the lawn.

She nodded but kept walking.

When Rory returned to Moya's house that afternoon, he was surprised to find her in the sitting room, polishing furniture. The room smelled of lemon oil and bread baking in the kitchen. She was wearing a pair of snuggly fitting, well-worn jeans, a man's red-and-blue plaid shirt that had seen better days, and her hair tied into a ponytail with a kerchief.

She looked up as he walked through and gave him a half-smile.

He thought she had never looked more beautiful.

Deciding not to push his luck, he continued on up the stairs to his bedroom. The first thing he did when he entered the room was to glance over at the dresser.

The earrings were gone.

She had come into the room, tidied up, and made the bed, but she hadn't returned the jewelry.

A lukewarm smile and no earrings. Two good signs.

Maybe by tonight they would be talking again. He could always hope.

But he decided then and there if they did get into a conversation, it would be best if he didn't mention one small fact: Bulldozing would begin on the property tomorrow.

Twelve

Moya stood at her bedroom window in her night-gown and robe and watched as the heavy machinery began to arrive on the property next door. Bulldozers, earth movers, and common tractors dragging vicious-looking equipment slowly made their way down the road and onto Angus's land, making the earth itself tremble below them.

The whole village had assembled at the property's borders to observe the action. Nothing so exciting as this had occurred in Gormloch since the building of St. Bridget's Church and that had happened long before anyone present at this event had been born.

There was a sense of celebration in the air, and Moya didn't know if that lessoned or increased her own pain. She was happy for her neighbors. If this was what they wanted, then she wanted it for them. It should have helped ease her sorrow, but it didn't.

She was glad to see them all so happy and exciting. But her own heart was breaking.

A soft knock sounded on her bedroom door, but she ignored it, hoping she could put off what was coming just a little longer. There was another, harder this time. She turned and, knowing who it was, she reluctantly said, "Come in."

Rory opened the door and took a step inside. He was wearing jeans, a long-sleeved denim shirt, and work boots. His face was a study in conflict. He didn't say anything, just stared at her. But she didn't need to hear him speak to know he was sorry to be causing her such sorrow.

That didn't help much, either.

"It appears today's the day," she said, motioning to the window.

He nodded. "Seems so."

"Gill told me that you had him clear everything of value out of Lios na Daoine Sidhe yesterday."

"I did."

"You have enough equipment out there to build Rome in a day. How long do you figure it will take you?"

"It depends on the weather. But most of the work should be finished by late fall."

"I see."

She turned her back to him and continued staring out the window.

He walked over to stand behind her. "Thank you for letting me stay here, Moya, in spite of our differences."

She shrugged. "You pay your rent on time. I couldn't rightly refuse you."

"You could have. I'm thankful you didn't."

Moya could hear the humility in his voice and she resented that, too. How dare he pretend to be a nice person, when he was about to . . .

Okay, she had to admit that he wasn't the Old Horned One incarnate, but she wasn't about to like him again. Never again.

"I'd like to ask for your blessing on this project before I begin, Moya. It would mean a lot to me if you were behind it."

She whirled around, her fists clenched tightly at her sides. "My blessing? Now it's my blessing you're after?! There's not a chance on God's green earth you'll be gettin' that, so don't even ask. You just don't have a clue, do you, as to how I feel. You're a lucky man that I didn't murder you last night in your sleep."

"Moya, this is for everyone. I can't back out after promising them a plant, not even for you."

"I know. I keep hearin' what a grand thing this is. And I'll not fight you on it any longer, Rory. I know why you're doin' it, and 'tisn't just to be contrary. Your heart's in the right place and you're doin' it out of kindness, not meanness. But I can't give you my blessing. I just can't. That's askin' too much o' me."

"I understand."

He reached for her and put his hands on her shoulders, drawing her closer to him. Looking into her eyes, he said, "Just tell me that you don't despise me for doing it. Give me that much. Because if you're really going to hate me forever, like you said you would, I won't go through with it. I'll walk down there right now and tell them it's all off. I'll come back in here, pack my bags, and go back to New York today."

For a moment, hope flared in her. He meant it. She could read the sincerity in his eyes, feel it in his touch as his hands squeezed her shoulders. All she would have to do was speak the words and Lios na Daoine Sidhe would be reprieved.

But she could hear her neighbors below, cheering as the work crew arrived. She thought of what Father Shea had said about how the added revenue would significantly improve their lives.

She choked on the words and began to cry. He pulled her against him and she buried her face in the soft denim of his shirt. Her own arms slipped around his waist, and she held onto him tightly, absorbing the strength that radiated from him.

"Do what you must, Rory," she finally said. "I may hate what you're doin', but I'll not hate you."

"Fair enough," he said. Pulling back, he looked down into her eyes. "Will you be all right, Moya?"

She nodded and sniffed. "I will. Away with you."

"Thank you," he said. "You're a fine woman, the best I've ever known."

Then he was gone.

By the time he reached the end of Moya's cobblestone pathway, Rory was feeling sick to his stomach. And when he reached Angus's property, the nausea was worse.

Within his own mind, he was sure that what he was doing was right. So, why was his head spinning and why did he feel like he was going to fall into the ditch at any moment and be violently ill?

He was heartsick, and his emotional upheaval was translating into physical symptoms. Whether he wanted to or not, he cared very much about Moya Mahoney and he was miserable at the thought of hurting her this way.

But he could see the villagers milling excitedly around the pub, eager for the groundbreaking of their new plant. He had promised them. Rory was well aware of his own shortcomings, but he was a man of his word. The process had begun and there was no turning back now.

He walked around the pub to the open field behind it where the crew was waiting, their heavy equipment rumbling, idle but ready to begin. Several of the villagers rushed to him, shook his hand, clapped him on the back, and wished him well. Suddenly, he was their favorite lad.

But from where he stood, he could see the back of Moya's house, her bedroom window . . . and he could see her standing in it.

He wished she would walk away, even leave town for the day and come back when the job was finished. The last thing he wanted was to destroy something she loved with her looking on.

"Is everything out of the pub?" he asked Jarlath Nolan, the crew foreman, a fellow from Limerick who was an expert in building demolition and earth moving.

" 'Tis all clear," he said. "We're ready when you are."

Rory looked again at the window and the figure standing there. The bitter taste welled up from his stomach and into his mouth. How could he do this? How could he do it to her?

But a hundred people were standing there, waiting—people who wanted nothing more than the opportunity to work hard and earn money for their families.

How could he not do it?

He looked at the giant earth mover and all the acreage that would need to be leveled before roads and foundations could be laid.

Abruptly he turned to the foreman. "Jarlath, I want to postpone the demolition of the pub, at least for today. Start leveling the land from here down to the river. That's several days' work. We'll worry about the building another time."

"Whatever you say, sir. Just show me where you want the lads to work and we'll get to it straight-away."

Rory began to walk in a line from behind the pub, straight back toward the river. "Right here is fine," he said, indicating the area with a sweeping hand. "It all has to be done, so I'd say start here and work back."

Jarlath stroked his chin thoughtfully. "Aye, that sounds like a fine plan. Everything from here to there, except the fairy fort, of course."

"The fairy fort? Oh, you mean that round bunch of trees? No, they'll have to go, too."

Jarlath's eyes widened in amazement and horror. "Surely, you don't mean it, sir. We mustn't touch the ringed fort! We can't!"

"What are you saying?" Rory shook his head, thoroughly confused. "Those trees aren't that large. If your equipment could tear down a stone building like that pub, it could surely take care of some trees."

"That's not what I mean, sir." Jarlath's face was turning red beneath his hard hat. "That's a special place, that fairy fort, thousands of years old. Sort of sacred, you know. It mustn't be touched."

"Well, it has to be touched. It has to be level. It's where the road is going to be that connects the airstrip and the plant."

"Then the road must go around the fort."

"The road has to be wide enough for trucks; it can't go around anything. And the fort's right in the center of everything. You don't understand. This isn't negotiable."

Several of the villagers, including Gill and Conn, had gathered in a curious circle around the two men. A few of the crew had turned off their machines and come over to see what the problem was.

Jarlath looked miserably uncomfortable, his face breaking into a sweat. "No, sir," he said, respectfully but firmly. "'Tis *you* who's not understandin'. We had no clue that you intended to harm the fairy fort, or we'd never accepted the job. We'll not do it. We can't."

Between Moya's illogical objections and now this, Rory had experienced as much Irish charm as he could stand. What was wrong with these crazy people?

"Are you telling me, Nolan, that you're refusing to do what needs to be done here? Is that what you're saying?"

"Aye. I'm sorry, Mr. O'Brien, but I must say no. And even if I agreed, there's not a man among my crew who would follow those instructions. 'Tis the height of disrespect and pure foolishness to desecrate an ancient place like that ringed fort. None of us would even walk through there, let alone drive a tractor through it."

"Is that true?" Rory turned to the crew members who were now all standing around, listening, hanging on every word of the argument. "Are you all superstitious? Is that what it is? You're afraid you're going to anger some leprechauns or fairies or something?"

They didn't reply, but the looks on all their faces confirmed the bad news for Rory. Even the villagers, who had been so joyful moments ago, were now wearing dejected expressions.

"We didn't know ye'd be wantin' to sacrifice the fort, Mr. O'Brien," Gill said softly. "If I'd known that was in yer plans, I'd have warned ye that it was an unwise thing to consider."

"Unwise? It's a bunch of trees and some round ditches! What's the matter with you? Whoever lived and died there has been gone for two thousand years. They don't care what we do now, believe me. They're long past caring."

Still the crew remained silent and motionless. The

villagers looked miserable. Rory's temper gauge climbed twenty notches.

"I can't believe this! I can't friggin' believe this insanity! It's just some trees. Come here, look at it. It's nothing."

He stomped across the field, the green grass nearly up to his knees. Some of the villagers and crew followed, but not too closely.

"I'm going to walk right through it and you'll see. It's just like any other piece of land. It's dirt. Plain old everyday dirt."

"Sir, don't," Gill said, grabbing for his sleeve. "Ye don't know what yer about."

"Oh, I know what I'm about. I'm about to build you a plant if only you'll all stop acting like stupid, superstitious . . ."

The bile rose higher in Rory's throat, until he could hardly breathe. His head spun as though he'd been drinking a dozen of Moya's whiskey punches.

He kept walking until he had almost reached the first of the circular trenches. "Come on," he called over his shoulder. "Watch me walk through it and see if any of your wee people attack me."

"Rory, don't," Conn said, nearly catching up to him. "Really, you shouldn't."

But Rory was beyond listening to anyone. He was too angry to listen to anyone who was spouting that foolish, superstitious crap that he had been forced to listen to all his miserable childhood. These fools were just like his father and—

He glanced back over his shoulder to see if they were following. And at that moment, he stepped into thin air. The next thing he knew, the ground was flying up to hit him.

It hit him hard. So hard that he couldn't breathe, couldn't see anything except a white light of blinding pain that started in his knee and shot up his leg and into his body, producing more agony than he had ever imagined possible.

Vaguely, as though from far away, he could hear someone say, "Holy Mary and Joseph, Mr. O'Brien has fallen into one of the rings, he has."

Someone else asked, "Is he dead?"

"I believe he is."

"No, he's not dead, he's moanin'."

"Why is his leg bent sideways like that?"

"Aye, he's dead. Dead entirely."

Then Rory O'Brien couldn't see or hear anything at all. Mercifully, even the white light of pain became a thick, suffocating blackness.

Thirteen

"*We can't possibly* get him and that heavy plaster cast up the stairs," Moya told Gill and Conn, who were supporting a drug-drowsy Rory on either side as they helped him through the doorway of her home. "We'll have to plant him in Angus's downstairs room for now," she said. "That seems to be the room reserved for wounded O'Briens."

"I can go up the stairs," Rory said, his speech slurred from the painkillers the Killarney clinic had given him to go along with the cumbersome cast that enveloped his leg from his foot to his hip. "Just leave me alone, and I'll do it myself," he told Gill and Conn. "I'm fine."

"Aye, ye may think yer just fine," Conn replied as he hitched Rory's arm higher over his shoulder. "But yer goin' to be in a mountain o' pain when that shot in yer arse wears off. I broke me leg as a lad, and 'twas no holiday, to be sure."

Gill grunted from the effort as they continued to follow Moya through the house to the bedroom in the rear. "True, and a broken limb takes a while to heal as well," he said. "Mr. O'Brien might become a permanent resident here, Moya, just like his uncle."

Moya didn't look back, but kept walking, afraid they would read the conflicting emotions on her face.

From her window she had seen Rory tumble into that ditch. That particular trench was at least six feet deep, and it had been a bad fall. For one horrible moment, she had thought maybe he had been killed. The intensity of her grief at thinking such a thing— even if it was only for the short time it took to run out of her house and to the ringed fort—had surprised Moya. The prospect of losing Rory forever had been a terrible pain, worse than the thought of the pub being destroyed.

And now, although she was sorry to see him in such pain, Moya had to admit that she was happy to have him under her roof for what might be an extended period of time.

But she had to admit, she was also glad that the property next door had received at least a temporary reprieve. A bad thing had happened, but it appeared at least some good would come from it.

"Ah, he's a tough fellow," she said. "He'll be mendin' quick enough. I'll feed him some good food to build him back up, and he'll be fine."

Conn cleared his throat. "I'm sure ye'll take good

care o' the lad," he said. "He's a lucky one, indeed, to be recuperatin' in yer house, Moya."

She detected a bit of jealousy in Conn's voice and realized she wasn't the only one evaluating the possibilities of this convalescence.

"Lucky?" Rory mumbled. "Broke my friggin' knee. That's lucky?"

"And ye've got some fine drugs in ye to drive away the achin'," Gill said with a chuckle. "I'd say right now, yer the most comfortable of us all."

They passed down the hall and jostled through the narrow doorway into Angus's room. Moya rushed to pull down the blankets and sheet, and she fluffed up the pillow. "There you go, boys, deposit the damaged goods right there, and I'll fetch more pillows to prop up his leg, as the doctor ordered," she said as she hurried from the room.

Gill and Conn carefully placed their burden on the bed as Moya returned with the extra pillows. Rory moaned as they wedged them beneath his foot. "Easy, boys," he muttered. "It feels like a shark's chewing on my knee."

"Drugs must be wearin' off," Conn said. "He's goin' to be in fine spirits when the hurtin' gets real bad," he added to Moya. "If ye need help controllin' him, give a holler."

"He'll be fine," she said. "I've been through this before with Angus, and he was a mighty cantankerous patient. I know how to handle an O'Brien with busted limbs. Shove the medication down their throat every four hours and threaten them with physical violence if they misbehave."

Rory opened one eye and groaned. "Did you hear that?" he asked Gill. "Don't leave me with her. I'm in enough misery already without the nurse from hell shoving things down my throat."

Gill patted his shoulder companionably. "She's only boastin' about the torture. She'll take fine care o' ye, and I'll trot over every few hours to help ye . . . ye know . . . visit the lavatory."

"Oh, yeah . . . that. Thanks, Gill. You, too, Conn, for getting me out of that ditch and to the clinic."

Both Irishmen shrugged and dismissed the acknowledgment. " 'Twas nothin' we wouldn't do for a poor ol' cow who'd fallen into a ditch," Conn said.

Rory chuckled in spite of his pain. "Here we go with the barnyard animals again."

Moya pulled the sheet up to his chin and tucked it around him. "Just be grateful we didn't treat you like a racehorse who'd broken his leg. You'd have been shot where you laid."

"I am," he said, drifting off into a drugged sleep. "I'm grateful. To all of you."

Moya was slumped sideways in the overstuffed easy chair that sat in the corner of Angus's bedroom, her legs thrown over one arm of the chair, a small pillow shoved under her head and a woolen afghan covering her. She was sound asleep and had been for an entire fifteen minutes.

On the bed, Rory groaned and tried to turn onto his side. But the pain made him cry out. Instantly Moya was wide awake.

"Hey, what is it you're tryin' to do there, lad?" she said as she tossed the afghan aside and hurried to him. "You mustn't thrash about like that. You'll harm yourself worse. And then we will have to put you out of your misery with a bullet between your ears."

She glanced at the clock. It was three o'clock in the morning—four hours since his last dose of pain medication.

"Ah, I see," she said. "Your last pill has worn off, and you're needin' another. Poor lad. I'll get it for you straightaway."

Rory opened his eyes and looked at her with an expression of raw misery that went straight to her heart. "It hurts . . . ," he said through gritted teeth. "It really hurts like hell."

"I know, love. I know." She took a bottle from the nightstand and shook a pill into her palm. Then she poured some water from a china pitcher into a tumbler. "But this will make it much better. Here you go."

Gently lifting his head up from the pillow, she placed the pill in his mouth and the glass to his lips. "Drink up, love. The sooner you have that in your bloodstream, the sooner you'll be gettin' relief."

"Thank you," he said as she laid him back down and brushed the hair from his forehead. His curls were damp from sweat, although the room was quite cool. Being in agony was hard work.

"You're most welcome." She sat on the side of

the bed next to him and continued to stroke his hair like a mother comforting a wounded child.

She could tell by the clear, alert look in his eyes that the absence of medication had sharpened him mentally, at least temporarily, until the dose she had just given him took effect. For the first time since he had been injured, she could tell that Rory was beginning to comprehend fully what had happened to him.

"I can't believe I did that," he said, shaking his head. "Falling into a ditch . . . how stupid."

"You mustn't be ashamed. It happens."

"Not very often," he replied. "How many people do you know who've fallen into ditches and broken their legs?"

She chuckled. "Oh, more than you might think. 'Tisn't altogether uncommon in this part of the world. Though usually not in broad daylight, and generally not when a body is stone cold sober."

"I had other things on my mind."

"I know. You were worryin' about me, and the villagers, and the new plant you'd promised to build for them. 'Twas enough to distract any man, truly. And it's sorry I am that I contributed to your misfortune."

Rory reached out, took her hand in his, and squeezed it. "Don't be sorry, Moya. It wasn't your fault, and you're very kind to help me now."

She grinned. "Ah, 'tis nothin'. I'd do it for any dumb animal."

Rory laughed, then grimaced from the pain the movement cost him. "I suppose those villagers and the crew think the fairies in the fort did this to me."

Moya said nothing, but shrugged and smiled.

"That's what I get," he said, "for walking on their sacred ground, right?"

"Could be," she replied. "You might have fallen because you angered the Good People. Or you might have taken that tumble because you're a clumsy oaf who can't keep his feet beneath him."

"Gee, thanks. Either the leprechauns are out to get me, or I'm a klutz. What a choice."

"Or, as I mentioned before, you were a person who was distracted by the fear of hurtin' another person."

His hand tightened around hers. "A person I've grown very fond of. I do like you, Moya. Probably more than you know."

She smiled. "You've grown a bit more appealin' to me, too, Rory O'Brien. And I'm sorry I said such unkind things to you that night at the pub and here. You were only doin' what you thought was right, and a man shouldn't be faulted for followin' his conscience."

"So, does that mean we're friends again, you and me?"

"We are."

He sighed. "Ah, good." He lifted his hand and stroked her cheek, then gently cupped her chin in his palm. "If we're friends again . . ."

"Yes?"

"Will you give me a kiss, then, Moya Mahoney?"

She looked down at his lips, full and as inviting

as the glow of desire in his blue eyes. "I will," she said, "but, if I give you a kiss, you must promise to return it straightaway."

"I will."

She leaned down intending to give him a soft, brief peck on the lips. But Rory apparently had other plans. He moved his hand from her face to the back of her head, and twining his fingers in her hair, he coaxed her into a long and luxurious kiss, much like the one he had first given her. Open, probing, warm, and moist . . . the kiss went through her body like liquid heat, making her want more. Much more.

Reluctantly, she reminded herself of the circumstances and pulled away. They both sighed in unison, then laughed.

"And I have another favor to ask you. Will you wear those earrings I gave you?" he said with a childish vulnerability that touched her. "I really enjoyed buying them for you, and I liked seeing them on you."

She nodded. "I will."

By the hazy look in his eyes and the slowness of his breathing, she could tell the medicine was filtering into his system. "Is that pill startin' to work?" she asked.

"It is."

"And are you startin' to feel better?"

"I am. And if you kiss me once more, I'll be even better."

She did as he asked, but this time he stopped responding halfway through the kiss. Pulling away, she smiled down at him. He was sound asleep.

"Good night again, Rory O'Brien," she whispered. "Sleep well, darlin', and mend as you rest."

Moya walked back to her chair, draped herself across it, pulled the afghan over her, and resumed her all-night watch.

Fourteen

After three weeks, Rory was beginning to feel better, and Moya was finding it more difficult to nurse him. He was no longer content to lie about on Angus's old bed, reading books, and having her bring him his meals on a tray.

He had talked her into setting up a phone on the desk and stocking him with pens, pads of paper, and a calculator. Assuring her that he would pay the astronomical bill, he spent hours sitting at the desk, talking on the telephone with someone he called Fredl and a couple named Mark and Darla.

"Are you conductin' great wheelin' and dealin' right in me very own house?" she asked him one day when she brought him a pot of afternoon tea and some chocolate-dipped biscuits on the copper tray.

"I don't know how great the deals are. But I'm trying to keep the ship afloat while I'm enjoying myself here at the world-famous Mahoney Bed and Breakfast."

"Enjoyin' yourself? Are you now? Well, I must be doin' this nursin' thing wrong then. You're supposed to be sufferin' through, not havin' a holiday for yourself."

She set the tray on the desk in front of him and propped her hands on her hips. "How long have you been sittin' there, chattin' on the telephone, when you're supposed to be in bed with that damaged leg of yours elevated?"

"Not very long . . . Mom."

"Don't you be 'Mom-ing' me, young man. Back to bed, before I take a strap to your backside."

He waggled one eyebrow suggestively. "If that's your idea of a threat, I think I like it."

"Well, you're not supposed to be likin' it; you're supposed to be tremblin' with fear and dread."

He smiled. "I am. Can't you tell?"

"No, I can't say that I can. Most folks don't grin from ear to ear when they're terrified."

"It's just a brave front. The truth is, Moya, it's very important to me that I stay on your good side, and not just because I'm dependent on you for food, water, shelter, and basic human companionship. I like you."

"I like you, too, Rory O'Brien, but you must get that leg up or I'll beat you soundly from head to toe . . . beatin' and likin' you all the while."

He stuck out his lower lip in a little boy pout that went straight to her heart, as she was sure it was supposed to. "I'm bored, Moya. I don't want to stay in my room anymore. And if you won't let me play with the telephone anymore, I—"

"All right, all right. You've surely worn me down. You'll come out to the sitting room this evenin' and help me entertain. The wee ones are comin' over at half seven for a bit o' storytellin', singin', and dancin'. 'Twill be a good diversion for you, and maybe then you'll stop your whinin'. 'Tis worrisome, hearin' a grown man wailin' like a cat with his tail under a rockin' chair."

"There are other diversions you could offer," he said, eyeing her lips.

"And *you* could behave yourself and not add fuel to the gossips' fire. The whole village thinks that you and I are . . . you know."

"Really? Well, if your reputation is in tatters anyway, we might as well have some fun."

She poured him a mug of tea from the pot and shoved it in front of him. "Of course we'll be havin' fun, Mr. O'Brien. Stories and recitations and singin'. 'Twill be more fun than you can bear."

Turning on her heel, she marched away to the door with pseudo indignation. "I can bear a lot," he called to her as she hurried down the hallway. "And by the way, nice earrings. Did some nice, generous guy give you those?"

"No!" she yelled back. " 'Twas some cheeky lad, who deserves to have his other leg broke!"

Three weeks later, Norah Delaney was sitting at Moya's kitchen table, stuffing scones into her mouth and washing them down with cup after cup of strong tea. "So, how is His Royal Highness this afternoon?" Norah asked, pouring herself another cup. Only a few minutes ago, the porcelain teapot snuggled beneath the knitted cozy had been full. Her last cup had nearly drained it, and the two women weren't even halfway through the day's list of gossip topics.

"Rory is much better, thank you for askin'," Moya said as she washed vegetables at the kitchen sink. "Conn and Gill hauled him off to Killarney bright and early this mornin' to get that big, ugly cast removed. Now he has only a smaller, brace-type of a thing on there, with straps and belts and buckles to bind him. 'Tisn't easy for him to put on and off, but gettin' about is far easier now. He's in a fine mood, like a man released from the jail."

"Has he said what he's goin' to do about buildin' the plant? Will he be doin' it after all, or has he abandoned the idea entirely?"

"I don't know. If he's decided, he hasn't told me."

"Well, the whole village is wonderin'. They want him to, but after him breakin' his leg and all, they're set against him even goin' near the fairy fort. They're sure he'll cause destruction to rain down on us all."

Moya shrugged. "Like I said, I don't know what he has planned. Since we must be under the same roof for a while yet, and since we've such different notions on the subject, we consider it best to keep our thoughts on the matter to ourselves."

"Aye. 'Tis a wise decision, I'd say. Especially on his part. Can't fight too well with a lame limb. And where is he now?" Norah asked, craning her neck and trying to see into the dining area.

"He's with the little ones in the sittin' room. Kevin, Shauna, and Sean come over every day now after school to provide the entertainment for him."

"Entertainment? What are they now, buskers?"

Moya laughed. "Aye, they'll be takin' off with the travelin' people any day now, doin' tricks and singin' at the fairs, hopin' for a coin to be thrown their way."

"What sort of entertainment do they provide?"

"Shauna sings for him. I think she's a bit in love with him, croons all these romantic songs to him, she does, with stars shinin' in her eyes. 'Tis very dear to watch."

"I'm sure it is. Give me some more tea, love. The pot's dry."

Moya walked over to the table and took the teapot from under its cozy. "Well, that one wasn't long for the world."

"I haven't eaten all day," Norah said, though Moya knew it was a lie. Norah Delaney had never missed a meal in her life. For such a wee person, she ate as though every day might be her last.

As Moya refilled the pot with hot water from the kettle on the stove, she continued her critique of the children's review. "And Sean is showin' him all the new dance steps he's been learning in Mrs. Mc-Givney's classes. Rory is convinced that once he has his feet back under him, he'll be prepared to join the Riverdance troupe, just with the knowledge Sean has imparted to him these last weeks."

"Is that second batch of scones about finished

bakin'? I think ye might be burnin' them, love, and
that would be a tragedy, sure."

"Two more minutes, Norah. Cinch your belt and
be patient. And Kevin has been regalin' him with
stories of yesteryear. I'm thinkin' he may be the village's next seanchai; he does have such a fine way
with the words. Rory's receivin' a scholar's educa-
tion in Irish history and culture, all from a ten-year-
old bard."

Moya's cooking timer rang, and Norah snapped
to attention. "'Tis the scones, all finished. Take them
out, love, before they're cinders."

Moya smiled and grabbed an oven mitt. "'Tis flattered I am that you enjoy my cookin', Norah. What
would I do without you to compliment me so?"

One by one, she popped the golden pastries from
the pan and placed them on the plate where their sib-
lings had recently sat before Norah had attacked them
with her voracious appetite.

"See if you can send these along to scone heaven
as you did the others," Moya said, presenting the full
plate to Norah. The old woman spent no time waiting, but dove right in.

"So, that lad of yers is practically healed," she
said with her mouth full. "The only problem with ye
nursing him so well is that once he's mended, he'll
be wingin' his way homeward, and then where will
ye be?"

"Here, where I was before he came along," Moya
said, turning her back to Norah and continuing with
her vegetables. Suddenly the sunshine of the older
woman's company had become dim. Why did she

have to speak the very words that had been nagging at Moya's mind, night and day, until she could find no rest?

"No," Norah replied. "Ye won't be the same. Losin' a love changes ye."

Moya whirled around. "A love? What are you talkin' about? Who said anythin' about love?"

"Haven't ye? Hasn't either one of ye uttered the word yet, whilst yer stealin' kisses there in Angus's room?"

Moya could feel her cheeks go hot. Of course, since that first night, when he returned from the hospital, there had been many kisses exchanged between herself and Rory, and a few other caresses, as well. But what did Norah know about what had passed between them? Did she have the gift of the fairies, knowing things no one had told her?

"Are ye surprised that I know?" Norah said, chuckling. "I was young once, too, Miss Moya Mahoney, and I did me share o' kissin' an O'Brien. Angus did a fine job o' it. And I'll wager his nephew does, too. Did ye think we were all as white as lamb's wool back then? No. There's nothin' in the matters of love and romance that ye young ones have invented yerselves."

"Well . . . I didn't . . . I mean . . . I . . ."

"Aye, the cat has bitten yer tongue, I see." She shook her head and clucked. "So, neither of ye have spoken of love. What a shame. Cowards ye are, the two of ye. Someone must be the first to say it, or there's a danger 'twill never be said at all, at all. And what a waste that would be."

"I don't know what you're goin' on about, Norah."
Moya wiped her hands on her apron and returned to
her vegetables, peeling the carrots with a vengeance.
"But I think you should put two of those scones into
your mouth at once and spend some time chewin'."

"Tell him ye love him, Moya, before he leaves. If
ye don't, ye'll live to regret it. I know. I've had me
own share of regrets to live with. And regrets don't
make good companions when ye get to be my age.
A livin', breathin' man is much better to have around
in yer latter days . . . especially if he's a good kisser."

Broken leg or not, Rory O'Brien couldn't recall a
time in his life when he had felt so content and right
with the world. Sitting in front of Moya's turf fire
that afternoon, listening to the children chatter as
they sat at his feet, hearing their peals of laughter,
made him think that maybe earth was a good place
to live after all.

This sort of thing had been missing in his New
York life. The softness of children, the gentleness of
a good woman, the simple pleasures of being in a
cozy room with people who wanted nothing from
him but his company.

The three children—Shauna, Kevin, and Sean—
touched his heart, melting his icy wall of cynicism
with their innocence, their naivete that was born of
kindness, not ignorance. They weren't loving because
they didn't know how to hate. They chose to extend
themselves for others and found joy in serving.

Every day of his convalescence, they had been
there, one or all of them, cheering him with little

poems, songs, and stories. Their mothers had sent baked goodies, and their fathers had smuggled in bottles of booze to lift his spirits. In those six weeks, Rory O'Brien had been the recipient of more generosity than he had been shown in all of his years combined.

When he had first arrived in Ireland, he might have thought he was being "buttered up" by these people with the sweet lilt to their voice. He might have been suspicious, thinking they were trying to assure the future of their new plant. But he had listened to them talk about each other—about the poor widow down the road who was given free milk every day; the sick priest who had his house cleaned while he was away at the doctor in Killarney; the young mother whose fussy, new baby was dandled on first one lady's knee and then the next, so that she could take a much needed nap; and he realized that generosity wasn't a tool for manipulation in the village of Gormloch. It was as natural to the people as the misting rain and the fragrant air, the blue lakes and the red rhododendrons that grew in profusion against mossy stone walls.

Rory O'Brien had discovered his ancestral home, and it was far different than he had expected it to be. He was in love with Ireland. And, whether he wanted to admit it or not, he was in love with a certain daughter of Ireland.

With his leg healing rapidly, the time would soon be coming for him to leave. And he didn't know how he was going to turn his back on either this beautiful island . . . or Moya Mahoney.

"Would anyone like a cup of me famous hot chocolate?" Moya asked as she entered the room with a tray of steaming mugs, interrupting Rory's thoughts.

The children cheered, excited over the simple treat, served in mugs which were their favorite colors: red for Shauna, blue for Kevin, and green for Sean. They were so easily pleased. It took so little to give them joy.

"Thank you, Moya," they said as she placed a mug in each of their hands. They sipped and their faces glowed with delight.

"Will you and Mr. O'Brien have a cup with us?" Shauna asked, arranging her skirt daintily around her knees and licking the chocolate mustache off her upper lip.

"We will, indeed," Moya replied. "This mug is for Mr. O'Brien." She handed it to him, her fingers brushing his with a touch that he found more sensual than any sexual experience he had ever had.

He took a drink of the chocolate and realized that she had added a splash of Bailey's Irish Mist to it. He smiled at her and nodded, acknowledging his "grown-up" version.

Moya took the last cup from the tray and sat down on the end of the sofa, where she usually did her reading or needlework. Rory had grown to love seeing her there. Night after night, she would be there, the firelight glistening in her copper hair.

Compared to his nights in New York spent poring over papers, writing proposals, and composing contracts, this was a bit of heaven.

Too bad it couldn't last forever.

Moya turned to the children. "Can anyone tell me why that cup was Mr. O'Brien's and no one else's tonight?" she asked them.

"I think I know," Rory said, grinning. "A dash of, ah, extra cream, right?"

She smiled back at him. "Extras aside, there's another reason. Who can name it?"

Loving any sort of puzzle or riddle, the children debated long and hard about the significance of the mug. Finally, Kevin exclaimed, "'tis the crest, the shield that's on it!"

"Aye," Moya said, "and why is that perfect for Mr. O'Brien?"

The children squinted, studying the red crest with its three golden lions. "Is it Brian Boru's crest?" Kevin asked. "I think he used the three lions on his battle flags."

"And you think right," Moya told him. "What a clever lad you are. Can you tell Mr. O'Brien what that crest has to do with him?"

"Oh, oh, I know!" Shauna shouted, barely able to sit still. "He's an O'Brien. Of Brian. The mighty Brian Boru was one of his great, great, great, great grandfa'rs."

"If you add a few more greats in there, you'll have it," Moya said. "After all, 'twas more than a thousand years ago that the great emperor of Ireland walked the earth."

"Brian who?" Rory asked. "Oh, you mean that old king. I think my da told me something about him. He fought the Vikings, right?"

Kevin was scandalized. "An old king? Ah, Mr. O'Brien, that's like sayin' the glorious Shannon is just some old river. He was the greatest king in all of Irish history. And yer a son of his. Ye should be as proud as a peacock with two tails, bein' descended from Brian Boru."

"What did he do that was great?"

Kevin swelled with importance, pleased to have his expertise questioned. "Brian Boru was the only man to ever unite all of Ireland under one kingship. Oh, he had his troubles, to be sure, with rebellions and the like. But he was able to gather the Irish clans together to mount an offense against the Vikings—fierce barbarians they were—and put an end to their pillagin' and plunderin'."

"Aye," Sean added, "Brian Boru was over seven feet tall, had the strength of twenty warriors, and could cleave a man in two with one stroke of a Viking battle-ax."

"Oooo, that's dreadful," Shauna said, covering her ears with her hands. "I'll be havin' bad dreams tonight and have to crawl into bed with ma and da, just from hearin' such a thing."

Rory turned to Moya. "Over seven feet tall?" he asked with a smirk. "The strength of twenty warriors?"

She shrugged. "Far be it from me to correct a bard, just because he's embroiderin' his story a wee bit to heighten the drama. Old Kevin there has kissed the Blarney stone, you know. Twice."

"Aye," Sean volunteered, "and swallowed it once besides."

They all laughed as Kevin blushed and Shauna took turns looking at him, then Rory, with love shining in her eyes. It was all too apparent—she was hopelessly smitten with them both.

But Rory—Rory, son of the mighty Brian Boru—was oblivious to her adoration. His attention and affections lay elsewhere, with the beautiful redhead who had joined the children on the floor in front of the fire and was beginning to tell them a story about some fellow named Cuchulain.

Again, the dilemma haunted him: She loved Ireland and would never consider leaving it; he knew that without even asking. And while he *was* growing to love Ireland and the Irish people, he was a New Yorker at heart. His life was there, his business was there and the company he had worked so hard to build was already suffering in his absence. If he didn't return soon, he was going to lose everything he had striven to gain.

And, although he kept turning the problem over and over in his mind, he still found no answer.

Moya lay in her bed, both embracing and fighting the images that flooded her mind: Rory sitting by the fire, talking with the children, laughing with them, telling them his own stories about growing up in New York. His stories had been poignant, funny for the sake of the children, but she had read the pain between his words. He was a different man from the one who had arrived on her doorstep, soaked, rude, and insensitive to the feelings of others. The Rory who had been sitting in her living room tonight would be an excellent father, a wonderful husband.

But as much as she wanted to cling to that dream—and to him—she knew better.

Rory wasn't the only one who had experienced a difficult childhood. She had suffered loss too many times to set herself up for one now.

A big one.

Losing Rory O'Brien—and she was bound to very soon—was going to be painful enough without her futile dreams adding to the misery of it.

So, she tried not to remember how the firelight played across his rugged, handsome features, how deep his voice was and how his laughter sounded as it filled her house, how sweet he had been to little Shauna and how he had teased the boys and bonded with them, like an uncle.

No, it didn't bear thinking about. But lying there in her bed, with the light of the full moon filtering through the delicate lace curtains and filling the room, she could think of nothing else. Norah's words from earlier that day flooded through her, mixing with her thoughts of Rory. The evening spent with Rory and the children had brought home Norah's message with an alarming force. That this, this type of evening, filled with laughter and happiness was what she stood to lose if she didn't take a chance—

A soft knock at her door interrupted Moya's thoughts. She had no guests in the house, so it had to be . . .

"Rory?"

"Yes," came the quiet answer. "May I come in?"

She threw back the covers and hurried to the door. In her shock that he had come upstairs on his injured leg, she didn't think to put on a robe.

When she opened the door, she saw him standing there, bare from the waist up, wearing a pair of pajama bottoms and a shy smile.

"What do you think you're doin', lad?" she said. "You're not supposed to navigate those stairs yet! Just because the doctor put that new brace on—"

She got no further. He reached for her, pulled her to him and held her so tightly that she could scarcely breathe. "Don't get bossy with me, Moya Mahoney. Not now." His arms tightened around her waist, and he buried his face in her hair. "I've been waiting to get that damned cast off for six weeks. Why do you think I haven't been up here before now?"

She gasped as his hands left her waist and slid downward to cup her hips. "Because you're a fine gentleman . . . ?" she said as she allowed her own hands to roam across his bare shoulders, loving the hardness of his muscles and the smoothness of his skin. "And because you didn't want to take advantage of me?"

He nuzzled her neck, his breath warm and moist against her throat. "No," he said, "that wasn't it at all. Okay, maybe that was a little bit of it. But I'm not *that* fine of a gentleman."

"And it appears . . ." she whispered, ". . . I'm not that fine of a lady." She twined her fingers in his thick curls and leaned her head back, offering him her lips.

He took them, kissing her long and hard, like a

hungry man who had denied himself for too long. As their tongues mated, he pressed her even more tightly against him, and his intentions became obvious, his desires all too apparent.

Every inch of Moya's body was aching with sweet needs of its own, more intense and demanding than anything she had ever felt. She knew that in seconds she would pass that crucial point and there would be no turning back. It was going to happen . . . a hundred fantasies were about to become real, if that was what she truly wanted.

In the back of her mind a voice whispered, reminding her of a vow she had made to herself years ago, a promise she had kept . . . until now.

She pulled back from him slightly and looked up into his eyes. "Rory, I don't know," she said, struggling to find the right words. "I want you . . . I want to be with you . . . but it should be . . . special. It should mean more than just. . . ."

He stared at her for a long moment, saying nothing. The look of raw desire faded from his eyes to be replaced by something softer, more gentle.

"Of course it should be special, Moya," he said. "This isn't just sex, really. *You're* very special to me. And I wouldn't say that if it weren't true. I *am* more of a gentleman than that."

He released her from his embrace and took her hand. "Come over here," he said as he led her to the window and into the moonlight that was streaming through the lace curtains. "I want to see your face when I try to tell you. . . ."

He reached up to touch her cheek, and Moya saw

that his hand was trembling. His vulnerability went straight to her heart. This wasn't the cool, collected, worldly New Yorker, standing here in her bedroom. The expression on his face was more that of an awkward adolescent; he looked the way she felt, young and inexperienced.

"I'm not that good with words, Moya," he admitted. "Especially romantic ones. For an Irishman, I'm actually pretty limited in that area. But I came up here tonight because I want you to know how much you mean to me. I want you to know how much I appreciate all you've done."

"I know that, Rory. You've thanked me often enough and—"

"No, I haven't. I *can't* thank you enough. You took care of me, Moya, when I was hurt and couldn't fend for myself. And you didn't make me feel weak, or embarrassed, or obligated. You just . . . you took care of me. Nobody's ever done that before."

She smiled and reached up to brush a wayward curl back from his eyes. "'Twas no bother, Rory. Truly. 'Twas only a pleasure."

"That's because you have such a good heart, Moya. You're the best person I've ever known, and I'm so grateful for all you've done for me, all you've taught me."

He cupped her chin in his palm and traced the edge of her upper lip with his thumb. "You're a beautiful woman, Moya, and I'm not going to pretend that I don't want you in a physical, sexual way. I've wanted you since the first night I met you. But it's much more than that. I don't know how to tell you in words how I feel about you, but I'd like to show you."

He bent his head and kissed her, softly, sweetly. "I'm much better at showing than telling," he said, his lips still against hers.

"Yes," she said breathlessly, "I imagine you are."

His hand left her face and trailed slowly down the front of her nightgown, his fingers dipping into the deep vee of her bodice. "I'm not *always* in a hurry, Moya. I'll wait if you want me to. I'll wait as long as you want. It's up to you."

His fingertips moved slowly across the rounded softness of her breast until they found the hardened peak. She caught her breath as he slowly circled, stroked, and stoked the fire that was building deep inside her.

"I don't want to wait, Rory," she said. "I've waited long enough."

"Ah, lass," he replied with that terrible, fake Irish accent she had grown to love, "that's what I was hopin' ye'd say."

He started to scoop her up into his arms, but the moment she realized what he was intending to do, she said, "Don't you dare be so foolhardy! And you with that leg still healin'!" Taking him by the hand, she added, "You come along with me now, Mr. Rory O'Brien. There's this spot I've been savin' for you . . . on the right side of me bed."

He followed her, all too willingly. "And what if we both wind up in the middle?"

She laughed and shrugged. "Aye, well . . . so be it."

Once they were in bed, her nightgown lying on the floor beside his pajama bottoms, Rory fulfilled his promise of slow, leisurely lovemaking. With patient, skillful fingers he explored her, stirring desires that he later satisfied with his lips and tongue. She had never known such pleasure as he revealed to her the wonders of her own body. At his touch she felt like a meadow daisy, opening to the warmth of a sunlit, spring morning, unfurling, then bursting into glorious bloom.

It was she, not he, who finally ended the sweet agony. At her urgent coaxing he moved over her, into her. With one stroke, he breached the fragile barrier and filled her more completely than she ever could have imagined. The ache of desire that had tormented her, day after day and night after night, was finally, completely, deliciously satisfied.

Later, as they lay side by side, he trailed his fingers down her arm and grasped her hand. Lacing his fingers through hers, he said, "You should have told me, Moya. I didn't know you were a . . . you know. . . ."

"A virgin?" She laughed. "You can say it. 'Tisn't a bad word. Everyone must have a first time."

"I know, but I didn't know this was going to be yours."

"Would you have done anything differently? Surely, you couldn't have done anything better!"

He chuckled. "Well, I don't know about that. But

I just hope I didn't . . . ruin anything for you. I mean, were you saving yourself for marriage or . . . ?"

"Aye, I was." She snuggled closer into the warm shelter of his arms, feeling more completely happy and contented than she could ever remember. Sighing, she closed her eyes, savoring the precious moment. "But you mustn't trouble yourself about it," she added. "Seems it wasn't a hard and fast rule."

Moya watched the moonlight fade into dawn while lying in the comforting circle of Rory's arms. He had fallen asleep hours ago, and so had she. But when she had awakened, just before sunrise, the warm contentment of lovemaking had disappeared, to be replaced by the chill of fear.

Now that the gray light of dawn had replaced the silver moonlight, she wondered why she had been so foolish as to have allowed it to happen. She should have sent him downstairs as soon as she had opened the door and seen him standing there with that sweet look of anticipation on his face.

Before their lovemaking, she might have been able to say good-bye to him with only a few days or weeks of grief to endure. But now, she knew him, loved him, so much more intimately. After having been joined together, their inevitable parting would be all the more wrenching.

Moya thought of his big hands caressing her in the night, the taste of his lips on hers, the bliss of feeling his hard, male body moving above her, inside her, the spiritual bonding that came when they both reached the peak of ecstasy.

Surely, it had been a great mistake. Because now she knew her grief at losing him wouldn't be over in a matter of days, weeks, or months. It would last a lifetime.

Fifteen

Moya was cleaning her kitchen furiously trying not to think about the fact that Rory was packing, getting ready to leave Ireland.

She had crept out of bed that morning, leaving him to sleep while she slipped downstairs to prepare breakfast. Waking with him, snuggling and whispering sweet lovers' words would have been more than she could stand. One more bond to sever.

When he came downstairs half an hour later, he looked as sad as she felt. He knew as well as she did that this wasn't going to work. Some problems didn't have a solution. And the problem of Rory O'Brien, New York entrepreneur, and Moya Mahoney, Irish bed and breakfast owner, had no answer.

He had returned to his room after breakfast and spent more than an hour on the telephone. While she changed the linens in the adjoining bedroom,

Moya overheard him talking to Fredl and several other of his board members. When he had finished speaking to them, he had solemnly told Moya he was leaving.

Moya was sure he had decided to return to New York earlier than originally planned because of what had happened between them last night. He, too, realized that they were traveling a path to even more heartache, and he was ending the journey.

And, although she knew he was right, she wished there was something she could say or do that would convince him to stay.

She left the kitchen and walked to the half-opened door of his room. He was taking his clothes from the armoire and placing them in the suitcase on the bed.

He paused when he saw her, and Moya saw her own sorrow reflected in his eyes.

Norah's advice came back to her: *Someone has to say it. Someone has to be the first to admit they're in love.*

But she couldn't do it. She couldn't make a sad moment even worse by admitting a truth that made no difference in the end.

"The sun is shining this morning," he said, nodding at the brightly lit window, but he didn't sound happy about it.

"So 'tis."

"Not at all like the rainy night I arrived."

" 'Twas a good night," she said, "rain and all."

"Yes. It was. I'll never forget it." He folded the charcoal gray suit he had worn that night when he had addressed the villagers and put it in the suitcase.

He closed his eyes for a moment, as though fighting back tears, and shook his head. "I'll never forget last night, either. It was wonderful. *You* were wonderful, Moya."

"So . . . were . . . you. I . . ." She choked on her words and sat down abruptly on the corner of the easy chair, afraid that her knees wouldn't hold her.

He walked over to her, knelt before her, and took her hands in his. "I'm leaving, but I want to be sure you know—it isn't because you aren't important to me. It's because I'm afraid you're becoming much too important to me."

She tried to speak, but couldn't for the knot in her throat. She nodded instead.

"Sooner or later, I have to go home," he said. "I love Ireland, but I can't live here in this village for the rest of my life, the way you want to. Do you understand that, Moya?"

She managed to say, "Aye, I do."

He pressed the back of her hand to his lips, then placed her palm along his cheek. "I'd love it if you'd come to New York with me right now—today. Nothing would make me happier. We've started something great here, and I'd like to continue it . . . there. Would you come, Moya? I'll take care of all the details, even find someone to look after your guest house here. All you have to do is pack a suitcase. What do you say?"

Moya felt as though someone was painfully ripping the fabric of her soul right down the middle.

She had never cared for any man the way she did Rory. It was so easy to imagine a future with him . . . but only if it were here in Gormloch, in her own house. She couldn't even imagine herself on the streets of an enormous, unfriendly, dirty, noisy city like New York. How could they continue to build on what they had started here in a place like that? It wouldn't be the same. It couldn't be.

"I can't, Rory. I wouldn't be happy there."

"How do you know? You've never been there. Forgive me for saying so, sweetheart, but you've never been anywhere. Give New York a chance. Give *us* a chance. Last night was the most fantastic night of my life. If you'll come with me, we can have more nights like that. Many more."

Tears burned in her eyes, then spilled hot down her cheeks. "You don't understand, Rory. I'm Irish. I'm a daughter of old Eire. Being here is like being in my mother's arms. I could never feel at home anywhere else."

He nodded and bowed his head. "I understand. I can't insist that you make a sacrifice I'm not willing to make myself. And I just can't stay, Moya. I can't."

"And I can't leave."

He stood and pulled her off the chair and into his arms. "Then I have to," he said. "And the sooner I do, the better it will be for both of us."

He kissed the tears that were flowing down her cheeks, then kissed her lips that were trembling so badly she couldn't even kiss him back.

"I love you, Moya Mahoney. And I'll never forget you."

A moment later, he was gone.

He had said it. He had spoken the magic words.

But there was no magic in it after all, Moya decided. Even though he had found the courage to say it first, he was still gone.

Rory sat in his first-class seat on the Aer Lingus jet and wondered for the seven hundredth time if he had done the right thing. He knew he couldn't be happy living in Ireland, but now, thanks to a certain red-haired lass, he wasn't going to be happy back in New York, either.

The flight announcements were made, the Fasten Safety Belt/No Smoking lights came on, and they were taxiing down the runway. Seconds later they were airborne, the emerald fields of Ireland spread out below them.

Rory's heart ached and he thought of what Moya had said about feeling as though she was in her mother's arms in Ireland. Safe in the arms of old Eire. And, to his surprise, in that moment, he knew exactly what she meant. He, too, felt it, the draw of the land itself. The acute feeling of loss that filled him as he left that enchanted, green land.

He thought of all the emigrants who had been forced to leave this peaceful place over the ages. How they had stood on ship decks and watched as the fog closed around them, shrouding their vessel, the sight of that breathtaking green becoming smaller and smaller.

With his face pressed to the window, he, too, watched as the clouds began to close behind him, and the last tiny patch of green disappeared. When he finally leaned his head back on his seat, he was only dimly aware that tears were streaming down his cheeks.

A hand closed over his arm, and for the first time he noticed the tiny, elderly nun who sat in the seat next to him. Her classic Irish face was a study in sweet empathy. "There, there, dear," she said, patting him with her soft, wrinkled hand. "Don't cry. Ye can return home soon."

"What?" he asked, not comprehending. Then he understood; she thought he was Irish. "That's the problem, Sister," he said with a sigh and a sniff. "I *am* going home."

Moya sat on the damp grass next to Angus's grave, oblivious to the rain that was starting to fall, and the fact that she had no coat or any sort of wrap to protect her. The chill she felt came from deep inside. She would have been cold had she been wearing a heavy Aran sweater and had the sun beating down on her head.

"I know you aren't here," she said to the newly carved gravestone that bore Angus O'Brien's name. "I know you're in a far better place, and from there you can't help me in my present circumstances, but I felt the need to come here. I hope you don't mind me burdenin' you this way, Angus. But I thought you might have special knowledge of my predicament."

Moya glanced around, feeling foolish for speaking her heart to a silent grave. She had spoken to her dead relatives before but never about anything quite so personal and she didn't want anyone to overhear her outpouring. She wasn't the only one who had visited Angus's resting place that day. A fresh flower lay at the base of the stone, a single red rose. Angus had been well-loved in the village; the humble gift could have been from anyone.

Seeing no one, Moya continued to unburden her soul. "He left today, Angus. Went back to New York. If you can hear me, you probably know that already. But I want to tell you how I feel about it."

A sob caught in her throat and she reached into her jeans pocket for a handkerchief. "Desperately bad, that's how I'm feelin'. Me house is so empty now, I can scarcely bear up."

She wiped her eyes and blew her nose loudly. "He told me he loves me. Said so plainly. But he left. He can't live the rest of his life here in this little village after seein' the big, broad world. He even asked me to come with him, but I said no. It was too much to ask, leavin' this place and everyone I love."

The rain began to fall in earnest, but Moya paid no attention as the drops mixed with her tears and streamed down her face.

"You know how I feel, Angus, better than anyone," she said. "You couldn't leave when Norah wanted you to. You gave up the love of your life rather than leave your home. Are you happy you did it? Was that the right choice? If you had your life to live over again, would you do it differently?"

A sudden chill shivered down her back and Moya wrapped her arms around herself, aware for the first time how wet and cold she was.

"I wish I knew your thoughts on the subject," she said. "I wish we had talked about it at least once before you . . . before you left.

"Was it enough, Angus, sittin' by the fire and tellin' the old stories all your livelong life? Will it be enough for me?"

A flash of lightning cut the sky almost directly over her head, and a clap of thunder shook the ground beneath her. Even in her grief-numbed state, Moya knew it was time to go home.

Besides, as she stood and slowly walked away from Angus O'Brien's grave, she knew that the answers she sought didn't lie there with her old friend. They were within her own heart. The problem was, her own heart felt as though it had been torn in two parts, one belonging to Rory O'Brien and the other to the village of Gormloch.

As Moya passed through the iron gates and started down the road toward home, a figure stepped from behind the O'Brien family's crypt, only a few feet from Angus's grave. It followed her from a distance and watched until she disappeared into her house.

Moya crept quietly into her sitting room, not wanting to disturb the nice young couple who were sitting on the sofa, holding hands and whispering sweet nothings to each other. She needed to place more turf on the fire, but she hated to interfere with what was, obviously, a much-needed romantic evening for the wife and husband.

No sooner had Moya returned from the graveyard earlier than the couple on holiday from Los Angeles and their two children, an infant and a toddler, arrived and asked for a night's lodging. The adorable little one had been in bed for an hour, but the toddler kept jumping up and down, demanding something to eat or drink, and trips to the lavatory.

Moya had replenished the fire and was discreetly taking her leave when the little boy bounded back into the room, wearing fuzzy, tiger-striped pajamas, complete with flannel claws for feet and a tail hanging from the back. He held out his bottle to his mother and said, "Mommy, want more. Want d'ink. Pe-e-eese!"

Moya's heart melted. "'Twould be my pleasure to fetch it for the young master," she told the tired mother. "Why don't you just sit there with your husband and keep his hand warm while I tuck Mr. Tiger Tails back into his bed."

"Would you?" The lady gave her a grateful smile. "That would be so nice."

"Come along," Moya told the boy, offering him her hand. "We'll head for the kitchen straightaway and fill that bottle with some nice fresh milk. Then it's to bed with you and nothin' else, do you hear me, lad?"

The child frowned. "Me not lad. Me Ryan."

"Ah, Ryan it is! Well, you're in Ireland now, Master Ryan, and every boy here is called a lad, even if he's ninety-seven years old. Now bring those wild pajamas along with me, and yourself in them. We've business to attend to, concerning that bottle of yours. Serious business, indeed."

A few minutes later, Moya was tucking the child into a small trundle bed next to the crib where his baby sister lay sleeping.

"Now, look at that," Moya whispered. "The wee one is already snorin' away, she is, and you still makin' a nuisance of yourself."

"What noos-an?"

Moya chuckled and knelt beside the bed. "A nuisance isn't really what you are. Truth be told, you're just the sort of bother I'd love to have meself. Which is no bother at all. You're a good lad, Master Ryan, a fine boy, indeed. And now 'tis time for all good boys to close their eyes and dream of their favorite things. What do you like, Ryan?"

"Ice c'eam."

"Ah, me, too. And what else do you like?"

"Ki'y cats."

"Then close your big pretty eyes and you'll see ice cream, mountains of it, waitin' for you to attack it with a giant spoon. And at your feet are two baby kittens, playing with a ball of string and—"

"No. 'Dis many." He held up four stubby fingers.

"All right, so 'tis four kittens, playing while you eat your ice cream. I want you to think of that ice cream and those kittens, Ryan. See there, right behind your closed eyes?"

He nodded. She reached down and stroked his soft curls.

"Aye, you just keep watchin' them, and eatin' the ice cream, and before you know it, mornin' will come and you can get up and play."

As she continued to stroke his hair, Moya could hear the child's breathing slow and feel him relax, drifting away into that peaceful sleep reserved for children and other pure souls.

She waited until she was sure he was deeply asleep before rising from her knees and slipping from the room.

As she walked back to the kitchen to get things ready for the next morning's breakfast, she thought of Rory and the children, telling stories beside the fire. She thought of how soft and sweet the little boy's hair had been and the smile on his face, painted there with her words about ice cream and kittens. She thought of the young couple holding hands in her sitting room and Rory's kisses as he had told her good-bye.

Moya decided to go on to bed. In a matter of seconds, she was going to be crying. And she didn't want to do it in the kitchen. That sort of sobbing required the privacy of one's own bedroom.

Tommy O'Sullivan was watching the evening news on the television, a half-drank Guinness in his hand, his feet pointed toward the warm turf fire on his hearth, his black Labrador retrievers on either side of his chair, when a loud, impatient knock sounded

on his door. The dogs sprang from a dead sleep to
furious balls of barking fur.

"Ehhh, damnation," he muttered as he hauled himself out of the chair and went to answer it, the dogs
at his heels. There were two more series of pound-
ings before he could get the door open.

"What is it ye want?" he said when he saw Norah
Delaney standing there in the rain, wearing a plastic see-through pancho and the usual frown on her
face.

"I want ye to open the post office," she said. "I
have business to conduct with you."

"I'll conduct no business with you or any other
person at this time of night, Norah Delaney. The
whole village is well aware of me rules on that subject."

"I'm well aware of what a lazy, worthless lout
ye are, but I also know ye to be a greedy one, so
open that store and I'll make it worth yer time. I've
a letter to post and a telegram that must be sent
straightaway."

"A telegram?" Tommy had perked up at the mention of compensation, but his face had fallen when
he'd heard what she wanted. "Now that telegram
sendin' is a very complicated procedure, Norah. It
requires that I—"

"Oh, shut up, Tommy, and stand back. I'm
comin' through. My shoulder is causin' me a world
of pain . . . me havin' stood in the rain most of the
day. I'll soon be dead if I don't get this business
done. And my demise will all be on yer head,
Tommy O'Sullivan. Yers alone and—"

"All right, all right. Come in, Norah." Tommy sighed. "Come in out of the rain and tell me what ye want that telegram of yers to say. The telegram yer willin' to pay so dearly for. . . ."

Sixteen

When Moya was most upset, she usually changed something. Drastically. And often, it was the color of one of the bedrooms: the walls, linens, curtains, art, accessories . . . everything. It gave her the feeling of a fresh start and a cleansed soul.

She was rolling powder-blue paint onto the walls of the smallest upstairs bedroom when she heard Conn calling out from downstairs.

"Moya, where are ye, darlin'? And what's that dreadful smell?"

"'Tis fresh paint, Conn," she said, climbing down off the splattered stepladder she had been standing on. "The smells of paint, varnish, and cleaning fluids are unfamiliar to most bachelors," she added. "Come upstairs and take a lesson on sprucin' up your habitat."

"Ahhh, ye are a mighty decorator, Moya, a whirlwind of a woman," he said as he entered the room and stepped gingerly from newspaper to newspaper that lay on the floor for protection. "Ye know how to make a house a home, and that's for certain. Ye'll make some man a happy husband one o' these days."

She wiped her hands on a rag and laughed. "Aye, well, he won't be so cheerful when I put a paint-brush in his hand and shove a ladder beneath him."

Conn gave her one of his sweet, broad-faced smiles. "I have to tell ye, Moya, I'll not be weepin' into me pillow tonight, depressed that the New Yorker has returned home. I was a bit worried that he was givin' me competition for yer affections."

"He's not a topic I care to discuss, Conn, if you don't mind."

"I don't mind at all, at all. Let's talk about the two of us and what a fine team we make, playin' music together. How long's it been since ye knocked the dust off that bodhran o' yers and brought it over to the pub? Me tin whistle is gettin' rusty waitin' for ye to appear."

"I'll be over soon, Conn."

"How soon? Tonight maybe?"

"Maybe. It depends on how far I get with this paintin'."

Conn glanced around the room, a look of soulish indecision on his face. She knew he was weighing the prospects of breathing paint fumes with her or sharing some political debate with the lads at the pub. She also knew which he would choose.

Although she might be the object of his affection, chatting with the lads was his obsession.

"I do hope ye'll make it out this evenin'. 'Twould make me eyes glad just to look upon ye again."

"We'll see, Conn. Thank you for checkin' on me."

"Checkin'? Oh, no . . . I had a reason for comin'. What was it?"

She nodded toward the envelope he was holding in his hand. "Were you intendin' to bring me my mail?"

"Ahhh, that's what it was, indeed. What a clever girl you are. I told Tommy I'd be callin' on ye, and he asked me to save him the trip."

"Thank you, Conn." For just a moment, she hoped it was from Rory. But he had just left, and a letter would take days to arrive. And this one was posted here in the village, though the sender hadn't written a return address on the envelope.

"Doesn't say who it's from," he said as he placed it into her hand. " 'Though it looks like a female's penmanship."

"So it does, Conn. So it does."

She knew he was waiting for her to open it in front of him, but something told her not to. Shoving it into the back pocket of her jeans, she said, "I'm in need of a cold glass of lemonade, Conn, so I'll be walkin' you to the door."

"I wouldn't mind a glass meself," he said, brightening.

She sighed. It wasn't fair for her to encourage Conn, when she knew he would never be more than a friend to her.

"And I'd be glad to sit meself down and share

one with you, Conn, but I must get this room painted, since I'm doin' it all by meself, and all."

Again, Conn decided to ignore the hint. "I understand. And I'll not be interferin' with yer work any longer."

"Thank you for bringin' the letter, Conn. 'Twas most kind of you."

"I'd do anythin' for ye, Moya," he said as he headed for the stairs and started down. "Yer the finest woman in this village, and ye know how I've always held ye in the highest regard."

"Hmmm . . ." Moya watched him leave and realized she felt nothing but relief to see him gone. Not at all the way she felt when Rory walked out of a room.

She had allowed the man she loved to leave and refused to go with him, because she had wanted to stay in Gormloch. But among the villagers, there wasn't one man she wanted for a husband. And to her knowledge there was only one man who wanted her.

And it was Conn. Conn, who hadn't had the courage even to kiss her, let alone ask for her hand in marriage in all the years they had known each other.

She thought of the darling children in her house the night before and how unlikely it was that there would be any wee ones in her future.

It seemed to her that the price she was paying to remain in her home became more dear by the moment.

• • • •

Once Conn had left, Moya had decided to sit down and take a break with her lemonade after all. After checking the seat of her jeans for paint, she sat down in her favorite chair and propped her feet on the ottoman.

Now that Rory was gone, she could sit in this chair again, having surrendered it to him so that he could keep his leg elevated. But she wasn't happy about her new liberty. She would rather sit on the sofa and have him sitting in the chair, listening to her stories, telling her some of his own.

Funny, before Rory had knocked on her door that rainy night, Moya hadn't realized how nice it was to have a man in the house. Not an older, fatherly sort like Angus had been, but a man her own age, whose eyes gleamed with an interest other than paternal. Rory had somehow made her home complete with his masculine presence. Funny, she thought, how she had never noticed anything was missing before.

Moya had drunk more than half of her glass of lemonade before she remembered the letter in her hip pocket. Setting her tumbler on a nearby table, she reached into her jeans and pulled it out.

The envelope was a simple white one, like the ones Tommy Sullivan sold in his store, giving no clue about the sender. Moya seldom received letters; in such a small village, if someone had something to say to another, he or she had only to walk down the road and do so.

Or, they could whisper it to a neighbor, who would

pass it along, and the message would arrive even more quickly than if it had been delivered personally.

Her curiosity piqued, she ripped open the envelope's sealed flap and peered inside. It contained two sheets of paper—one white, one blue—folded together. Moya read the few words scribbled on the first page, the white one first. It said simply:

> *Moya,*
> *Angus wrote this to me, but I think he would want you to read it. So, read it. And stop acting like a turkey's arse. You're a smart girl. Act like it.*
>
> *Norah*

Time seemed to slow for Moya, as it did when she had the premonition that she was about to learn something that would change her life forever. She also had a strong sense of Angus's presence as she began to read his familiar, oversized and scrawled handwriting. She could almost smell his blackberry tobacco smoke in the air and could somehow feel him rest his hand lightly on her shoulder, imparting warm, fatherly comfort, as he often had over the years when they had talked about something important.

Slowly, she read the message, sent to her from beyond the boundaries of the grave, knowing in her spirit that this letter—written more than three years ago as evidenced by the date on the top of the page—contained the advice that she pleaded for yesterday at his gravesite.

My Dearest Norah,

Today, as I watched little Moya here in her house, attending her guests, I thought of you. I thought of how different she is from the way you were at her age. If you had been like her, happy to live out your days here in Gormloch, we could have been together. But you were the wild one, always eager to see what was beyond the next horizon.

Perhaps I should have gone with you on your journeys. If I had, you'd have been mine instead of that lout, Delaney. The last I heard, you two were living in Paris, like aristocracy. I suppose you're happy. I'm not. I hate wondering how different our lives would have been if I'd only found the courage to take more chances.

I wish I had told you I loved you, because I do, so very much.

I wish I had asked you to be my own wife. We would have been good together, much better than you and that Delaney bum. Much better than me lying alone every night thinking of you. Wondering.

I wish I had taken you to Paris.

Always,
Angus

By the time Moya had finished reading, tears were streaming down her face and dripping onto Angus's blue stationery. She had also decided what she was going to do about Rory.

Having asked for an answer, for direction, she knew she had received it. She also knew that if she didn't reach into her soul and summon the necessary courage to do what she must, she would never forgive herself.

She didn't ever want to write a letter of regret like the one in her hands. If she failed in her life, it would be the result of chances taken, not opportunities forsaken. If she was going to suffer from regret in her later years, it wouldn't be because she had been a coward. She would reach out with both hands, and if she failed to grasp happiness, she would take comfort in the fact that she had tried.

Holding the letter tightly against her chest, she left her sitting room and walked up the stairs. With each step she felt lighter, as though a burden were being lifted from her heart and mind.

And, by the time she reached the top, she was running.

Seventeen

As Rory guided his Jaguar XJR through the crowded, crazy streets of midtown Manhattan, he cursed the taxi drivers who cut him off and wondered how he could ever have considered this city stimulating. He was dead tired, and he had been since he had come back from Ireland.

When had this town become so blasted noisy? When had the people gotten so damned rude and insensitive? Hurry! Hurry! Hurry! They were in a rush even when they weren't going anywhere in particular. Everyone wanted to be first . . . first in a line, first through a door, first to speak, first to have their bagel smeared with lox-flavored cream cheese at the deli counter. First! First! First!

No one seemed to understand the quiet satisfaction of patiently standing aside and allowing someone else to go ahead of them.

He missed Ireland. He missed those peaceful green fields. He missed Moya. He—

He couldn't even enjoy his memories of Ireland and Ireland's lovely daughter, because his stupid cell phone was ringing.

Of the forty-eight hours he had been back in New York, forty-two of those had been spent unraveling the tangles that had developed in the fabric of Nova Tech during his absence. Fredl, Mark, Herman, and Darla had done an excellent job, keeping things going. But Rory had never realized before how much he contributed to his own company. His presence and input had been sorely missed.

"Yeah, what now?" he barked into the phone, as he turned the corner at Thirty-fourth and Fifth Avenue and nearly crunched a delivery boy on a bicycle who darted across the road in front of him trying like everyone else to be first no matter what the cost.

"Good evening to you, too." It was Fredl's soft German accent on the other end. "I was hoping your Irish friends had taught you some manners."

"They tried. They didn't succeed. What's up?"

"I just got a call from the car service," she said. "They have some sort of problem and can't pick Darla up from the airport. She's flying into JFK from London tonight about eight-thirty. Could you go get her? I'd call another service, but you know how she is about riding with people or services she doesn't know."

"No, I don't know how she is about that. What's wrong if it's an established, licensed service?"

"I don't know. She's just got a thing about it—
'

heard about some woman who was attacked by a
rabid taxi driver. You didn't have plans this evening,
did you?"

Rory could hear the sarcasm in Fredl's voice, the
implication that he had no life outside the office. Of
course he didn't have anything planned. How dare
she be right! He *hated* it when she was right.

"Why don't *you* go get her?" he snapped. "You
live closer to the airport than I do."

"Because, unlike you, *I* have a date . . . theater,
dinner, dancing, drinks . . . probably wild and crazy
sex afterward. What's your excuse?"

"I'll get her," he said with a sigh. "Give me the
friggin' flight number."

Once Moya had gotten over her initial panic and
queasiness brought on by her first airline flight, she
had quite enjoyed herself. The attendants had been
solicitous, supplying her with ginger ale and words
of encouragement. They had assured her that the jet's
miscellaneous squeaks, creaks, vibrations, and occasional dips were all perfectly normal.

She tried to strike up a conversation with the businessman from the Bronx who was sitting in the seat
next to hers, but he made it clear early in the flight
that he was going to use the time to catch up on
some much-needed sleep. So she stared out the window hour after hour, at the dark Atlantic Ocean, and
thought of what might be awaiting her in the big,
scary city of New York.

She knew many people from around the Killarney
area that traveled frequently between the States and

Ireland. With plenty of relatives in the New York area, they commonly hopped a flight and flew across the sea to visit their loved ones, and returned with interesting stories of their adventures there. She honestly had to admit that she didn't know anyone personally who had been mugged, molested, or murdered in New York. She didn't even know anyone who *knew* anyone who had been.

It would be just her luck to be the first.

But, even worse than the thought of being a victim of mayhem in the city, she was even more concerned about what she would do if no one was there to greet her at the airport.

She had made the call earlier to Rory's office, having rehearsed her little speech about how much she missed him and how she was willing at least to pay a visit, if it would mean seeing him again. But his secretary, Fredl, had told her he was out of the office . . . on a luncheon date. She hadn't mentioned if his meal companion was male or female, but Moya had assumed the worst. After all, he was back home again, and they had made no commitment to each other. Why shouldn't he go out to lunch with a beautiful, glamorous, sophisticated New York woman if he chose to?

Fredl had asked if she could be of assistance, and Moya had blurted out her plans to arrive that evening, as well as her misgivings about what to do once she arrived, as far as transportation and lodging. Sounding sympathetic, Fredl had assured her that she would arrange to have someone meet her as soon as she disembarked, someone who would take care of everything.

Fredl hadn't mentioned who that might be. She also didn't say whether she was going to mention Moya's call to Rory. For all Moya knew, he might be spending the rest of the afternoon, and evening, with his "luncheon date."

A hundred disturbing scenarios flooded Moya's mind, making her doubt the wisdom of booking an impromptu flight like she had. But having spent every carefully saved punt on the nonrefundable airline ticket, she was reluctant to throw it away . . . along with any chance of continuing the relationship.

And as she stared into the blackness of the night sky and the dark sea below, she had ample opportunities to scold and congratulate herself for both her stupidity and her courage in taking this step.

When the captain of the airliner came on the speaker and announced that they were thirty minutes away from landing in New York, her heart leapt into her throat and she could hear her pulse pounding in her ears.

The Bronx businessman next to her awoke and began to thumb through a stock investment magazine. She took her purse from under the seat in front of her, freshened her lipstick, and checked for mascara smears under her eyes.

Then she continued to watch out the window, peering into the darkness for any sight of land.

Finally, she saw them—twinkling lights—lots of them, in the distance.

It was the United States! A country she had heard

so much about all her life, and now she, Moya Mahoney, was seeing it with her own eyes!

"That's it!" she exclaimed, gouging the man in the ribs with her elbow. "I can see it!"

He gave her the sort of wide-eyed, cautious look that was usually given to escapees from a mental asylum.

"What?"

"New York City! I can see it there in the distance. There, look out the window and you'll be seein' it, too. 'Tis a glorious sight, indeed!"

Cautiously, he leaned across her and glanced out the window. "That's not Manhattan, " he said flatly. "Not yet."

She deflated. "No? Is it sure you are?"

He nodded, bored, and sighed. "I'm sure. I've traveled this route three times a month for seven years. That ain't it."

"Oh." She leaned away from him and stared out the window for two more minutes, watching the lights grow nearer and brighter. But she couldn't contain her excitement. She turned back to him. "Beggin' your forgiveness, sir, but would you please tell me when New York City is within sight?"

His gruffness faded and he gave her a half-smile. "First time to the Big Apple, huh?"

"Aye, 'tis me first time to anywhere."

"Mmmm." He stuck his nose back into his magazine. "Don't worry about it, when you see Manhattan, you'll know. You won't have to ask."

She pondered his answer, as well as his seemingly brusque demeanor. He growled like a bear, but she saw the twinkle in his eyes. She knew he was secretly enjoying her enthusiasm for her new experience.

Having recently spent considerable time with a New Yorker, she was beginning to see through this facade of theirs. Their words were curt, their observations uncomfortably perceptive, the fuses on their tempers short and easily ignited. But underneath, they were sweethearts. And she found she liked them.

The jet banked steeply to the left and the engines' whine changed in pitch. Moya's ears began to pop, and she felt the queasiness rising in her stomach again.

"Don't worry," her neighbor said without looking up from his magazine. "Descending. No sweat."

"Thank you, sir. I *was* wonderin'. You're most kind to reassure me."

"Humpf. Just don't want you urping on me."

She laughed. "No. I won't do that. You're safe enough."

"Good."

Her pulse pounding in her stuffed-up ears, she turned to look at the window as the jet leveled out. What she saw took her breath away.

Below her—but barely below—was the glorious city of New York, its world-famous skyline a forest of sparkling steel, glass, and lights. Skyscrapers of every style, shape, and size lit the black night sky like a thousand giant Christmas trees, glittering in myriad shades of silver and gold. Necklaces of deep blue lights shone like sapphires, outlining the graceful dips and arches of magnificent bridges.

"All the saints in heaven preserve us," Moya whispered. " 'Tis too beautiful to be real. 'Tis like a dream, a grand and splendid dream."

"What? Oh, yeah, I guess so," said the man next to her.

"And you've been blessed with such a sight three times a month for the past seven years. What a fine thing, fine, indeed. You must be most grateful for such a gift."

"Huh? Well, sure. It's pretty neat, I suppose." He leaned across her and pointed out the window. "See the building over there with the lit arches, the pretty lines to it—that's the Chrysler Building. And the big pointy one is the Empire State Building. They change the lights on it all the time—red and green for Christmas; red, white, and blue for the Fourth of July; green for St. Patrick's Day."

"Green for St. Patrick? Really?"

"Yeah, really. St. Patrick's Day is a big deal around here. Everybody's Irish for a day."

"Truly?"

"Uh-huh. And those two buildings down there at the end, those are the Twin Towers. They make up the World Trade Center. You'd probably like it, lots of places to shop."

"Oh, thank you, sir. But I haven't much money— spent it all gettin' here."

A look of concern crossed his face. "You *do* have friends or family here, don't you? I mean, this ain't a city for a girl alone, especially one right off the boat . . . er, plane . . . from another country."

"Aye, I know someone. But thank you for askin'. You're most kind."

"Hmmm. Just wonderin'. Got enough bums on the street as it is. Don't want you begging me for change in Penn Station."

She gave him a sweet smile. "You're a dear man, if I do say so meself."

He glanced around suspiciously. "Well, don't say it so loud. You'll ruin my reputation."

She patted his arm. "'Twill be our little secret. Now, tell me . . . what is that place up ahead, with all the blue lights shinin' in long rows?"

He looked out the window. "That, my dear, is John F. Kennedy Airport. Our destination. We'll be on the ground in less than five minutes."

"Oh, goodness," she said, pressing her hand over her mouth. "I think I might be gettin' sick after all!"

Eighteen

As Rory stood at the railing that separated the arriving international passengers from those waiting to receive them, he was glad that the information posted on the electronic monitors around the room indicated that the flight was only ten minutes late.

Even ten minutes was an eternity to him. He hated to wait—for anything. But during his stay in Ireland, he had seen something: the virtue of patience in practice.

As loudly as New Yorkers proclaimed their impatience with delays—whether caused by incompetence, disorganization, or the occasional natural disaster—the Irish prided themselves on being flexible, tolerant, and understanding.

Before his convalescence, Rory had considered those who are patient, weak people who lacked the courage to speak their minds and let their wishes be known. But in Ireland he had seen strong people—confident, articulate individuals—quietly accept the many minor delays of daily life, choosing to use the moment for a bit of conversation, observation, or meditation.

Now, as he looked around the room filled with anxious individuals waiting for the arriving passengers and antsy chauffeurs holding signs with names scrawled on them, he made a conscious decision to enjoy the moment, to do a bit of people watching and appreciate the fact that—at least for a few minutes—nothing special was expected of him.

This wasn't a delay.

It was a much-needed break in a busy day.

A new flood of people swept by on the opposite side of the railing. They walked the length of the barrier to the other side of the large room, dragging their luggage with them, looking weary but relieved to have arrived at their destinations. Relatives and friends called out to each other, and hurried to the opening where the railing ended to kiss, embrace, and chatter.

He shifted from one foot to the other as he watched those coming out of the door in the far wall, exiting Customs. Darla was only about five feet tall, a tiny woman with a cloud of beautiful silver hair, and Rory was afraid he might miss her in the crowd.

Funny, he had never heard her mention any taxi phobias. In fact, he was pretty sure he had seen her flagging cabs outside their office building after a day's work. *Oh, well,* he thought, *it just goes to show how little you really know about people.*

The stream of people began to slow to a trickle. He was surprised he hadn't seen Darla yet; she liked to fly first class and should have been one of the first to disembark.

He checked his watch, then glanced up at one of the overhead monitors to make sure he had the right gate. A stylishly scruffy young man, carrying a battered guitar case and a stuffed duffel bag, walked by him and Rory said, "Excuse me, but were you on Flight 8091 from London?"

"Aye, but 'twas a connectin' flight. I'm from Shannon meself."

From Shannon? A connecting flight?

At that moment, he saw her . . . a vision of fiery copper hair, wearing a cream-colored Aran sweater, blue jeans, and a broad smile.

"Moya?" he whispered, thinking this couldn't be true. A dream? A hallucination? Someone who looked just like his favorite Irish lass, someone who had thrown her suitcase to the floor and was running toward him, a look of rapture on her lovely face?

"Rory! I was so hopin' 'twould be yourself come to collect me!"

He reached for her, lifted her, and not too gracefully dragged her over the railing and into his arms. "I don't believe this," he said between kisses and laughter. "I don't friggin' believe it! This is awesome! When did you . . . ? How did you . . . ?"

She pulled back and looked up into his eyes.

"What do you mean? Didn't she tell you? That secretary of yours, Fredl . . . didn't she mention it was meself?"

"No. She mentioned it was a woman I work with."

He saw the smile disappear from her face in an instant. "A woman . . . you work with?"

"An older woman. A sweet, elderly, grandmotherly type with silver hair who is our chief accountant."

The smile reappeared. "Ah . . . I see. I think your secretary was havin' you on a bit, tellin' you it was the grandmother and not me."

"I think so, too. And the next time I see Fredl, I'm going to kiss her."

Another frown.

"On the cheek, Moya. On the cheek. Now let me hop over this barrier and go grab your bag that you dropped. You certainly can't leave it lying on the floor here for two weeks. Sorry, love, but you're not in Ireland anymore."

When Moya slid into the black Jaguar with its soft, dove gray leather seats that smelled classy, masculine, like Rory, she felt like Princess Niamh who was climbing onto a magical stallion's back, ready to soar away to Tir na nOg. And she had her own Ossian at her side.

He climbed in beside her, his nearness making her deliciously, deliriously happy. Sliding his right arm around her shoulders, he pulled her to him and kissed her. "I can't believe you're here," he said. "I'm afraid I'm going to wake up in a minute and find myself alone in bed."

She grinned impishly. "Now, there's no reason for you to be sleepin' all alone tonight unless that's what you want to—"

"That's *not* what I want. I don't want that at all, at all . . . as you Irish say. I want you beside me tonight. I want you beside me *every* night from now on."

"Well, I don't know about every night from now on, but I have a couple of weeks. My return ticket is for two weeks from tonight."

He lifted her hair, baring the nape of her neck, and placed a quick kiss there. "Two weeks? Why only two weeks?"

She laughed. "Because, if you hadn't been happy to see me, and I'd had to stay in a hotel, two weeks is about how long my money would have held out."

"A lady with a plan." He sighed. "So, I only have two weeks to sell you on New York."

"Oh, I saw it from the air and it was grand! Absolutely grand! I'm sold already."

"Yeah? Well, you wait until you're on the street looking up at those skyscrapers. Your eyes are goin' to be sore, lass," he added with a dreadful attempt at a county Kerry accent. "This is my town, and I'm very proud of it. You'll soon see why."

Moya's eyes *were* sore, as well as her feet, by the time Rory took her to his brownstone town house on East Seventy-fourth Street and walked her up the stone steps to his front door. He had taken her on a whirlwind mini tour of the city, up Fifth Avenue and down Park Avenue, past Radio City Music Hall and Carnegie Hall, Grand Central Station and Madison Square Garden, Rockefeller Plaza and Trump Tower.

Moya Mahoney was utterly, positively dazzled. And in love. With Rory, with his city.

But, like a windup toy that had run in circles all day, she had wound down. She had enjoyed quite enough big city glamour and glitz for one evening.

She was surprised at how cozy his neighborhood was, how peaceful in contrast to all the hustle and bustle only a few blocks away.

"What a lovely street," she said, "with all the pretty trees and the old brick buildings. In my imagination I can see the horses trottin' by, pullin' carriages filled with ladies in long dresses, wearin' cloaks with fur collars, and gentlemen wearin' elegant jackets and top hats, carrying canes and—"

"Boy, you do have a vivid imagination," he said, slipping his key into the lock. "To me, it's just my place on seventy-fourth Street. Somewhere to crash and burn at the end of the day. I don't spend much time here. Just a few hours each night to sleep. It doesn't really feel like home, the way your house does."

Moya felt a sharp stab of pity. "How very sad," she said, "to never feel as though you're goin' home, to feel the house waitin' to welcome you. Your soul needs a home, Rory O'Brien; everyone's does."

"Until I met you, I might have disagreed," he said, opening the door and ushering her inside. "But I think you've domesticated me, Moya, my dear. I've discovered the simple joys of spending the evening watching a fire burn on the hearth."

"And who would have thought that walking down a city street could make you feel so alive?" she exclaimed. "Why, I can feel the energy just bubblin' up through the sidewalks and into me! It has a pulse, this town, a throbbing heartbeat of its own. And I can feel it in my own body and spirit!"

He reached over and tweaked her nose. "Like I said before, Miss Mahoney, you have a very vivid imagination. Come inside and let's put all that fantasy potential to good use."

She laughed and allowed him to lead her through the foyer with its black-and-white checked marble tiles and walnut wainscoting. The house was obviously very old, but in excellent shape. The walls had been freshly covered with a simple but elegant cream-colored cloth with a jacquard embossing. The moldings had been recently restored to their original beauty and gleamed richly in the carefully orchestrated lighting that came from subtly placed, recessed spot lamps and a few contemporary, graceful lamps.

In what he called his living room, Rory had contemporary furniture—ebony wood pieces with clean, sharp lines, inlaid with precious hardwoods like rosewood, tulipwood, and purple heart. The sofa and chairs were oversized and cushiony, covered with leather that was black, gray, or white. On the walls hung examples of black-and-white photography, pictures of the city and its inhabitants: an elderly bag lady feeding pigeons in the park, a street musician playing a saxophone with a crumpled hat on the sidewalk in front of him to collect his coins, a child laughing gleefully, sitting on the back of a beautiful carousel horse.

"What wonderful pictures," she exclaimed. "They have such character! Wherever did you find them?"

"Oh, here and there," he said, shrugging off the compliment. "If something catches my eye, I snap it."

"You . . . ? I meant, where did you find them, as in, *buy* them, the pictures. You mean you took these yourself?"

"I thought you meant where did I find my subjects. Photography is one of my hobbies. Or at least, it was. I haven't had much time to devote to it since the business took off. I'd like to get back into it again."

"You should, indeed. You should do whatever feeds your soul, Rory, and I can tell just by lookin' at these pictures that they do."

"*You* feed my soul, Moya," he said. "In fact, you're a delicious feast for my soul."

He reached for a lock of her hair and curled it around his forefinger. "And speaking of feasting . . . would you like to see the rest of the place?"

"Were you intendin' to show me the kitchen, then?"

He shrugged. "Actually, I was thinking of the

bedroom. I'll show you the kitchen tomorrow morning when *I* make breakfast for *you*."

"You cook?"

"Not exactly, but I pour a mean glass of orange juice, and there's a diner around the corner."

Nineteen

Every time Rory looked through the viewfinder of his camera and clicked the shutter, he knew he was falling a bit more in love. And he had already tumbled so far down that rabbit's hole into Wonderland that he was a dead duck.

He laughed at himself and his silly, childish thoughts. Moya had rubbed off on him; he was thinking in terms of fairy tales and barnyard animals.

Rory couldn't help himself. He loved the little girl in her, and she brought out the child in him.

Although he had visited Washington Square Park hundreds of times, admired the magnificent, commemorative arch, walked the peaceful paths among the old trees, and listened to the musicians, he had never paid much attention to the dog run, filled with mongrels and purebreds of every size, color, and temperament. But Moya was ecstatic, thrilled just to stand outside the fenced off play area and watch the frisky canines romp.

"Oh, look at the little dachshund, nipping the big fella's belly. What a spirited little lad he is! And see the face on that bulldog! What a wonderful mug it is, all full of wrinkles and teeth!"

Rory snapped another picture and wondered if there was anything sexier on the planet than a female with a shapely woman's body and a child's enthusiasm for life. With the sun setting fire to her copper hair and the light of excitement shining in her eyes, she was a wonderful subject to photograph. And for the first time in years, Rory felt the warm flood of creativity washing through him, making him feel as alive as the beautiful woman in his sights.

"Ahhh! Do you hear that, Rory? They've struck up a band over there. Let's go have a listen!"

He had to run to keep up with her as she flew across the park to an area by the fountain where a trio of folk singers were belting out sixties tunes. Two men and a woman, two guitars and a tambourine, gave pleasant renditions of Peter, Paul, and Mary songs, a few Bob Dylan favorites, as well as a few of the Kingston Trio's hits.

He was surprised that Moya seemed to know the words to most of the tunes and she sang along with no inhibitions, her clear, alto voice blending beautifully with the others.

A half a dozen preschoolers, herded by several young nannies, raced across the lawn and headed straight for the fountain in the center. Wearing rubber sandals and bathing suits, they splashed about, dodging squirts of water and squealing with glee.

"Oh, aren't they precious, those wee ones!" she exclaimed as she left the musicians and hurried over to watch the children—another ring of the amazing circus that was Washington Square Park.

"Don't you love them, Rory?" she said as one of the larger children grabbed a younger one's hand and coaxed them to run through a stream of water. "Little ones are the best people on God's green earth, unspoiled by the bitterness of livin' too long. Aren't they a treasure, sure?"

"They are, Moya. Apparently there are treasures everywhere. Sometimes it just takes a special person to point them out."

But she didn't hear him; she was busy watching the children.

So, he took some more pictures . . . more clicks of the shutter . . . and fell a little deeper down the rabbit hole.

O'Leary's Pub on Second Avenue had been serving Guinness to transplanted Irish folk for four generations. A continuous flow of stout and tradition ensured that it was a home away from home for many a lonely immigrant, and Pat O'Leary, great-grandson of Padraic, the founder, made certain there was a constant supply of everything Irish within those dark green walls.

"How about a pint, love?" Rory asked as he parked the Jaguar in front of O'Leary's. "I hear they keep their Guinness on tap icy cold."

She gasped, scandalized. "No, tell me 'tisn't true! Who would be so foolhardy as to serve an icy pint of Mr. Guinness's finest?"

He laughed and switched off the car key. "Don't worry, Moya. I'm sure they can find a Guinness in the place that's room temperature. Just the way you like it."

Once inside, Moya found that far more than just the Guinness was to her liking. A rowdy game of Gaelic football was on the television in the corner over the bar, which was lined with patrons engaged in heated political debate. The traditional folk tunes of Makem and Clancy were playing on the sound system. And on the back wall was a dartboard near where several big, strapping lads with broad, ruddy faces and gentle Irish brogues were in the midst of a fierce competition.

Other than the absence of a turf fire, it felt a lot like Lios na Daoine Sidhe.

"Hey, Rory! How are ye, lad?" shouted the red-haired, round-bellied bartender. "Can I pull ye a proper pint, or will ye be havin' yer usual weak cat piss—oh, excuse me. I see ye have a lady friend with ye."

"Yes, Pat, this is Moya Mahoney from county Kerry," Rory said as he seated Moya on a barstool and sat on the one next to her. "Moya, this ruffian is Patrick O'Leary himself, and you'd better keep your eye on him or he'll rob you of your purse, your reputation, and your virtue."

"And not in that particular order," Pat added with a wide grin. "So, are ye on holiday, Moya from

Kerry? Or have you taken up with this rascal O'Brien and ruint yerself already?"

"I'm only on a holiday, but destroyed nevertheless. Hopelessly smitten, I am."

Pat shook his head sadly. "I thought as much the moment the two of ye crossed me threshold. Now there's a couple that's sipped from the well of passion, and they're thirstin' for more."

"Pat," Rory said impatiently, "cut the Blarney and draw this lady a Guinness. I'll take care of any other thirsts she might have."

Moya sat, watching, listening, absorbing the ambiance. The sights and sounds of home were more quenching to the soul than any beverage could be to the tongue. The chats up and down the bar were same as in Gormloch, only they included references to "that bloody mayor" and the "cursed transit authority" along with discussions about peace in Northern Ireland.

By the time they were ready to leave, more than two hours later, Moya had made friends with Irish folk from five different counties, and they had received invitations to two dances, an Irish music festival, and an evening of storytelling and music-making in the upstairs room of the pub that weekend.

"Who would have thought," she mused as they left the pub and walked east toward the river, "that we Irish would come to this country—'the great melting pot' it's called—and remain so like ourselves."

"Eh," Rory said, "you throw a handful of Irishmen into a pot of ethnic stew and they'll rise to the top every time."

As they neared the river, the sun was sinking, setting the windows of New York's skyscrapers afire with crimson light. Moya stopped in the middle of the sidewalk and soaked in the glorious sight, filing it away forever in her memory to be savored in years to come.

"Many of these buildings were built with Irish hands, you know," Rory told her. "In the mid-1800s, during the famine, when the emigrants arrived by the shipload, they found work building the great cities of the East Coast. Skyscrapers, bridges, canals, tunnels, railroads . . . they raised them, dug them, laid them. When you look at this magnificent skyline, Moya Mahoney, you can be proud that your people built so much of it."

She turned to him and searched his eyes. "And what of you, Rory O'Brien? Are you proud to be Irish?"

He opened his mouth, as though to answer her quickly. Then he seemed to reconsider. "The easy thing would be to say, 'Sure.' But I wasn't always proud, Moya. Growing up where I did, the way I did . . . I wasn't happy to be Irish. But then I visited Ireland. I met you. I met the villagers there in Gormloch. And now I'm proud. Fiercely proud to be Irish, to be an O'Brien. Descended from Brian Boru himself, I am," he added with the dreadful impression of an Irish brogue that only a lad from the Lower East Side of Manhattan could accomplish.

"We have to work on that Irish tone of yours," she said, slipping her arm through his.

"Pretty bad?"

"'Tis nothin' less than a tragedy. An utter tragedy."

Rory sat at his desk, holding Norah's telegram, reading it for the hundredth time and wondering if he should tell Moya about it.

With her return flight scheduled for tomorrow evening, he knew she was deeply troubled, their relationship at a critical point. Why else would she have asked to be alone this afternoon, to wander about the city and think?

He knew she was weighing the balance, with him on one side of the scale, Ireland and everything she loved there on the other.

If he showed her this telegram, would it tip the scale in his favor? Maybe. Maybe not.

Either way, he knew that the problem that lay between them had less to do with geography than with fear. If they were willing to take the chance on love, willing to risk their hearts on a future together, the logistics would take care of themselves. They had to.

He knew that Moya had concerns, and he had plenty of his own. It was no easy gamble, this game of love.

Would he be a good husband? A good father?

How much of his own life, his freedoms, his dreams would he have to surrender if he tried to combine her plans, goals, and hopes with his? Rory was old enough and wise enough to have learned that nothing comes without a price. Not even a loving, committed relationship.

A person's life was a finite receptacle with walls, boundaries. It couldn't contain limitless choices. One had to choose carefully what existed inside those confines. To take something else in meant that something had to go.

Yeah, and what have you got that's so wonderful right now that you can't let go of it for her, he thought as he laid Norah's telegram aside and picked up the photos he had taken of her in Washington Square on their first day together in New York.

What do you have right now that wouldn't be even better if you could share it with her? he asked himself. He listened to his heart and heard no reply.

What was all of this for anyway? The business, the money, the property? He'd proved himself long ago. There needed to be a new reason.

Moya. What better reason could there be?

And a family, a family of their own. That would be the best reason he could think of.

It was reason enough for him. But would it be enough for her?

Moya stepped from the bright glare of the sunlight on the city streets into the cool dim interior of St. Patrick's Cathedral. She had seen pictures of the building and its interior, but nothing had prepared her for its grandeur.

The cavernous sanctuary with its soaring arched ceilings, magnificent stained glass windows, and ex-

traordinary craftsmanship in the form of ornate wood-
working and stone masonry took her breath away.

Along the side walls were the altars of the saints,
each with a hundred or more glimmering candles,
left as a symbol of the ardent prayers offered there.
Although no mass was being said at that moment,
worshipers sat or knelt in the pews, heads bowed
reverently, while tourists and sightseers strolled quietly, respectfully, up and down the great aisles.

Moya slipped into one of the back pews, folded
her hands, and prepared to quiet her mind and spirit.
It wasn't difficult to assume an attitude of reverence
in such a place, and Moya felt a sense of destiny
had led her to that spot at that moment of her life.

She thought of what Rory had told her about St.
Patrick's Cathedral—how it had been built with the
meager offerings of the common Irish folk of New
York. It hadn't always been easy, being Irish in New
York. The immigrants had been the target of ridicule,
bigotry, sometimes even cruelty. With few skills to
market, they had taken the jobs of common labor-
ers, the women as house servants for the wealthy,
the men as workers in construction.

But as Moya sat and looked up at those amaz-
ingly beautiful gothic arches and the stained glass
windows, she wondered how many of her fellow
countrymen and women had come here after a difficult day of work, sat here in the very pew where
she sat, and felt that—because of their hard-earned,
if meager, donations—they owned some small part
of this marvelous structure.

Her heart swelled with pride. It was a fine thing, this being Irish. A very fine thing, indeed.

Bowing her head, she gave thanks that she was here to see this sight, something most of the people of her village would never see. She whispered words of gratitude that Rory had come into her life, that he had shown her a depth of affection that her heart had never experienced and had needed to so badly.

"And while I'm sayin' me thank yous," she added, crossing herself again, just for good measure, "could you give me some sign of what I should do about Rory O'Brien? I'm to go home tomorrow, and 'twill break me heart surely to leave him behind. I'm afraid to leave, but I'm more afraid to stay.

"The problem with livin' here or in Gormloch," she continued, "'tisn't the real problem, I've decided, but an excuse. 'Tis the fear of lovin' someone the way I loved my parents—even more—and thinkin' he might be torn away from me as they were. 'Tis easier not to love than to love and risk losin'.

"Easier . . . but not necessarily better," she added, echoing the words that she could hear so clearly, words spoken by her own heart.

"Father Shea tells us that perfect love casts out fear. But I'm only human and not even close to bein' perfect most of the time. How can I have that sort of love and courage . . . unless you give it to me?

"The good father says we need only to ask for heavenly gifts. So, I'm askin'. And I'm tryin' to do it humble, like you're supposed to, so that I can get it. I'd be oh so grateful if you'd take away some of this fear and replace it with more love. Maybe then

Mr. Rory O'Brien and I can find a way to work out this bit of a problem we have—bein' separated by the great, wide sea."

She started to stand, then dropped back onto her knees. "And I just want to say, that whether you answer this prayer or not, I, Moya Mahoney of county Kerry, will remain your friend, and I'm still most grateful for all the fine things you've brought into me life. Amen."

Twenty

By the time Moya walked back to Rory's town house, it was nearly dark. She hoped he would have returned from the office and be waiting for her, so she was disappointed to find no one at home. But when she went into the kitchen to get a glass of water, she did find a large note taped to the refrigerator door. Rory had scribbled across it with a thick red marker:

Moya,
At eight o'clock sharp a driver will come by to pick you up and bring you to me. I'll be waiting for you at the Plaza in the Oak Room. See you soon.

XOXO
Rory

The Plaza? How exciting, she thought. She had loved the movies *Arthur* and *Crocodile Dundee* and could hardly wait to see the famous landmark, where some of the scenes had been filmed. Glancing at the clock on the microwave, she realized she had no time to dawdle. If she was going to be looking and smelling pretty for her darlin' boy, she'd better get into the bath straightaway.

Sitting in the black limousine, wearing her best little black dress, high heels, and her tourmaline earrings, Moya felt like a princess, and a bit like a little girl dressed up in her mother's clothes, pretending to be a grown-up. In a town as glamorous as New York City, she couldn't claim to be "one of them," but she was having a lovely time playing the part.

And when the car pulled up in front of the elegant Plaza at the southern end of Central Park and the driver offered her his hand to help her alight from her Mercedes "carriage," the fantasy was complete.

Ornate, gilded lampposts with glowing globes lit her way up the stair where doormen in elegant livery opened the door and ushered her inside. In moments, she had found her way to the spacious Oak Room with its dark paneling and old gentleman's club decor. Rory was sitting at the bar, looking gorgeous in the same suit he had worn for the ill-fated village meeting.

Their quarrel of that night seemed a thousand years ago. In light of what he meant to her now, she couldn't imagine cursing him the way she had that day on her stairs. Though he *had* laughed in her face, so he probably wasn't permanently damaged.

"There she is!" he shouted, rising from his stool and opening his arms wide. "There's the woman I love! Right there! Isn't she gorgeous?"

Moya blushed furiously as a dozen well-dressed patrons turned to stare at her. Several of them smiled, others nodded in agreement. A few of the women looked jealous.

She flew into Rory's arms, more to hide than for any other reason.

"Don't you dare do that to me again!" she whispered against his collar. "I still owe you a beatin' for teasin' me the other night."

"I just want the world to notice what a beautiful lass I have on my arm tonight. You don't mind that much, do you?"

She giggled. "Not too much, I suppose." Glancing up and down the bar, she saw that most of the patrons were sipping glasses of wine, martinis, or other exotic drinks she didn't recognize. "I don't suppose the fellow in the tuxedo behind the bar would pour me a Guinness, if I ordered one," she said.

"I suppose he would, but I have a little something for us already." He reached down and lifted a shopping bag from the floor beside his feet. Opening it, he showed her the contents: a bottle of champagne wrapped in several snowy white towels, and a crystal champagne flute.

"Only one glass?" she said.

"Yeah, I figured if I got lucky, we could swap slobber."

"I see. How very romantic. When you put it like that, how's a lass to refuse?"

He tucked the bag under one arm and offered her the other. "Let's get out of here, Miss Mahoney. I have something much nicer planned."

"A carriage ride?" she asked when she saw where he was leading her—to a white carriage decked with garlands of roses, pulled by black horse and a driver dressed in red livery with a black top hat. "Are you after takin' me on a carriage ride around the park?"

"Around Central Park, in the moonlight," he said, "sipping champagne and trading bodily fluids at every opportunity. How does that sound?"

"It sounds positively splendid!"

"Oh, good. I was so afraid you'd refuse."

She grinned at him. "I doubt that. There aren't too many women who would turn down such a ride with you, Rory O'Brien, handsome lad that you are."

"Well, I'm not thinking about 'too many women,' just one. Get up there, darlin', and make yourself comfortable on that seat. I'll speak to the driver and we'll be on our way."

Rory waited until the ride was half over and the champagne half gone before he made his move. They had settled into the soothing cadence of the horse's clip-clop, enjoying the balmy breezes that wafted through the park, carrying the fragrance of spring, rich and fertile. The light of the full moon played on the trees, gilding their leaves in blue silver.

Slipping his arm around her shoulders, he drew her close for a long, intimate kiss. With her reaction more than positive, he decided to forge ahead.

"I went shopping a little earlier this afternoon," he said. "Around that corner."

"What corner?"

He pointed. "The one up there."

She leaned forward to see. "And what's up there?"

"Tiffany's."

He thought he heard her gasp. Her mouth was definitely hanging open for a moment before she recovered her composure. "Tiffany's has lovely things, I hear, like my earrings, but they're most dear. I wouldn't go shopping there so often if I were you."

"Well, I'm not going to be going there every other Friday. But once in a while . . . for special occasions . . ."

She raised one eyebrow and snuggled closer into his arms. "And is this a special occasion?"

"It could be," he said.

He reached into his pocket and produced the small ring box. Pressing it into her hand, he added, "It all depends on you, Miss Mahoney."

As she opened the box, he could feel her trembling beside him. At that moment, the horse passed from shadow into the golden light of a streetlamp and the emerald ring glimmered brightly against the velvet of the box. The diamonds set around the center stone caught the light, too, and sparkled like fairies' dust.

"Oh, my," she whispered, lifting the ring carefully from its box. "'Tis the most beautiful ring I've seen in all me livin' life. Rory, love, you shouldn't have."

His face fell. "I shouldn't have?"

"Oh, no, I mean, you shouldn't have spent so much o' your hard-earned money. I would have been content with far less."

"Really, well, I still have the receipt if you want to take it back and—"

"No!" She clasped it in her fist and held it tightly against her chest. "You've given it to me now. There'll be no takin' anything back."

"There's just something I have to ask you, and then I'll slip it on your finger."

She looked up at him and he could see the silver moonlight and golden streetlamps shining on her tears. "So . . . ask," she said softly.

"Just a second." He leaned out the window of the cab and shouted to the driver, "Hey, could you stop that horse for minute? I gotta get down on my knee here, and this damned thing is rocking around too much."

The carriage halted. He shouted, "Thanks, buddy," then turned his attention to her. "Now, where were we? Oh, yeah . . ."

Summoning every ounce of drama and elegance in his Lower East Side soul, Rory O'Brien got down on one knee in the cramped carriage, took the ring from her hand, and said, "I want you to wear this ring, Moya Mahoney, for the rest of your life. If you like, I'll place it on your right hand, and that will mean that you and I will be loving friends until the day we die, seeing each other as often as we can, you visiting me here in New York, me coming to Ireland to be with you. And if that's all we can have, I'll gladly accept that. Because the most important thing to me is that I have you, in some capacity, in my life."

"Aye, aye, get on to the next part," she said, nudging him with her foot. "And if I decide to let you put it on me left hand . . . ?"

"Well, we can't have you running around with a ring like this on your left hand unless it's an engagement ring. It wouldn't be proper at all. If you want to wear it there, you're going to have to marry me."

He saw the fear in her eyes and for a moment he was afraid. Then he saw the love come shining through. A battle of the heart had been fought and won in the space of one heartbeat.

She held out her left hand. "Slip that ring on me finger, lad, before you're a minute older."

He did.

Moya sat straight up in bed, suddenly wide awake. "Saints preserve us," she exclaimed. "We're gettin' married, but where are we goin' to live?"

Next to her, Rory groaned and pulled the blankets over his head.

"No, really," she said, nudging him. "You must wake up, Rory; this is a dire emergency if ever there was one. I was so happy about you proposin' and the lovely ring and all that I forgot—we are, indeed, sittin' on the horns of a dilemma."

"You may be," he said sleepily. "I'm on my side of the bed, trying to—"

"No, wake up. This's somethin' urgent we must discuss."

He growled and came out from under the blanket. "Why do you Irish have to be so melodramatic? Everything is always fierce, urgent, desperate, or a tragedy with you."

She grabbed her pillow and smacked him across the head with it. "I'll give you tragedy. I've no hope at all of goin' back to sleep until we've settled this. And if I'm not sleepin', Rory O'Brien, you'll not be lyin' there snorin' like Murphy's hogs."

"Who's Murphy?"

"Doesn't matter. Turn on that light and let's talk about this."

Grumbling under his breath, he switched on the lamp that was sitting on the nightstand beside him, flooding the room with light. He squinted and shielded his eyes with his hand. "There, are you happy now that I have scorched retinas?"

"Who's playin' loose with their words now? Scorched, indeed." She flounced around, like a hen settling in her nest until she was facing him squarely. "Let me repeat: Once we're wed, where are we goin' to live? Here? Or Ireland?"

He leaned over and placed a quick kiss on the tip of her nose. "'Tis a pain in the arse ye are, lass," he said. "I was going to tell you all about it tomorrow, but being an impatient female, you can't wait."

"Wait for what? And what does bein' a woman

have to do with patience? I've the patience of St. Bridget herself compared to you. And what is it you were goin' to tell me tomorrow that you can't tell me now?"

"Hang on," he said as he crawled out of bed and stumbled across the room, looking deliciously bedraggled with rumpled hair, wearing only his boxer shorts. "I'm going to go get something," he said. "I'll be right back."

"I'll not be bribed with ice cream," she called after him as he walked out of the room. "Or sex, either, for that matter. Though you might try a bit o' both," she added, "if all else fails."

He returned a couple of minutes later with a bright yellow paper in his hand. Climbing back into bed, he said, "I received this telegram the day before you arrived here in New York. As soon as I read it, I knew we had a solution to this 'horns of a dilemma' you were talking about. But I had to wait until you had seen New York, spent some time here, and gotten over your fears, well, your misgivings about whether we could make it as a couple. Since you said, 'Yes,' tonight, I assume you're pretty sure about us."

"About you and me? Absolutely. But we're birds of a different feather. Where are we going to build our nest?"

"We'll have two nests."

"Two? You mean live in Ireland and in New York?"

He nodded. "Why not? At the moment, we have two houses between us. Why not keep them? We'll spend part of the year in one and part in the other. How does that sound to you?"

Moya didn't have to think long. She had already decided in her heart that if she had to live in New York for the rest of her life to be with Rory, she would. Half of the time in a city as exciting as this, and half in her beloved Ireland was literally the best of two worlds. But . . .

"It won't work," she said.

"Why not? You wouldn't be happy doing that?"

"Aye, happy as a duck in a rainstorm, but you wouldn't. If you were stuck in Ireland for six months with nothin' to do, you'd be bored to death and probably cranky to live with, too. You'll be a grouch, you'll snap at me, then I'll be forced to strike you about the ears with kitchen utensils. It will be domestic violence the likes of which Gormloch has never seen. I tell you, it won't work."

"There you go with the melodrama again. I told you, I have a plan. And it's based on this telegram."

He handed her the paper. She unfolded it and began to read.

"It's from Gormloch," she said. "From Norah!"

"That's right. Keep reading."

As Moya's eyes skimmed over the brief, but concise message, they began to mist with tears. "What a kind soul she is. What a dear, kind soul. Who would think such a cantankerous old hen like Norah would do such a thing?"

"She cares about her community," Rory said. "And she wants them to have their plant."

"Obviously, if she would donate most of her land

to you for that purpose. You don't know what you have here, Rory. Norah is a very wealthy woman. Her property extends from Gormloch to the foot of Carrantuohill. And it says here you can have it all except the bit around her house and gardens."

"I do know," he said. "I sent Mark Giordano and Herman Irving to Gormloch last week to check it out and see if it's suitable. They sent back rave reviews. It will serve our purposes even better than Angus's property would have."

He snatched the telegram out of her hand, dropped it onto the nightstand, then threw her back onto the bed and rolled on top of her. "Now, I don't want to hear any more about how bored I'm going to be in Ireland. I'll be building, then running, the plant. And when I've got a spare moment, I'm going to be strolling down beautiful, peaceful country lanes with my camera in hand, trying to recapture my soul, as you would call it, on film. And I'm going to need you to come along as my model."

"And I'll mind my bed and breakfast just as I always have, only then I'll probably have more guests because of all the new commerce the plant will bring to the area. And the same with Lios na Daoine Sidhe; it'll be full of patrons, keepin' ol' Gill hoppin' behind the bar."

"And when we're here in New York, you'll have someone manage your guest house in Ireland, and I'll run my business as I always have," he said. "And you—"

"And I'll visit the wonderful museums, and go to the theater, and to mass at St. Patrick's, and I'll pop into O'Leary's Pub for a pint and a game of darts whenever I feel homesick."

He began to nibble her earlobe. "Sounds like a good life to me."

"And to me, too. Let's live it!"

"Let's do!"

Epilogue

" *'Twas a brave* thing you did, Norah, givin' away your land like that," Moya said as she stood beside her elderly neighbor and the two of them watched with the rest of the villagers as bulldozers and earth movers sculpted the land to make it ready for the new plant. Clouds of dust billowed, teams of men milled about, shouting to one another over the mechanical din. And in the midst of it, barking orders, wearing a hard hat and an extremely satisfied look on his face, was Rory O'Brien.

"'Twas a brave thing *you* did, Moya O'Brien," Norah replied, "marryin' the man ye loved. Looks like both of our decisions turned out to be good ones in the heel o' the hunt."

"There's nothin' especially brave about gettin' wed."

"Are ye coddin' me? 'Tis one of the most difficult tasks a body can undertake, lookin' at the same man every mornin' and every night for the rest of your days, puttin' up with all of his moods and oddities, and trustin' he'll be willin' to tolerate yours. If that doesn't take courage, neither does lion tamin'."

Norah wiped the dust off her forehead and squinted up at the noonday sun. "'Tis hot as a smithy's oven out here. Come into the house with me. I need a glass of lemonade and so do you."

Moya waved good-bye to Rory, who blew her a kiss right there in front of everyone. The man was impossible; he loved making her blush.

She shook her head, turned, and followed Norah down the road to her house.

Once inside, sitting in one of Norah's comfortable, overstuffed chairs, with Wolfe the Ferocious Fur Ball on her lap, Moya savored the glass of cold lemonade Norah had given her and took a moment to think about how happy she was, how good everything had turned out.

It was wonderful to be home with the green fields beneath her feet and warm turf fires on chilly nights. It was also grand to know that when summer and fall passed, they would be spending Christmas in New York, when the city was alive with winter magic, the stores decked out in red and green holiday cheer, and the smell of roasting chestnuts filled the frosty air.

Then it would be spring in Central Park, with the trees blossoming yellow, pink, and lavender, and tulips and daffodils carpeting the centers of the avenues in crimson and gold. And when the spring turned to hot summer in the city, it would be back to the cool, green meadows of Kerry.

"You look happier," Norah said. "Marriage agrees with you."

"Marriage to Rory agrees with me."

"Mmm . . . that reminds me. Do you know what today is?"

"Yes," Moya said. "One of the saddest days of me life. 'Twas one year ago today that dear Angus passed away."

"That's true. And I have somethin' for you . . . it bein' the anniversary of his departin' and all."

"What's that?"

"A letter." Norah reached over and picked up Angus's wooden box, which she had set in a place of honor in the center of her coffee table. "Doesn't say who it's to, but I suspect he'd want ye to read it."

She placed the blue envelope into Moya's hand, then bent down and gave her a light kiss on the top of her head. Moya nearly fainted. It was the first time in her life she had ever seen Norah Delaney express affection physically. What was the world coming to?

"I'm goin' to go take a nap," Norah said, suddenly curt. "Ye get tired quick when yer old like meself. I'll see ye later tonight at the pub."

"Aye, we'll be there for the singin', sure. Have a fine nap for yourself and thank you for the letter."

But Norah was already gone . . . to give her some privacy as she read it, she suspected.

Gently, she scooped the sleeping dog off her lap

and deposited him on the rug at her feet. Then she turned her attention to the letter.

On the outside of the envelope, Angus had written instructions that it wasn't to be opened until he had been gone for one year. She smiled when she turned it over and saw rings where moisture had been used to steam it open. Good old Norah. Good old, nosy Norah.

When she opened it, she found a single sheet of paper inside upon which Angus had written:

Dear Moya,

I feel I should write one more letter before I lay down my pen. I want to tell you why I have chosen to dispose of my property in the manner which I have done. Moya, I thought long and hard about leaving the pub to you. Certainly, you are the one who loves it most. And you are the one who deserves it, having done so much for me.

But I know that if you have yet another tie to this village, besides your own home, you'll never, ever leave this place. And while you may choose to return home, you should leave, at least for a while, and see the wide world that lies beyond.

It's something I should have done and now regret. I don't want you to suffer from regrets as I have.

I'm leaving Lios na Daoine Sidhe to my nephew, a fine young man who I spent some time with a few years back. I was most impressed with his business sense, and with him as a person. It is my wish, Moya, that when he comes to Gormloch to claim his heritage, perhaps you will be impressed with him, too. Something tells me you will be, and him with you. I think that would be very good for you both.

Forgive an old man for doing a bit of matchmaking, but I feel like a father to you, and I'm trying to watch out for your best interests. I hope, when you read this letter, that you'll agree I did the right thing.

Love and gratitude,
Angus

Moya folded the letter and pressed her lips to it as tears filled her eyes. "You did the right thing, Angus. Indeed, you did. Thank you for lookin' out for me in such a dear way. I love you, too."

Then she stood and slipped the letter into her pocket. She walked out of the house and down the walkway, but by the time she reached the road, she was running.

She ran all the way back to the construction site and looked everywhere among the flying dirt and the noisy machinery and dusty men for her husband. "Rory!" she yelled. "Rory, where are you?"

A deep voice boomed out of the haze. "There she is! There's the woman I love! Isn't she gorgeous? And eat your heart out, lads, she's allllll mine!"

The cloud of dust parted for just a second and she saw him, hard hat, plaid shirt, blue jeans, mischievous grin and all.

She flew to him, threw her arms around his neck, and gave him a long, hard kiss. She didn't even bother to blush when the rowdy cheers rose around them. St. Patrick himself could have been standing there, getting an eyeful, for all she cared.

This man was her husband. And she was positively, fiercely, desperately daft about him.

Life didn't get better than that!

Introducing a new romance
series from Jove...

Irish Eyes

From the fiery passion of the Middle Ages...
to the magical charm of Celtic legends...
to the timeless allure of modern Ireland...
these brand new romances will surely
"steal your heart away."

The Irish Devil by Donna Fletcher
0-515-12749-3

To Marry an Irish Rogue by Lisa Hendrix
0-515-12786-8

Daughter of Ireland by Sonja Massie
0-515-12835-X

All books $5.99

Prices slightly higher in Canada

Payable by Visa, MC or AMEX only ($10.00 min.), No cash, checks or COD. Shipping & handling:
US/Can. $2.75 for one book, $1.00 for each add'l book; Int'l $5.00 for one book, $1.00 for each
add'l. Call (800) 788-6262 or (201) 933-9292, fax (201) 896-8569 or mail your orders to:

Penguin Putnam Inc.   Bill my: ☐ Visa ☐ MasterCard ☐ Amex _____ (expires)
P.O. Box 12289, Dept. B   Card# _____
Newark, NJ 07101-5289
Please allow 4-6 weeks for delivery.   Signature _____
Foreign and Canadian delivery 6-8 weeks.

Bill to:
Name _____
Address _____ City _____
State/ZIP _____ Daytime Phone # _____
Ship to:
Name _____ Book Total $ _____
Address _____ Applicable Sales Tax $ _____
City _____ Postage & Handling $ _____
State/ZIP _____ Total Amount Due $ _____
This offer subject to change without notice.   Ad # 868 (3/00)

TIME PASSAGES

❑ CRYSTAL MEMORIES	*Ginny Aiken*	0-515-12159-2
❑ ECHOES OF TOMORROW	*Jenny Lykins*	0-515-12079-0
❑ LOST YESTERDAY	*Jenny Lykins*	0-515-12013-8
❑ MY LADY IN TIME	*Angie Ray*	0-515-12227-0
❑ NICK OF TIME	*Casey Claybourne*	0-515-12189-4
❑ REMEMBER LOVE	*Susan Plunkett*	0-515-11980-6
❑ SILVER TOMORROWS	*Susan Plunkett*	0-515-12047-2
❑ THIS TIME TOGETHER	*Susan Leslie Liepitz*	0-515-11981-4
❑ WAITING FOR YESTERDAY	*Jenny Lykins*	0-515-12129-0
❑ HEAVEN'S TIME	*Susan Plunkett*	0-515-12287-4
❑ THE LAST HIGHLANDER	*Claire Cross*	0-515-12337-4
❑ A TIME FOR US	*Christine Holden*	0-515-12375-7

All books $5.99

Prices slightly higher in Canada

Payable by Visa, MC or AMEX only ($10.00 min.), No cash, checks or COD. Shipping & handling: US/Can. $2.75 for one book, $1.00 for each add'l book; Int'l $5.00 for one book, $1.00 for each add'l. Call (800) 788-6262 or (201) 933-9292, fax (201) 896-8569 or mail your orders to:

Penguin Putnam Inc.
P.O. Box 12289, Dept. B
Newark, NJ 07101-5289
Please allow 4-6 weeks for delivery.
Foreign and Canadian delivery 6-8 weeks.

Bill my: ❑ Visa ❑ MasterCard ❑ Amex _____ (expires)

Card# _____

Signature _____

Bill to:

Name _____

Address _____ City _____

State/ZIP _____ Daytime Phone # _____

Ship to:

Name _____

Address _____ Book Total $ _____

City _____ Applicable Sales Tax $ ____

State/ZIP _____ Postage & Handling $ _____

_____ Total Amount Due $ _____

This offer subject to change without notice.

Ad # 680 (3/00)

DO YOU BELIEVE IN MAGIC?

MAGICAL LOVE

The enchanting series from Jove will make you a believer!

With a sprinkling of faerie dust and the wave of a wand, magical things can happen—but nothing is more magical than the power of love.

□ *SEA SPELL* by Tess Farraday   0-515-12289-0/$5.99

A mysterious man from the sea haunts a woman's dreams—and desires...

□ *ONCE UPON A KISS* by Claire Cross

0-515-12300-5/$5.99

A businessman learns there's only one way to awaken a slumbering beauty...

□ *A FAERIE TALE* by Ginny Reyes   0-515-12338-2/$5.99

A faerie and a leprechaun play matchmaker—to a mismatched pair of mortals...

□ *ONE WISH* by C.J. Card   0-515-12354-4/$5.99

For years a beautiful bottle lay concealed in a forgotten trunk—holding a powerful spirit, waiting for someone to come along and make one wish...

VISIT PENGUIN PUTNAM ONLINE ON THE INTERNET:
http://www.penguinputnam.com

Prices slightly higher in Canada

Payable by Visa, MC or AMEX only ($10.00 min.), No cash, checks or COD. Shipping & handling: US/Can. $2.75 for one book, $1.00 for each add'l book; Int'l $5.00 for one book, $1.00 for each add'l. Call (800) 788-6262 or (201) 933-9292, fax (201) 896-8569 or mail your orders to:

Penguin Putnam Inc. **P.O. Box 12289, Dept. B** **Newark, NJ 07101-5289** Please allow 4-6 weeks for delivery. Foreign and Canadian delivery 6-8 weeks.	Bill my: □ Visa □ MasterCard □ Amex _____ (expires) Card# _____ Signature _____

Bill to:

Name _____

Address _____ City _____

State/ZIP _____ Daytime Phone # _____

Ship to:

Name _____ Book Total $ _____

Address _____ Applicable Sales Tax $ _____

City _____ Postage & Handling $ _____

State/ZIP _____ Total Amount Due $ _____

This offer subject to change without notice.   **Ad # 789 (3/00)**

Penguin Putnam Inc.
Online

Your Internet gateway to a virtual environment with hundreds of entertaining and enlightening books from Penguin Putnam Inc.

While you're there, get the latest buzz on the best authors and books around—

Tom Clancy, Patricia Cornwell, W.E.B. Griffin, Nora Roberts, William Gibson, Robin Cook, Brian Jacques, Catherine Coulter, Stephen King, Jacquelyn Mitchard, and many more!

**Penguin Putnam Online is located at
http://www.penguinputnam.com**

PENGUIN PUTNAM NEWS

Every month you'll get an inside look at our upcoming books and new features on our site. This is an ongoing effort to provide you with the most up-to-date information about our books and authors.

**Subscribe to Penguin Putnam News at
http://www.penguinputnam.com/ClubPPI**